the unknowing

a novel

K E N G A G N E

ALSO BY KEN GAGNE

You're Gonna Miss Me Someday: A Memoir

Wave Her Home

To my parents,
and to Annie

If you want to keep a secret,
you must also hide it from yourself.

—George Orwell

There is no pain so great as the memory of joy in present grief.

—Aeschylus

I kept five pet snails in an aquarium at my grandmother's house when I was a kid, named them after every member of my family. They were happy, I thought, and lived longer than expected. But after one died, they all died. Nana Joan said the first dead snail released a bad smell, called ammonia, which killed the others. Instead of throwing them out in her garden, we placed them in a tide pool on the beach behind her house. "When their bodies decompose," she explained, "hermit crabs will inhabit their empty shells. After they outgrow them, they'll find bigger ones to move into." I asked if the shells were like houses; she said they were the souls of the snails. According to my grandmother, a dead snail would get another life whenever a crab crawled inside its shell. I liked thinking my pets would live forever, but there were thousands of empty *souls* scattered on the sand, and I worried about them. "Those will stay here, Devan," Nana told me, "until they get a new life, or the tide comes and takes them away."

THE END

My lungs locked at midnight.

I sprung out of bed. The kitten hopped onto the floor. I fought to breathe, knocked over the lamp. Inhaler on my nightstand, empty. Ran to the bathroom, to the cabinet, the drawer. My other inhaler, not there.

Rushed down the hall, wheezing, panting, and woke up my dad. "It's bad," I said.

He threw on some clothes, grabbed the keys, sped through red lights, stop signs.

A six-mile drive, I knew how far, we'd done this before. Struggling, begging, I clutched at my chest, writhed in my seat. Shaking, gasping. "Stay calm," he said. "Stay—"

My body tightened, breathing slowed. Dizzy, fading.

"Don't worry, Dev. Almost there."

Two miles left, long stretch of road, woods on both sides. No houses, no lights. The car lost speed. Sputtered, jerked. Pops slapped the dashboard. "No, God! No!"

He pulled over, and I forced out the words: "Please. Don't. Leave."

꩜

I took my last breath, weak and shallow, in the back seat of a stranger's SUV.

"Stay with me, son!" my father pled, cradling my head in his lap. "C'mon, Dev!" He stroked my hair, patted my cheek, clung to the hope he had left.

I didn't want to die, tried to hold on, couldn't. My grip on his shirtsleeve loosened, and I slipped away.

Darkness. Then light.

My spirit rose, and I watched Pops lug my lanky body through the double doors of Milford Hospital. He limped into the emergency room. "Somebody help!"

It was too late, he knew. A doctor arrived, and my dad released me.

But he never let go.

꩜

When I first crossed over, the line between life and death was blurred, shadowy at best; I couldn't tell where one began and where the other ended. Somehow, I still felt attached to my physical form, and I wasn't ready to leave my family, but I had no choice. Not yet.

My soul—a flowing vibration moving everywhere and nowhere at once—merged into a greater collective, and as the light around me grew more powerful and enveloped me, an overwhelming love consumed me. That's when I met my soul usher, Simone, an ageless, genderless beauty, four or forty, eighteen or eighty, male or female. I couldn't tell and didn't care, but I chose to see her as a young woman.

Simone had a golden aura of pure compassion, and something about her was familiar. Surrounded by warm light, I felt comfortable, safe in her presence. "Am I really dead?" I asked.

"You are, in the biological sense."

"But how can we be here talking now?"

"Well, *now* does not exist *here*."

"Huh?"

"On earth, you were like a snail with a shell," she said as the light engulfed us. "Now, you're no longer a snail, but your shell remains."

I thought of Nana Joan.

"When you died," Simone continued, "your consciousness moved on. Now it lives outside of your body, infinitely, as a soul. This is the real world now, Devan Jacoby, controlled by thought alone. The physical world you left behind? *That* was an illusion."

"So, I'm a ghost?"

"No," Simone said. "But you're not exactly a spirit either. You're still in between. Ghosts and spirits are variations of souls, with significant differences. Spirits are omniscient and godlike, free and at peace. Ghosts are unknowing wanderers, stuck, and never satisfied."

"What do I do now?"

"You have three choices. Either ascend into the spirit world—or, as it's called, the heavenly realm—or become earthbound and stay closer to your family."

"What's the third choice?"

"Enter a new body, with no memory of who you were, and play the game again."

I feared that my passing might rip my family apart, and I didn't want to abandon them. Simone cautioned me about the risks of staying earthbound, said it would sap my soul's energy force and imperil my chances of ever "moving on." She proposed I enter the spirit world, raise my frequency, and construct any form of heaven I dreamed of. But how could I find happiness in the afterlife with my family suffering on earth? Simone said if I crossed over into the heavenly realm, I could still look after them and communicate by sending special signs, like a favorite song or a rare bird or a familiar scent. To put it plainly, I could've been their guardian angel, but I wanted to make a real difference. They needed me close.

"I'll move into the spirit world after I help them," I said.

"Very well, Devan."

I chose to stay in the earthly realm, at Nana Joan's house on the beach in Old Saybrook, Connecticut, where my family and I laughed and loved for two months every summer. Both my parents, Jake and Iris, had been schoolteachers, and they took my siblings and me to my grandmother's from mid-June till mid-August each year. Old Saybrook was less than an hour away from our house in Hopedale, a suburb of New Haven, but I always felt different at Nana's place than I did anywhere else. Felt safer there, braver and free, more myself. My grandmother's love, the enormity of the ocean, and the comfort of an anonymous life in a town where no one knew me combined to make Old Saybrook, not Hopedale, feel like home.

I belonged there.

In a flash, Simone and I were on a familiar beach, a magical place that seemed to extend forever, where beauty and perfection surrounded me, straight out of a fantasy. I felt all the happiness and joy of a homecoming, all the promise of my heart's desire. Indescribable colors, like from one of my sister's paintings, full of light and hope, were splattered in the sky. The tide was out, impossibly far away, and pools of cool water lay everywhere, pure and clear like snow melted in the hands of a pretty girl. Giggly children ran on clouds of sand, collected snail shells, chased hermit crabs. Older folks laughed and danced, their tanned skin kissed by an endless summer. Everyone was filled with peace; everyone was Love.

As the sun shined on and on, I thought, *This must be heaven.*

I could've stayed in that blissful existence forever, but I missed my family, and they missed me, so I turned away. Facing me then were five steps that led to the sliding door at the back of Nana's house. Simone pointed to them, and I started my climb. When I got to the top, I hesitated and began to cry before crossing the threshold. Once I stepped inside, the door sealed shut behind me with an awful screech and snuffed out the light from the beach.

The old seaside house on Plum Bank Road had four small bedrooms, two bathrooms, a kitchen, a living room, and an attic. But the interior wasn't how I remembered it, looked dreary, felt sullen. No bright sunshine bouncing off the walls, no salt air filtering through the halls. The furniture seemed flimsier, the appliances dustier. My dad's favorite possession, a clock he built from an old ship's wheel, hung broken in the living room. But that clock had always been broken.

The darkness of the rooms, deep and sooty, bothered me the most. Each window in the house was stained and fractured, and I couldn't see outside—not the beach or the sea or the sun. In the glass, I only saw the members of my family living their everyday lives, as if I were spying on them with surveillance cameras or watching them on murky TV screens. I felt so near to them, read all of their thoughts and emotions, followed their words and actions, knew everything about their yesterdays and todays. It was as if Simone had granted me exclusive access to their souls, an all-knowing perspective. There were no mysteries about them in that new dimension, no secrets; that was the gift of death. My parents and siblings couldn't hide from me, not like before, but part of me wished they could. Knowing too much was a burden, and it hurt.

My *gift* was a curse.

My father and grandmother lived in that house, and I watched them go about their routines, day after day, through a clouded prism, a gray veil draped between our worlds.

In every room, Jacoby family photos were on display. When I was alive, I never realized how many of our memories my parents had documented. Now, as I moved around the house, I gazed at pictures from another lifetime, foreign yet familiar. Like the one in the kitchen of Gia as a toddler searching for sea glass on the beach with Nana Joan, the one in the living room of Mom and Russell raising his two MVP trophies from middle school basketball, and the one on my father's nightstand of him reading to me when I was four or five.

Each evening, for years, my dad and I snuggled in a big blue chair in the corner of my room and read together before bed. We went on wild adventures with Harry Potter when I was in elementary school, then Percy Jackson as I aged. Eventually, we grew out of our habit, coinciding with when he got busier. For extra cash, Pops tutored high school math students a few nights per week when he wasn't at one of Gia's travel soccer games or driving Russell back and forth to basketball practice in New Haven. I knew our reading ritual wouldn't last forever, but it was tough to surrender our special time together. For both of us, I thought.

In death, I couldn't speak to my father or Nana, not directly, and they couldn't see me as I roamed around them. But from the instant I returned to Old Saybrook, I became the pulse of the house and attempted to communicate with them, to make them feel my presence. I turned lights on and off, switched on the radio. Knocked books to the floor, opened doors and slammed them shut, broke pictures and dishes. I commanded the floors to creak, conjured the wind to sneak through drafty, darkened windows and relay a message for me.

I'm still here, the wind said.

Sometimes Nana Joan heard the whispers and told my father. But he couldn't see or hear past his pain, didn't entertain his mother's theories, or the truth, anymore. And I couldn't change that. He ignored my signs, had an excuse for each flickering light, falling book, and broken dish, blamed everything from faulty wiring to ocean storms to roadwork outside the house. He had lost me and didn't need any reminders.

From the moment we parted, I lamented the life Pops would live without me, the tragedy that took me away from him, and how he wouldn't know me in the years to come. As time passed, I prayed he'd find the courage to say goodbye, to let me go without understanding. But I vowed to stay close to him, hidden in the walls of that house, and in the shadow of his memory.

PART I

THE DAY BEFORE THE WEDDING

❧

Death is not the opposite of life,
but a part of it.

—Haruki Murakami

ONE

Ashes, or me

After my death, my parents and siblings drifted apart like boats in a fog, rudderless on a vast sea, each fading toward an invisible, opposite horizon. Beyond the flowers and hugs and sympathy casseroles, all they had left was what waited on the other side of sadness: a distinct and foreboding mystery for each of them.

The last time they were in the same room together was at my memorial service in a crowded funeral home in our hometown of Hopedale. The last thing they said to one another was "Goodbye," later that March afternoon on a desolate, windswept beach in Old Saybrook, after they flung my remains into the Atlantic. That was a brutal day for my family, impossible for any of us to imagine how much worse things would get.

Before my ashes dissolved in the saltwater, my older sister, Gia, donated her frumpy funeral dress to Goodwill and coaxed her used Kia back to the Rhode

Island School of Design to finish her freshman year. In the following decade, she dropped out of college, kept her festering opioid addiction quiet, and stayed in the Ocean State. Gia never returned to Hopedale, not even to get Mr. Paws, the kitten I named, and Pops planned to surprise her with on her nineteenth birthday—which no one celebrated forty-eight hours after I passed, except for our neighbor's eight-year-old daughter, who got a free cat that day.

A month later, my mother, Iris, told my father she wanted a divorce. "This isn't about Devan," she said. "This is about you, Jake. You and your fuckin' inability to deal with any of the shit life throws at you." She could've meant anything by that; they'd been through a lot. I wasn't even the first child they lost. I never knew my dead sister, none of us did. She was a stillbirth, and my parents kept the story to themselves. What was there to tell?

In typical passive fashion, Pops didn't argue with my mother when she served him the divorce papers. Though he factored opposing viewpoints into all equations, by his calculations, every problem had a black-and-white solution; the collapse of his mixed-race marriage was no exception. Twenty-four years of depreciating happiness added up to a bitter ending. Even when my twin brother, Russell, urged him to fight for whatever love our parents had left, our father refused, just didn't have the will. My death had taken that from him as well. In no time, Mom had moved into a condo an hour away in West Hartford, leaving Russell and Pops, sole survivors of the Jacoby family disaster, washed ashore with the wreckage, stranded together for two long years. During that span, Gia went MIA for months on end, while my mom got remarried to a high school principal named Tom Hyde, inviting no one from our family to the wedding, which took place on a yacht in Barbados.

Russell graduated from Hopedale High as the best point guard the city had ever seen. Then he headed west, rode the pine at Texas Tech, earned a degree in hospitality management, and spent three years as a cook and bartender in Las Vegas before relocating to New York City. Though Russ kept in regular touch with our family— texted Gia and Mom monthly, called Pops weekly, made more of an effort than anyone—it wasn't enough; we'd never again be who we were, the tight-knit clan who held silly sing-alongs on car rides, camped out under the stars in their backyard every Fourth of July weekend, and raced inflatable tubes down the steepest, scariest snow hills in town. Even in the lowest moments of Russell's brotherless life, when he wanted to give up on all of us, I wouldn't let him, my voice echoing in his head, clamoring about a plan to bring our family back together.

Reaching my father wasn't as easy.

For over a decade, Elliot "Jake" Jacoby considered giving up twice each day. At six in the morning, when he lifted his bathrobe off the hook in his bedroom closet, and at ten thirty in the evening, when he hung it up again. In those small moments, as the closet door creaked opened and closed, it spoke to my dad in a demonic whisper. *The shoebox is on the top shelf*, the door said. *Open it, pull that trigger, and all your pain will disappear.*

For a time, Pops fended off the voices. He couldn't leave Nana Joan, his eighty-four-year-old mother, whom he lived with in Old Saybrook and had taken care of since glaucoma stole her sight five years after I died. And he couldn't leave Dewey, the muscular black-and-white mutt, a pit bull mix, who showed up on our porch in Hopedale the day Mom walked out and never left my father's side. Some days, caring for his mom and Dewey was enough to distract Pops from blaming himself for destroying our family, for not saving me, or for not keeping me alive long enough to be saved. But most days, the blame haunted him. Mom, Gia, and Russell didn't suffer less than my father; they just suffered differently.

My dad didn't buy into the theory of God, never sank so low as to pray, and my death solidified his cynicism. Though my grandmother was a devout Catholic when Pops was growing up in rural Stockbridge, Massachusetts, he refused to believe in an "unnecessary delusion" and a bogeyman who'd torture him forever if he didn't live up to an impossible standard. When Nana forced my dad to attend church, he didn't get into the ritual, he just got into nicer clothes. To him, weekly mass meant sad music, bad poetry, ugly architecture, and crowds. In 1976, after my father left home and enrolled at Southern Connecticut State College, his mom sold their house in Stockbridge and moved to Old Saybrook, closer to her son. They were all each other ever had and glorified their sacred relationship. Pops worshipped his mother, not his maker.

Way back when, "Young Jake" could let go of anything. But now at sixty-five, "Old Jake" clung to his guilt, gripped it tight like a miser. Kept the pain locked deep in his heart while he replayed our last minute together, ran it on a constant loop in his head, both of us gasping for air in the back of an SUV. On the night he watched me die.

I'd been gone nearly eleven years—3,948 days, to be exact, but it felt like forever. During that time, as the weeks and months passed, my parents and siblings thought of me less and less. Whenever they succumbed to the siren song of the past and revisited a heart-tugging memory, they just got more upset with each other, or with themselves. Year after lonely year, I waited and yearned for my family to find a different way forward, but I couldn't make it happen, could only witness them floundering and fumbling through the days, their isolated reflections torturing me in the muddied, mystical windows of Nana's beach house. As I tracked their thoughts, past and present, and traced their movements, stride for stride, fate rendered me helpless to bring them together.

Then I got my wish, in the form of a small purple envelope. On Thanksgiving night, by the floating flames of Providence's WaterFire display, my sister's boyfriend, Luke Potter, professed his love and presented Gia with a modest diamond. She accepted his proposal with a bursting heart. Seven days later, wedding invitations appeared in a half dozen mailboxes throughout the Northeast.

Please Join Us in a Celebration of Love
Who: Gia Grace Jacoby & Luke William Potter
When: Friday, December 31, 2022, 6:30 p.m.
Where: The Cozy Cove Inn, Wickford, RI

The invitees: my mother and her second husband, Tom Hyde; my father and Nana Joan; my twin brother Russell and his girlfriend, Izzy Dominguez; Luke's parents, Bill and Beth Potter; Luke's brother and best man, Brodie Potter; and Gia's maid of honor and closest friend, Mara Morrigan.

The limited guest list guaranteed a quaint and quiet affair. That's what Gia wanted; she and Luke couldn't afford much else. My sister had refused to ask my father to chip in—she stopped leaning on him for money after she got clean. Despite offers from his folks, Luke and his bride-to-be were determined to finance the occasion themselves. So the wedding, as my mother put it, would be "intimate."

TWO

Gia, or ghosts

Ten o'clock in the harbor town of Wickford, Rhode Island, two days till 2023. The bright morning sun, unaware of the blizzard gaining strength off the coast.

A village locked in time, Wickford housed the souls of the living and the dead. Locals strolled past colonial landmarks, returned sweaters at boutique stores, sniffed out post-Christmas discounts at art galleries, while brushing by phantoms of Revolutionary War soldiers, Native Americans, and sea captains.

Bundled up and freezing, Gia and her friend, Mara Morrigan, hustled down patterned brick sidewalks, frozen and slick like hockey ponds throughout New England. In my sister's pocket: a two-hundred-dollar gift card for a salon called Nova, a wedding present from our mother. Before tying the knot, Gia hoped a deep-tissue massage would relieve her stress. Attempting to reunite our family was like toying with the gods, but for a former addict ready to heave her sketchy past into Wickford Cove, a chance at reconciliation was worth the risk.

I watched my sister from the attic window at our grandmother's house in Old Saybrook—sixty miles from Wickford, but more than a world away. From that window, resembling a ship's porthole, I used to look out over Long Island Sound. But that old view was inaccessible now; my soul usher, Simone, only let me see the people in my family, their fears and hopes, their every desire. In my life, the attic window was a porthole. In my death, a portal. I wanted to leave the house and be with Gia, but since I'd decided to remain earthbound, I couldn't move as freely as the spirits who'd crossed over into the heavenly realm. Their energy was higher than mine, allowing them to travel anywhere at the speed of thought. They could visit their loved ones whenever they wanted, but they never stayed on earth long.

"Why do I feel like we've been here before?" Mara asked and blew into her hands.

Gia grabbed her friend's arm. "Not sure, but I'm glad we're here now."

The surrounding air, crisp and sugary in my sister's lungs, delivered a shiver down to her toes as she breathed in the stillness sweetened with the subtle scent of frozen flowers. Gia had seen Mara only twice in three years and was looking forward to catching up. After COVID, the public relations firm Mara worked for let her stay on remotely. She moved out of her apartment outside of Boston and into her parents' home in Virginia. She didn't mind the setup, loved her folks even more than the free meals.

"I really have missed you," Gia said.

"Whatever," Mara joked. "Once you met Luke, you didn't need me anymore."

"I'll always need you."

My sister had enlisted her friend's help to survive the day—like Mara had helped Gia survive so many days before. Two hours of spa bliss preceded an aggressive agenda: lunch at noon with Luke and his brother, Brodie; an hour-long appointment at two with our mother and the owners of the Cozy Cove Inn to complete plans for the next day's ceremony; then a thirty-minute meeting with the wedding photographer; followed by a dress fitting and dinner with her future in-laws.

"One phase at a time," Gia said, trying to sound convincing. "It's all good."

"Except for that creepy inn we're staying at." Mara's hot breath vanished in the cold air like a runaway phantom. "No way you have sex this weekend without your bedroom walls drooling over your every position."

Gia laughed. "The Cozy Cove just needs a little face-lift."

"Yeah, right, the place is available for a group of eleven on New Year's weekend because of peeling paint and outdated appliances."

"Remind me again why I'm still friends with you."

Like the suspicious inn, Mara and Gia were complete unknowns when they met at RISD. Opposites, in lots of ways, they gravitated to each other through an inexplicable magnetic force. After my death, Mara's spunk and audacity pried my sister out of her shell and away from the spirals of addiction. She excelled in her role as best friend, replacing the family Gia had lost.

For the first seventeen years of her life, my sister had everything. Then she got hooked on prescription pain pills after a sports injury, then I died from an asthma attack. Then she had nothing, then she had Mara, then Luke. Now, by inviting our parents and Russell to her wedding, she hoped to get almost everything back again. In her cloudy past, Gia's days on the streets had blended together in a disturbing haze of mildew and urine and desolation to where she sometimes couldn't recall what year she was in—and only after meeting Luke did it matter.

The friends hurried into the salon, shook off the chill, and waited for a stocky woman at reception to pull her nose out of a magazine article.

Mara tapped her nails on the desk. "Ahem."

The woman lifted her head, eyebrows first. "Oh, sorry. Can I help you?"

My sister unzipped her coat and noted the receptionist's name tag. "Hi there, Amanda. We have reservations for Gia Jacoby."

Amanda set aside her magazine, opened a laptop, and scanned the screen. "Hmm, don't see anything here under that name."

"My mom called it in," my sister said. "It might be under Gia Potter or Iris Jacoby."

The receptionist clicked her tongue and twirled her hair. "Nothing under those names, but I see an Iris Hyde."

"That's the one." Gia's face glowed.

Mara rolled her eyes. "Nothing's easy with your mother."

They undressed in a back room and lay face down on adjacent tables, their bodies covered with white towels. Lemon-scented candles mixed with cinnamon incense coils while the multilayered, jazz-infused music of Fiona Apple wafted in the air. Gia lowered her face into the headrest. "Why do I feel like they're gonna bake us into a pie?"

Two masseuses entered, one male and one female. "My name is Joseph, and this is Kira," the guy said. "Who wants who?"

"Kira's kinda cute, but I should take you." Mara winked at Joseph, and a lock of her tangerine hair flopped in front of her face. "You know, just to keep the bride pure."

Kira worked on my sister's neck, shoulders, back, and legs. "Gawd, you're really tense." She dug her stiff fingers into Gia's right hamstring, below the hip, near a stick-and-poke tattoo of an oyster shell. "Cool tat, what's the meaning?"

"Just makes me think of the ocean, sort of my happy place." My sister didn't explain that she got the ink the day after she left rehab, that the oyster shell symbolized resilience and strength. A reminder that she could withstand more than she thought, could recover from turbulence, and resurface stronger than she was before.

"Okay, flip over," Kira said in a thick Rhode Island accent.

"Can you take it easy on my abs, please?" Gia turned onto her back, snuck a peek at the masseuse. "Took a tough Pilates class the other day."

"Sure." Kira readjusted my sister's towel. "Hoping a last-minute workout's gonna help you squeeze into a gown?"

"Something like that."

"Where's the wedding?"

"The Cozy Cove Inn."

Kira turned to her coworker. "Hear that, Joe?"

"Yeah." Joseph parked his meaty hands on Mara's shoulders, and his voice dropped. "Lots of history in that big colonial by the harbor, used to be called Hayle House, built centuries ago, survived the Revolution when most buildings around here got destroyed."

"Don't leave out the best part." Kira kneaded her palms into Gia's quad. "Tell 'em about the dead kid walkin' the halls."

"Hold up," my sister said, face white, glow gone.

"It's just a stupid legend," Joseph said, "but folks claim a little girl in a green dress wanders around the place, sometimes in broad daylight, comes and goes, doesn't make a sound." He squirted oil into his hands and rubbed Mara's forearms. "And I sometimes hear about pranksters hanging a noose from the oak in the yard."

My sister shuddered. "Please tell me you're joking."

"Hey, I grew up in Wickford." Kira's accent flipped the *ford* into *fud*. "And all I'm sayin' is that before Hayle

House became the Cozy Cove, or whatnot, us kids called it 'Hell House.'"

"Okay," Mara said with a cringe, "end of subject."

I knew the legend might be true, and if Gia believed in the ghost of Hayle House, then maybe she'd believe in me too, and in all of us. Could my sister be the bridge our family might use to return from the dead?

Outside the salon, the temperature had fallen to sixteen degrees, and the ladies had zero interest in walking the half mile to lunch. Huddled next to Mara on a frosty wooden bench, Gia texted Luke for a ride. She chewed on a fingernail, tore off part of the cuticle. The blood on her lips, salty and warm.

Mara rubbed my sister's back. "Relaxed yet, G?"

"My family's getting together for the first time in ten years," Gia said. "It'll take more than a massage to loosen me up."

"You know what they say?" said Mara. "Can't escape family, right?"

"It's crazy." Gia studied her bloodied finger. "I want them all here, but it's probably better if my dad and brother don't show."

"Last week my birth mom came for Christmas," Mara said. "I thought it'd be really awkward, but it gets easier every year."

"Your parents did the right thing by telling you the truth when you were young."

"They're not the secret-keeping type," Mara said. "My

dad swears that secrets have evil powers. But once you share them, the power decreases."

"What is he, a witch doctor or something?"

"Close," Mara said. "Podiatrist."

My sister sprung to her feet and hopped in place. "God, it's freezing."

Mara jumped up, mirrored her friend's movements. "Are we cold or nervous?"

"I don't even know." Gia stopped and stared at the bleak sky. "I just feel like something bad is about to happen. It hasn't reached us yet, but it's on its way."

"Let's cheer you up, Donna Doomsday." Mara latched on to Gia's jacket sleeve and reeled her in. "Okay, girl, gimme your all-time favorite memory."

Gia chuckled. "You sound so wannabe when you call me 'girl.'"

"You rather I call you 'ho'?"

"Nah, you good." Gia smiled her dimply smile, the same one Russell had, the same one I used to have. Across the street, the clock on a church steeple struck twelve. "One of my best memories," my sister said as the chimes began, "was when I was probably eleven, and Dad took me and the twins to the Trove, an antique shop in Old Saybrook, where eccentrics buy stuff no one else wants."

"Gimme twenty years," Mara said, "and I might be on those shelves."

My sister snickered. "Anyway, Dad bought an old wooden ship's wheel and a vintage copper clock that day." Gia mindlessly rubbed a tiny blood stain on the sleeve of her thick white jacket. "When we got back to the house," she said, "my brothers and I hosed down the wheel while Dad fixed the gears on the clock, replaced the hands, and installed a new mechanism for the chimes. He attached the clock to the wheel and hung it in the living room. It was so tacky, but he was really proud, you know?"

"Your mother must've *loved* that," Mara said.

"It was in my Nana's house, so Mom didn't really have a say." Gia stared at the steeple. "Dad told us we needed a name for the clock, gave each of us kids a vote. We could either call it The Wheel of Time or the Captain's Clock."

"And the winner was?"

"It was unanimous," Gia said. "The Wheel of Time."

"How meta."

"Funniest part though, that clock *never* worked, ever, ran way too fast. Dad took it down constantly and turned back the hands, but never figured out the problem. The chimes rang at noon and at midnight, but never twelve times, always eleven. Drove my mother crazy, but the rest of us thought it was hysterical."

"Is it still at the house?"

"Yep, been hanging above Nana's TV for seventeen years."

"With his big math brain and nothing but time," Mara said, "you'd think your dad would've fixed the thing by now."

My sister laughed. "I know, right?"

I sensed Gia's guilt as she poked fun at our father. He took pride in building things, found peace in tinkering, never met a household task he didn't tackle himself; electricians and plumbers be damned. Gia loved him fiercely when she was a kid, the same as she loved herself back then, before drugs turned her into someone unlovable. She wanted to tell Pops about the stranger she'd accidentally become, and that she'd changed back, that she was better now. But how would he react to the ugly truth? Knowing the severity of her addiction would challenge him more than any leaky faucet or loose doorknob. And she wondered if—*Beeeeeep!*

Luke pulled up in his black Grand Cherokee. On the passenger side, Brodie Potter lowered the window and stuck out his beach ball head. "You hotties looking to get lucky?"

Mara snared Gia's hand. "Too late to elope?"

"Way too late." As my sister licked her finger, she imagined drips of blood slowly creeping backward into the tiny crevice where her cuticle had been. Imagined the skin melding together, the cells finding one another again, and closing completely like nothing ever happened.

Outside Jocelyn's Cafe, a soulful brunch spot at the far end of town, the foursome climbed out of the Jeep. My sister gritted her teeth, and her cheeks went numb.

Thirty-year-old Brodie, wearing jeans and a fraternity sweatshirt, no coat, sprung ahead of the others and raced into the place. Gia didn't know her fiancé's older brother well. They'd met only once before, last May, when she and Luke drove to Chicago for a friend's wedding and spent a long night at Brodie's showy town house in Pittsburgh on the way home. Her first impression of him: shallow and arrogant. Her second impression: the same.

Luke opened the door for the women, then positioned himself behind my sister, hugging her while they waited at the counter for a hostess. "Let's warm you up." He nuzzled the back of her neck. "Can't be catching cold before your big day."

Gia closed her eyes, breathed in his body wash. "You mean *our* big day," she said as his beard rubbed against her cheek. "Mmm, you know I love that."

Though Jocelyn's was half empty, a sign near the entrance read: *Please wait to be seated.* They hadn't been there twenty seconds before Brodie bulled his way to a booth. "Not a ton of urgency out here in the sticks, huh?"

Mara slid in opposite Brodie, and my sister took a seat beside her. A middle-aged server named Mary Ellen wiped down the table, handed out menus, and filled four plastic cups with water. "Can I start you off with some drinks?"

"Thought you'd never ask." Brodie tossed his menu toward Mary Ellen. "I'll take a Manhattan, no ice, and eggs Benedict with extra hollandaise."

Luke glanced at Gia and Mara as they scanned a shared menu. "The rest of us need a few minutes," he said to the server. "Thanks."

Gia extended her leg under the table, stroked Luke's calf with her foot. She recalled the day they met, nearly three years earlier, though the details were still foggy; Oxy will do that. It was early March, and she was working the ticket counter at a contemporary art gallery in

Providence, when Luke walked in with a cute young woman. After my sister took his money, she handed him two brochures, and their eyes linked. The next day, he visited the gallery alone. When Gia's shift ended, they hit happy hour at Xaco Taco, had too many margaritas, and stayed till closing.

"Wanna get out of this place?" Luke asked her then.

"And go where?"

"Wherever people go to get out of places."

They strolled along the river, guided by a full moon, and talked till dawn. He made her laugh—a sound she'd almost forgotten how to make. Those first few hours were like magic, a fairy tale under a curtain of stars. It seemed too good, too soon. And one day later, right on cue, a pandemic shut down the world.

The couple spent the next three months exploring Providence with fresh eyes. Holding hands as they beat a path along Thayer Street, taking lunch breaks in the park with grinders from Jolly Roger's, and drinking beer on the rooftop of Luke's Federal Hill apartment, while a neighboring Italian bakery teased their nostrils with homemade focaccia.

Gia had dated white guys before but hadn't felt what she felt with Luke, described it to Mara as feeling "less alone." She jumped *heart*first into her new addiction while keeping her old one hidden. Something about him stirred her spirit, and she ached for him when they were apart. As they got more serious, she felt compelled to tell Luke about her struggles. Her drug use had been a kind of armor to protect her from reality. Now she had a choice: either unbuckle the armor or leave it on. She unbuckled. On the first of August 2020, she revealed her problem and asked for his help. Four months later, she checked into a rehab facility in Westerly for a five-week detox program.

Mary Ellen balanced two platters of food like she was part of a circus act. She set a glass of chardonnay next to my sister's plate of avocado toast. "Here's your wine, sweetie."

Gia grabbed the edge of the table, bracing herself. "Excuse me, but I just ordered a cup of coffee."

The server reached for the glass. "Oh, I'm sorry. Let me take—"

"Leave that there," Brodie interrupted, his mouth full of Canadian bacon. "Someone will drink it, probably me."

Mary Ellen shot him a look and focused again on Gia. "I'll be right back with your coffee, dear. Would you like any milk with that?"

"Half-and-half, please."

Brodie snickered and winked at my sister.

She knew what he was thinking: *Just like you, huh?*

The Potter brothers were opposites. Luke quiet and creative, clear-minded and calm, steadiness personified with a dash of spontaneity, much like Pops used to be. Brodie reeked of ambition and agita, smugness and ego—a pigeon adorned in peacock feathers, much like our mother had become. The brothers grew apart once Brodie got his finance degree at Penn State, landed a job at a wealth management firm—owned and operated by his college roommate's father—and moved to western PA. Luke, an occupational therapist with a bachelor's from URI, heard from his older brother every few months— whenever Brodie called to brag about a salary bump or bonus. The weekend's "best man" never skipped a chance to prove it.

Luke reached across the table and put his hand on Gia's. She smiled and shook her head, bringing her kinky curls to life.

Mara raised her Stella. "To a long and happy marriage. Love y'all bitches to death."

Brodie swigged his Manhattan and smirked at Luke. "Yeah, and good luck surviving on fifty grand a year, little bro." He looked at Gia. "I doubt Georgia O'Keeffe here is gonna help much with the bills."

"G's got more talent in one earlobe than you'll ever have," Luke said.

"Oh, I'm sure she's got mad skills," Brodie said before belching. "You can tell me all about 'em after your wedding night."

My sister squirmed, face flushed, tugged on the collar of her sweater, and lowered her eyes. Her abstract art had never garnered much interest. She had a weeklong exhibit in Boston last summer, a favor orchestrated by a former RISD professor, but only sold two pieces for eight hundred dollars. Luke supported her effort and set up a studio in his spare bedroom, which was cramped and dimly lit. He encouraged my sister to give her passion another year before looking for other work.

From the time Gia first held a pen or a brush, our

mother fostered her creativity, praised her poetry, pushed her painting. At some point, Mom stopped praising but kept pushing. Her own creative dreams had stalled with her position as a high school art teacher, and she hoped Gia would gain greater success. But now those hopes were dying.

"I'm sorry." Mara tucked a lock of hair behind her ear and leered at Brodie. "I know we just met, but have you always been an asshole?"

"Don't worry, babe," Brodie said, "we got the entire weekend to get acquainted."

When Gia brought her coffee to her lips, Mara leaned forward and accidentally elbowed the cup, spilling hot liquid onto my sister's lap.

"Shit!" Gia yelled.

"I'm so sorry," Mara said.

"Good one, Morrigan," said Brodie with a cruel chuckle. "Or should I say *Moron*-igan?"

Luke grabbed two cloth napkins, soaked up the spillage. "You okay, G?"

"I'm fine," Gia said, and it sounded like a lie. "I'll be right back."

She hurried into the restroom, turned on the faucet, and wet a paper towel with warm water. Dabbing the stains, she avoided her reflection in the mirror, knowing what she'd see: the image of a porcelain doll who'd been dropped and shattered, then glued together again, showing no evidence that she'd ever been damaged, not a single crack across her vacant, smiling face. How could people not see her brokenness? To Gia, it was evident, something she felt in her soul more than she saw with her eyes.

As she headed back to the table, Brodie stood at the counter with the bill. When she tried to tiptoe past him, he grabbed her arm. "Not so fast."

"Ow, what's wrong with you?"

His sly grin contained a dash of sympathy. "I heard about your little problem."

"What problem?"

"Let's just say if you feel like jumping off the wagon this weekend, I got whatever you need." Brodie put a finger to his nose.

"I don't know what you're talking about."

"Oh, I think you do," he said. "I also think your perfect little Lukie isn't the steel trap of trust he claims to be."

Gia drew a fake smile, letting Brodie sketch his own conclusions. She couldn't imagine that Luke told his brother about her addiction, couldn't believe *anyone* would confide in Brodie. "It's almost two o'clock," she said. "I have to go."

"Hold on a sec," he said.

"No, Brodie." She hustled away, both saved and doomed by the time, trading a minor problem at the cafe for a giant one back at the inn, where our mother awaited.

✧

At a window in Old Saybrook, I watched Gia and Mara scoot into the lobby of the Cozy Cove, slalom around a corner, and burst through the library door. The room was chilly and quiet, in organized disarray, crammed from floor to ceiling with antiques and books. For a second, my sister thought being ten minutes late was no big deal.

But to our mother, Iris, it was a big deal. "Have we no regard for punctuality?"

"Sorry, Mom, lunch went longer than expected," Gia said.

"Hmm." In a statement-making black pantsuit, our mother posed, prim and proper, in the room's corner next to a dusty marble bust of the Narragansett tribal leader Canonchet.

Stanley and Helen Nielsen, proprietors of the Cozy Cove, stood stiff against the wall. The Nielsens, a loving couple in their seventies, hardworking but frail, had bought the historic home forty-five years earlier, converted it into an inn, and funneled every earned dollar back into the place. But the mansion's decaying outward appearance and eerie reputation kept customers away and prevented the Nielsens from turning a profit.

I recognized Helen's soul but couldn't remember from where or when. After watching my family for years, I'd seen familiar souls from my earlier lifetimes. But I had no memory of who I was before and couldn't place them. As for Helen's body, it was slight and withering. Despite her prune-like face and pearl white hair, she looked younger when she smiled. Her raggedy outfit: window drapes reincarnated as a blouse and skirt. Stanley slouched quietly next to his wife, timeworn chestnut eyes taking in every movement in the room, aware but not outright staring. He had badly cut, thinning hair as though trimmed by a distracted barber. Clothes pressed and mismatched. Black-and-white checked flannel shirt. Faded blue jeans exposing his ankles. Red suspenders.

Gia planned to hold the wedding ceremony in the library, the largest of seventeen rooms, with striking features. Red and gold rug, with tassels on the corners, sprawled across dark hardwood. An enormous crystal chandelier. Three separate conversation areas furnished with ornate loveseats, plush maroon chairs, and coffee tables with golden lion's feet. Alongside a tall wall on the left, a thousand books perched on dozens of shelves. Above the fireplace at the front, a massive wooden mantel with another fifty-odd hardcovers lined in a row. On the wall opposite the books, two large double-hinged windows with heavy curtains that matched the chairs.

"Damn." Mara locked arms with Gia. "This will be perfect tomorrow, G."

"Let's hope so." My sister glanced at our mother. "I'm only getting married once."

Mom ignored the comment and paced the perimeter of the library, disturbing every molecule in the air while scanning for imperfections. From across the room, Gia noticed for the first time in years how much she resembled our mother. The same dark, tight curls bouncing above their shoulders. Same curvy shape and wrinkle-free skin, belying their thirty-six-year age difference. Same height and weight. On the outside, the women were carbon copies.

Our mother paused in the middle of the room and glared at the Nielsens. "Could one of you please take my daughter's coat?"

Helen snapped to attention. "Oh, gosh, I'm sorry about that. How rude of me." She stretched out her matchstick arms like a sinner waiting for communion. "Please, ladies, let me take those for you."

"Thanks so much." Mara offered her thigh-length mink.

"I appreciate it," Gia said, down jacket in hand, cheeks blushed.

As Helen took the coats, my sister wondered, *How can a sweet couple like the Nielsens operate an inn called "Hell House?"* But Gia wouldn't ask directly, partly out of respect, mostly out of fear.

"Stanley, move this furniture to the side," Mom said. "I need to visualize what I'm dealing with here."

Stan cleared the area, aided by the bride-to-be and maid of honor, who moved two chairs apiece. My sister kept her smile to herself when the "Jacoby Family Musical Chairs Challenge" crossed her mind. Another lifetime ago, on rainy summer afternoons at Nana Joan's house in Old Saybrook, our mother would arrange kitchen chairs in a circle and play her favorite Motown CDs, while I marched around the ring with my father and siblings. When the music stopped, Mom would fall into hysterics as Pops scrambled around like a jittery jester, pretending he couldn't find a seat. If it weren't for our father, I would've been out first every time.

"We'll hold the vows in front of the fireplace," Mom said, "with six large candelabras evenly spaced along the walls, and guest chairs in a semicircle right here." She waved her hand above the red and gold rug. "Let's take this up. I hate the colors."

Stan yanked the rug away, revealing a detailed carving in the dark wood: a giant green serpent twisted in the shape of an infinity symbol, and swallowing its own tail.

"My goodness," Mom scowled. "Cover this eyesore."

"That's the Ouroboros," Helen said, "an ancient emblem of eternal destruction and rebirth, a unique piece of artistry, original to this house."

Iris scoffed. "It's horrid."

As Stan pulled the rug over the snake, Gia cleared her throat and tucked her hands into her pockets. "Mom, I think we should separate the chairs so I can walk down the—"

"Baby, don't worry," our mother said. "I'll take care of everything. You just focus on being gorgeous tomorrow."

"Okay, but maybe—"

"Did I hear you booked a DJ?" Mom went to the front of the room. "I still don't know why we didn't get a string trio."

Our mother had always criticized Gia more than me or Russell, because she was the oldest child, and she was a girl. Mom's slights squashed my sister's spirit, led her to believe she was a disappointment, unable to be trusted. Gia grew up fearing failure, being imperfect, and making dubious choices that proved our mother right—like getting herpes from Joey Sardinia and quitting drama club in high school. She second-guessed herself and struggled with identity, while Mom played puppet master, crushed Gia's confidence, and pointed her down a path of lies.

Mara stepped forward. "The DJ was my idea, Mrs. Jacoby."

"It's Hyde." Mom hated it when people got her name wrong and suspected her daughter's friend hadn't made an honest mistake.

"Sorry," Mara said. "But Gia deserves her favorite music for her wedding. Plus, it's New Year's Eve tomorrow!"

Our mother smacked her lips, dismissing Mara's rationale. "I guess we'll stick him in the corner by the Indian head."

Gia smiled. "The DJ can play songs you like too, Mom." She did a little dance and snapped her fingers. "Some Chaka and Gladys, maybe some Aretha."

"Fine then."

That was our mother's way of ending a conversation. *Fine then.* Two small words Gia heard on the phone every three weeks. Eight simple letters which, like a Pavlovian bell, caused my sister to regret letting the woman back into her life. But when Gia got clean, she promised to restore her tainted relationships. Mom was first on the list.

Our mother never realized the extent of my sister's addiction, only that she had "experimented" during college. Gia's adult life had been littered with petty crimes, emergency room visits, multiple eviction notices, and a two-week stay at a homeless shelter in Providence. But Mom didn't even have an address for her daughter until two years ago. And she'd never know the hollowness in Gia's heart, the helplessness in her soul, the night my sister sat on the ledge of an overpass above Route 95, bony legs dangling, staring at the traffic below. Ready to plunge into a river of headlights.

When Tom Hyde walked into the room, Gia's stomach flipped, and bile gurgled up in her throat. She'd been to dinner with Mom and her second husband a couple of times and liked him well enough, but he was a little *extra* and our mother stomped on him like a bath mat. The nausea had nothing to do with our stepfather though, everything to do with my sister's morning sickness.

"Hey, how's our little girl?" Tom said as he adjusted his glasses and crept toward Gia with open arms.

"Hi, Tom." Her hug was more duty than greeting.

"You know, sweetie, I was telling your mom this morning, if Jake decides not to come tomorrow, I'd be honored to walk you down the aisle."

"Pretty sure my dad will show up," Gia said. "But thanks."

"Well, don't rule it out." He brushed lint off the lapel of his tweed sports coat. "I'm here if you need me."

Gia forced a grin, caught Mara mid eye roll.

"Am I the only one drinking here?" The question barreled into the room just before Luke's parents, Bill and Beth Potter, stepped in. Fondling a tumbler of Dewar's with one hand and his wife's waist with the other, Bill gifted Gia and Mara a distinguished and disarming smirk.

"God, he's hotter than George Clooney," Mara whispered and nudged my sister. "Like a frickin' rich man's George Clooney."

Beth, an ordained minister and the officiant for the wedding, guided her husband to where Mom stood.

"You must be Gia's mother," the clergywoman said. "It's a pleasure to meet you."

Mom nodded, eyeballed Beth's royal blue dress and beige sweater. "Likewise."

My sister sidled up to her in-laws-to-be and hugged them lightly. "I'm so happy to see you guys."

Gia wasn't sure if they were happy to see *her* though. She'd met them two Novembers ago, before she got sober, at the Potters' timeshare in Vermont, an hour from their home in Burlington. My sister was high all three days of that ski trip, distant and aloof, had embarrassed Luke for certain. He'd cleared the air with his parents since then, only because they trusted him. *Will they ever trust me?* Gia wondered, and her stomach flipped again.

"Great to see you too," Beth said, and kissed my sister on both cheeks.

Mara stepped in front of Gia. "Hi, I'm Mara Morrigan, the twenty-eight-year-old who's *not* getting married this weekend."

Bill took Mara's hand. "If I were thirty years younger, Ms. Morrigan, you wouldn't be single for long."

Beth laughed and cut in. "We've been together for thirty-*five* years, Bill." She tilted her head and smiled. "Delighted to meet you, Mara."

Mom leered at Beth. "We just finished discussing the plan for tomorrow."

"Oh, I'm sure we'll figure it out," Beth said, her short sandy blonde hair shining under the chandelier. "These quaint ceremonies always seem to take form in the moment."

Bill wiggled in his jean jacket, stirred his drink with a finger, and winked at Mara. "I've taken a few forms in my day."

She winked back.

Gia swayed, the world spinning around her, and zoomed in on Mara. "Really?"

"Honestly, Beth, it's settled," our mother said. "Nothing more to discuss, is there, Gia?"

My sister flinched. "No, I suppose that—"

"When the flowers get delivered," Mom said, "Gia and I will display the arrangements, then meet with the photographer to run through the itinerary."

Bill took a gulp of whiskey and snickered. "If anything's wrong with those arrangements, Mara will tell me, and I'll do the deflowering."

Mara didn't blush, she purpled. Then she licked her lips.

Gia burned and hushed, "Seriously, Mar?"

"It's a joke," Mara said. "Relax."

Mom glared at the Nielsens as they stood near the hearth. "Stanley and Helen, maybe the Potters would like a tour of the house."

"No, thank you, we're fine," Beth said.

"Already found the bar," Bill added. "Nothing else I need to see."

Pulled a thousand miles away, Gia caught only echoes of the conversation. She wished she had the guts to tell Mom to back off, to stop controlling everything, to let her daughter have the sweet and civil wedding of her dreams. She wished our mother would admit that starting over was scary, that healing was hard, that fixing oneself didn't happen overnight.

I wished Mom still missed me like she did ten years ago, wished she'd say so aloud. But no one in my family talked openly like that. Not anymore.

Gia's belly gurgled again. "Excuse me, everyone." She put a palm over her lips, bolted from the library, stepped into the foyer and whirled. As the sourness rose, she swiveled and searched for the restroom. It wasn't where she thought. She glanced down the hall. Nothing. Ducked into the dining room. Nope. She'd never make it upstairs in time. *Oh God.* My sister pushed open the front door, staggered onto the porch, leaned over the railing. She gagged and coughed and threw up so violently, it seared her throat. A tear streamed alongside the curve of her nose. And she shivered.

THREE

Iris, or diamonds

MY MOTHER RAN a rigid finger along the mahogany mantel. "Hmm," she said, loud enough for the Potters and Nielsens to hear.

With Gia gone, and Mara chasing after her, the library took on a darker tone. The meager midafternoon sun, straining against thick windowpanes, promised to slink away soon. A quietness settled into the bookshelves, and the glass chandelier swayed as if trying to avoid the uneasy air.

"I'll put a kettle on for tea." Helen wiped her palms on her apron and displayed a flat smile. "Would anyone like to see the dining area?"

Mom led the way, chin first. She'd written off the Nielsens' ability to pull off the wedding, couldn't believe they'd kept the inn afloat for nearly half a century. The place was severely run-down—stained ceilings from water damage, drafty windows, wallpaper shedding in every room. The house didn't meet my mother's standards, and neither did the Nielsens. On top of it all, Mom couldn't open the closet in her bedroom. Stan had told her there was no key; the door had been locked since he and Helen bought the place.

Across the foyer, opposite the library, the dining room boasted four round oak tables with four chairs each and yellow lace tablecloths. Cylindrical sconces, two per wall, produced a low glow, while heavy curtains draped the windows and splintery wainscoting surrounded the perimeter. As Mom walked around, the pinewood floor creaked.

Beth surveyed the room, showed off a broad grin. "What a classic space."

Stan tipped an invisible hat. "We appreciate that, ma'am."

Scanning the area, my mother planned the seating arrangement in her head, recalled the dinner menu, mentally ran through the itinerary. *Something's missing*, she thought and tossed a glare at Helen. "You have the centerpieces, correct?"

Helen looked at Stan, then at Mom. "Um, I didn't know about those."

Behind the kitchen's double doors, the teakettle whistled.

Stan looked at Helen, then at Mom. "Were we supposed to get a delivery?"

"I sent you an email last week," my mother said. "The Waterford vases were ready for pickup at Brennan's in Newport ten days ago. You confirmed you would handle it."

"Oh dear, now I remember," Helen said. "I am so sorry. It must've slipped my mind with everything going on."

The kettle blared.

"I should get that," said Helen, and she scurried off.

Stan grumbled, "I'll head out to Brennan's now, catch 'em before they close."

Tom took a half step forward. "That's okay, Mr. Nielsen. I'll go."

"No you won't," said Mom. "We're going to the jewelry store this afternoon. I need something nice to wear tomorrow."

"C'mon, Iris," Tom said. "I'll be back in under an hour."

"You and I are leaving for that store in twenty minutes."

Stan shuffled past Tom and nodded. "Thanks for the offer."

Mom's relationship with her second husband hadn't always been one-sided. In 2009 Tom Hyde became the principal at Pathway Regional High in New Haven, where my mother taught art, where Pops used to teach math before switching to a local community college. Riding high after the country elected its first Black president, Mom saw some of Barack Obama's charisma in Tom. The coworkers spent an increasing amount of time together: green tea in the teachers' lounge, martinis after work. He was five years younger, which excited my mother, and Tom made her laugh, as my father once had. Plus, she was attracted to his principal's salary, which was twenty grand more than my dad's. Mom had claimed she leaned on Tom for support only after my death in 2012, but she'd slept with him at a Holiday Inn a year earlier.

"You know, Iris, if the vases don't work out," Beth said, "a simple votive would make a pretty centerpiece."

"The vases *will* work out," my mother snapped.

Bill slung an arm around Tom's shoulder. "Can I buy you a pop, my main man?"

"That doesn't sound too bad," Tom said.

Mom scowled, couldn't envision a world where Tom would be Bill Potter's "main man." And she let them both know with her loud silence.

Tom caught her staring, cleared his throat, dislodged a sigh. "Maybe later, Bill."

Beth smoothed the wrinkles on a tablecloth and smiled at my mother. "Actually, a celebratory drink sounds wonderful. Why don't we all meet up for a glass of wine after dinner?"

Beth's gentle tone sparked special memories in my mother. The kindness in the minister's cadence, the calmness in her voice, reminded Mom of someone. It was the same way Ruby Reed, her grandmother, used to talk to her when young Iris needed to escape a terrifying reality. When her parents and seven siblings called her a "piece of shit." When their pinches and slaps became punches and slugs. When Philadelphia—and everyone in it—were too big and too mean for a pudgy, blue-eyed Black girl to battle by herself. On those dark days, Grandma Ruby would set a plate of pecan cookies in front of my mom, unbraid her hair, and sing old church hymns for hours, as if fate could be turned with the wave of a wand. Then she'd re-braid the little girl's hair until the cookies, the hymns, and the hurt were all gone.

The conversation in the dining room lapped back and forth, from candles to tables to vases. When a young family of five appeared in the doorway, Mom craned her neck, and her penciled-on eyebrows narrowed. The father and mother, fair-skinned and blond, in their mid-twenties, looked exhausted. Two of their disheveled daughters darted away, zipped around the room, giggled and squealed. Mom followed their movements. The youngest child had a head of blonde curls, nursed a pacifier, and spun in circles, while the towheaded middle girl held a stuffed rainbow pony close to her chest and skipped to a made-up song. The eldest daughter wore a tattered green dress and was almost invisible against the wall. My mother assumed the girls were two, four, and ten years old.

"Excuse us," the young woman said in a voice that sounded like it could nap for days. "Do you have an available room for two nights?"

The question skirted past my mother as she sized up the older of the three sisters. The child's shoulder-length hair was windswept and wayward, not quite black, the color of dusk. Clothes appeared borrowed, face looked ashen, like she'd eaten a bowl of cinders for lunch. Bruised eyes, from a lack of sleep, perhaps. A dark red burn mark around her neck.

"Well, good afternoon." Helen straightened her paisley skirt and walked toward the couple. "We do have one room that—"

"I'm sorry," my mother interjected, "we're holding a private event here this weekend. I'm sure there's a vacancy elsewhere in the area." Mom had a talent for cutting others down, a nose for picking out the meek; she went straight at them like an experienced commuter went for the best seat on a train.

"That's just the thing," the man said, "we've checked five other hotels, but they're all booked. We were on our way to Maine, didn't want to go any farther with the storm coming. Hoped we could wait it out here."

Mom scoffed.

"Right this way," Helen said and danced toward the lobby. "I'll check you in." She peered back at my mother and wagged her head.

Lagging near the door, the young woman called out, "Katie, bring Maura please!"

When Katie, the middle daughter, took her little sister's hand and headed for the exit, the rainbow pony slipped from her grip and fell next to Mom's black boots. Both girls stopped in their tracks, looked up at my mother like she was a mountain to climb—a terrifying, unclimbable mountain. Mom crouched and snatched up the pony, inspected it for a second, then held out her hand and smiled. "Here you go, Katie."

Off to the side, the eldest daughter in the green dress stood perfectly still against the wall with her hands folded before her. Gazing downward with blank, desperate eyes, she focused on her scuffed-up shoes, which didn't quite touch the floor.

∽

Dense clouds gobbled up the three o'clock sun and spewed out a murky haze, under which Wickford lay hidden, protected by a thousand Narragansett spirit-warriors who'd taken the form of fog. "Free spirits," the ones who'd crossed over into the heavenly realm, were unlimited and unstoppable in their movements and desires. By staying with my family in the ghost world, I'd rejected those powers.

Some shops on Main Street had shuttered early, braced for the storm, their blinds covering windows like drowsy eyelids. At the end of town, Tom Hyde parked his Range Rover in a gravel lot next to the Silver Lady jewelry store. After he exited and opened my mother's door, she stepped out and pulled up the collar of her faux fur. There was no wind, but the cold stuck to her cheeks.

When the couple pushed into the Silver Lady, the bell above the door jingled. An elderly manager, sleepy-eyed and spindly, arose from a chair behind a long glass case. "Good afternoon, folks." He wore an eager grin, like he hadn't seen a customer in weeks. "My name is Raymond. How may I help you?"

"We're somewhat pressed for time but in the market for a necklace," Tom said, holding his glasses up to the light, checking for rogue smudges. "Something to match my wife's beauty and elegance."

My mother glared at him, and he cut his compliments short. Mom had packed several necklaces for the weekend, had other options for the ceremony, but she always wanted more.

Raymond tilted his head, smiled, and snapped his fingers. "Let me guess, it's your ruby anniversary?" He scuttled to the far end of the counter. "Forty years of bliss deserves a gem like this right here." From the display case, he removed a gold chain with a blood-red teardrop pendant that spun and shimmered in the track lighting overhead.

"We've only been married seven and a half years," Tom said. "But that's a gorgeous piece, don't you think so, dear?"

"Not exactly what I had in mind," Mom said.

She hated it when Tom told anyone how long they'd been married, thought people would make wild assumptions and fabricate scandalous stories about a handsome Black couple in their sixties, well off and recently wedded. Stories about infidelity and divorce—stories that actually told the truth. My mother imagined herself under oath, accused of treason against her own family, arguing her side of things, waiting to be judged and sentenced.

Raymond produced several other exquisite necklaces, delicate and dainty, with price tags north of eight hundred dollars. Affordable? Of course. But for Mom, the *ability* to spend trumped the act of spending itself, and nothing of average value satisfied her.

Thirty minutes passed.

The manager sighed. "I'm afraid we'll have to wrap this up, folks." Outside, an angry flurry announced a dangerous prophecy, fierce flakes falling quietly, one by one, and all at once, like the stealthy boots of an approaching army. Raymond hung the last of his samples on a plush purple perch. "Closing up shop early before the nor'easter."

In a nook at the back of the store, my mother peered into a small case on a pedestal and knocked a nail on the glass. "Show me this one, please."

With nimble fingers, Raymond withdrew the necklace from the case and held it up to the light. "Ah yes, our interlocking double-heart diamond necklace set in fourteen-karat gold with matching eighteen-inch chain."

"It's stunning," Tom said. "Try it on, dear."

Raymond flinched. "This is quite an expensive item," he said before handing it over to Mom. "I insist you handle it with extreme care."

My mother coiled the chain around her neck, secured it in place, and flattened the interwoven hearts against her skin. "How much?"

"Twelve hundred eighty-five," Raymond said like a proud papa.

"I'll give you nine fifty," she replied.

"We don't negotiate, ma'am."

"One thousand."

"I'm sorry."

Tom inched nearer to his wife. "Let's buy it, babe," he whispered. "Consider it a late Christmas gift. We can put it on the Visa." Her second husband didn't come from money, nor was he made of it, but he never balked at a chance to make Mom happy.

My mother grabbed the neck of a looking glass, held up the mirror. "It's the principle, Tom, not the price." But it *was* about the price. Though Mom had her share of regrets, none annoyed her more than taking a lump sum from my father in the divorce settlement. Had she made other arrangements, she'd still be collecting alimony. Those arrangements, however, would've included not marrying Tom.

She fiddled with the clasp on the chain, contorted her face, and bit her lip. The necklace wouldn't come off and got twisted in her hair. "Jesus Christ."

Sweat formed on Raymond's furrowed forehead. "Let me help you with that, ma'am." He balled his hands into fidgety fists and raised them in front of his bow tie.

My mom glowered, almost snarling. "I'm good." She tugged at the chain, untwined it from her hair, and swiveled the clasp to the front. Chin on her chest, she stared into the neckline of her black blouse and flicked the stubborn clasp with a nail.

"Here, honey, let me try." Tom put his hands on hers, tried to separate them.

She held fast. "I've got it." She spun the chain around again.

"Hold on a sec." Tom moved behind her and grabbed at the necklace.

Mom shrugged and jerked away from him.

The clasp broke, and the chain loosened. Interlocking hearts slid off, cascading onto the carpet. My mother picked up the pendant and scrutinized it in her palm. Connected but not identical, the two hearts stared back at her. The larger one sported the diamonds, while the smaller one, made of plain gold, lacked luster and clung to the other. Mom thought of me and Russell, our similarities and disparities. And then she thought of Gia, the fragile connector who, once upon a time, before she broke and slipped away, had tied our family together.

My brother and I weren't identical, though most people couldn't tell us apart, specifically those who thought all light-skinned Black boys looked alike. We were inseparable as kids, but once we hit middle school, he outgrew me in every way—aided by an unfair four-inch growth spurt. At Hopedale High, we didn't take the same classes and never hung out. He had tons of friends, while I only had a few. Russell was Mr. Popular, the star athlete with a gleam in his eye and a surplus of swagger, while I was his twin with asthma. Pops and Gia treated us the same, as if we were at all alike, but Mom looked at us differently, had more time for my brother, more smiles, more hugs. Limited by shyness, the coordination of a newborn giraffe, and frequent emergency breathing treatments at the hospital, I was a disappointment, worthless in my mother's eyes. Some nights, when she came home late, she petted my head while I pretended to sleep. Other times, she ignored me entirely. After I gained the wisdom that came with death, and had the ability to read her thoughts, I discovered the truth behind her callousness: she saw weakness in me, and too much of herself. We were breakable, she and I, like brittle pieces of jewelry, susceptible to the softest touch. But only one of us could fit under her protective glass case.

The store manager pried the pendant from Mom's grasp. "You'll need to leave right now," Raymond said, his old eyes on fire.

"Our apologies," said Tom.

Out on the sidewalk, an anchor of cold weighed down the day, and the mad flurry whipped, while the wind wailed warnings of the worsening storm. My mother held out her gloved hand and let the flakes settle onto the leathered palm. The crystals dissolved into the material, vanished as though they had never been there. She got into the car and gazed into the pure white windshield, her snow-flecked lashes unblinking. She hated winter, but not as much as she loathed spring.

When I was alive, my pollen allergies sprung up in early March, and the changing of seasons filled Mom with anxiety. On its own, my asthma was a challenging, yet manageable, fact of life; allergy season, however, was the wildcard. For most people, blooming daffodils and budding elms signaled hope, a sign of better days ahead. For me, they sounded an alarm. If my mom didn't keep my nightstand drawer stocked with pharmaceuticals, I'd be doomed. Those pills, inhalants, and liquids were my white knights. Without them, lethal allergens freely pelted and pierced the tissue-paper lining of my lungs every spring, like swarms of diamond shards. My family knew I was hyper-allergic to pollen. But not to cats.

My mother hustled onto the rickety porch of the hulking old inn, which seemed to lurch and croak whenever anyone approached, and her boots left footprints on the snowy steps. She made a mental note: *tell Stan to shovel and salt.* Downy flakes had speckled her curls, matching her graying roots, and she ordered Tom to pick up a box of Dark and Lovely hair color at CVS, hoping to knock ten years off her appearance after her next day's appointment with Gia's stylist.

In the foyer, Mom hung her fur on the rack and shrugged away the cold. She peeked into the library and dining room, found no one. Checked her watch: ten past four. *Gia should be here.* Their meeting with the wedding photographer was supposed to start in five minutes. She took her phone from her bag and—

"You must be Gia's mama."

My mother wheeled and faced a slim woman in her mid-forties. The stranger wore a jean jacket and had a silver nose ring shaped like a horseshoe pierced through her septum. Eyes were puffy and red, like she'd been rubbing dreams out of them. Short pink hair, a web of live wires. Mom stared three seconds too long before speaking. "And you are?"

"Chrysalis." The woman extended her hand. "The photographer."

My mother stared at the hand like she'd been offered a liverwurst sandwich.

"I'm Gia's friend." Chrysalis plucked a business card from her back pocket.

Mom confirmed the information and lightly grasped the photographer's fingers. "Good to meet you. My daughter will be down in a minute."

The ladies stood apart, wedged by an awkward silence.

Mom texted Gia: *GET DOWN HERE NOW.*

Chrysalis removed her jacket, tossed it onto the seat

of an antique chair. She sported a ripped black tank top that read, *Is It Gay in Here, or Is It Just Me?* My mom pursed her lips, tried to decipher the colorful tattoo sleeves coating the photographer's arms, made out Bob Marley's face on one shoulder, a cobra on the other.

While Chrysalis filed through her equipment bag, my mother pretended to check her phone. Around the corner in the dining room, the ticking grandfather clock conversed with the creaking floorboards. Mom sighed and, against her instincts, begrudgingly broke the ice. "So, how do you know my daughter?"

Chrysalis looked up from her bag. "Oh, we met at Brightstar last year."

"Brightstar?"

"The rehab center."

The ice: obliterated.

Mom and Gia had discussed rehab only once, after my sister graduated from RISD and promised our parents she'd pull herself together. But when the issue died, nobody followed up on the conversation. Pops remained concerned while Mom simply moved on, and Gia spent the next six years hiding the truth from them both.

My mother coughed, expelling a lump of surprise. "And how long have you been taking pictures?" Changing the subject was her superpower.

"Since I was a kid, really." In the photographer's eye, a tiny spark jumped and clicked its heels. "Feel like I've always had an ability to, you know, just point my camera and find the honesty in a person, kinda capture their soul on film."

My mother shifted her weight, glanced over her shoulder at the staircase, listened for an unheard noise. "Gia should be down soon."

"It's fine, we can start without her," Chrysalis said. "Where's she holding the actual ceremony?"

"*We* are holding the ceremony in the library," Mom said. "This way." She started down a short hallway with the rehabilitated shutterbug in tow.

As my mother thought ahead to the wedding, she imagined having to face my father and brother again, suspected they'd always known about her affair with Tom, figured my grandmother had told them. Since the divorce, Mom had put her infidelity behind her and buried her guilt in a forest of bygones. She sneered at a memory: an August weekend in 2011, when my dad took Gia and me to one of Russell's basketball tournaments in DC, when Nana Joan "stopped by" our Hopedale home unannounced and stumbled upon Tom Hyde zipping up his fly outside the hall bathroom. My mother hoped Nana fell for her excuse, that Tom was there on school business. Joan Jacoby, however, was no rube.

The photographer stepped through a grand doorway and into the library. Flames danced in the fireplace, while a chorus line of lights flickered on the bookshelves. "What an incredible room," Chrysalis said as she spun, camera clicking. "Absolutely perfect."

Clip-clop. Clip-clop. The sound emanated from the hallway, and Mara Morrigan clamored in. "Oh my God, you guys, I am so sorry."

My mother narrowed her eyes at the tangerine blonde,

had never been fond of Mara's tight-fitting wardrobe, country club upbringing, or the sisterly relationship she shared with Gia.

"Okay, so our girl still feels like crap," Mara announced, "and asked me to represent." She handed Chrysalis a sheet of paper. "I heard you're the most amazing photographer. So, like, here's a list of stuff G wants you to shoot, and also sort of an itinerary for tomorrow."

"May I see that?" Mom said and grabbed the paper. She perused the list and itinerary, shaking her head. "No, no, no. This is all wrong."

"It's what G wants," Mara said. "She told me to make sure—"

"My daughter doesn't know what she wants," Mom snapped, slaying Mara with a murderous smile. Then she turned to Chrysalis. "Let me show you the dining area, where we'll give the speeches and cut the cake."

After the three women ambled through the foyer and into the dining room, my mother stopped in the spot where the young girl had dropped her rainbow pony earlier. As Chrysalis scouted the space, Mom paid her no attention, but after a minute she said, "We can stage some nice color portraits there by the corner window."

"Sorry, Mrs. Jacoby." Chrysalis put a finger to her lip. "For weddings, I shoot only black-and-white and hardly stage anything. It's kinda my rule."

"It's Mrs. Hyde," my mother said. "And tomorrow you can make an exception to your little rule."

"If you don't mind," the photographer said, "I'll check with Gia on that."

"Hmph." Mom brushed past Mara, ignoring her as if she were a houseplant. "Let's look at the sunroom."

My mother disregarded her art students in the same manner, demanded they take her personal approach, curbing their creativity. When teaching landscapes, she picked the panorama and the palette. When teaching cubism, she selected the figures and the fragments. Her talent, tenure, and temper held the school administration at bay, and complaints levied against her by parents and students fell on frightened ears. Time and again, Tom had urged her to retire, citing Mom's bucket-list desire to spend a winter in Paris, but she wouldn't give up her post.

The women entered the sunroom—a spacious area at the rear of the house with wall-to-wall windows—where the Nielsens would set up a post-ceremony cocktail station; Stan and Helen had already cleared the room and moved a portable bar into the corner. By the doorway, an ancient radiator hissed and spit, while Iris turned up her nose at the sound and smell, approached the widest window on the longest wall. The view out back extended past an expansive yard and into a desolate harbor. Coating the wide lawn and short beach: a thickening layer of snow.

"The wedding will begin at six thirty sharp," my mother told Chrysalis. "Then cocktails at seven fifteen, dinner at eight, and the reception from nine till midnight."

Mara slid between the two women. "Gia said she wants the party to go into the New Year, till at least one o'clock."

Iris ratcheted her head, alternated her gaze from

Chrysalis to Mara then back to Chrysalis. "You should take photos of the entire day," she continued with calculated coldness. "Starting at three when my daughter and I will get ready."

"Like I said," the photographer replied, "I'll check with Gia on all of this."

"You'll do what I ask." Iris stiffened. "I doubt you appreciate one-star online reviews."

"I don't read reviews."

"Well, I'm sure you'll read the amount on the check I write for you tomorrow."

Chrysalis smiled. "Actually, I won't."

"Excuse me."

"Your daughter helped me through some pretty shitty days," Chrysalis said, "convinced me I could change when no one else cared." She ran a hand through her pink hair. "This gig is on the house, a favor for her and Luke. The least I could do, really."

My mother nodded, gazed out at the harbor then back at the photographer. "Actually, the least you could do is clean yourself up tomorrow and pretend to be a normal human being."

As Mom left the sunroom, the radiator hissed and spit again.

FOUR

Russell, or voices

As my brother held his breath and shoved his forearm into a restaurant kitchen grease trap, fats, oils, and assorted liquids glazed his skin. Cleaning the trap was the worst part of his life, and he had to tackle the chore every four weeks.

His general manager position at the Blue Moose, a trendy New York City brunch spot, tested his stamina and patience. Early mornings, late nights, and a steady serving of aggravation filled his weeks. But the restaurant offered significant benefits, his boss was a good friend, and the casual dress code came in handy when it was time to clean the grease trap.

At the bathroom sink, Russell wiped the slime and stink off his sinewy forearms with a wet paper towel and peered into the mirror; my twin spent a lot of time looking at reflections in mirrors. He shook his headful of loose brown curls until the rat's nest settled into its natural form. Smiling his perfect smile, he pointed at his perfect image. "Still the man."

Between me and Russ, he had won the fraternal twin lottery, receiving our mother's flawless features, while I got our father's "rough good looks," which Pops said meant, "good-looking for an ugly guy."

As my brother dried his hands in the restroom, he heard voices from inside the restaurant, where a crowd had congregated for happy hour. But one voice, louder than any customer's, came from within. Since passing away, I'd put words in his head, but none more essential than what I said now: *You need to go.*

Russell squeezed his eyes shut, as if that would make me leave. *Shut up*, he thought.

We'd always shared an unspoken bond, a silent communication, sort of like mind reading. When we were kids, we used our ability for silly things—like guessing how many fingers we held behind our backs, finishing one another's sentences, bringing each other snacks without needing to ask. We called our power "twin magic." But no matter what I said to Russell now, his conscience told him he was nuts. He wanted to move on, wanted peace.

After my brother left the restroom and moved to the front of the restaurant, a middle-aged man wearing a beret and a cardigan stepped in front of him. "Are you the manager?"

"Yes, sir. Can I help you?"

"Do you control the music here?"

"I do."

"My wife and I are trying to enjoy a late lunch, and we're highly offended by the song that's playing right now."

Russell tilted his head. Over the din of the crowd, Kanye West's "Gold Digger" pumped through the ceiling speakers, taking its turn on Blue Moose's upbeat and eclectic playlist. It was the clean version, no N-words, no cursing. "Is it the artist or the lyrics that you find offensive?" Russ asked.

The man raised a brow. "Does it matter?"

My twin gave in. "No, it doesn't. Give me a second." He received annoying complaints like this every day: the music too loud, the service too slow, the food too cold. And whenever customers lost control and got heated, he didn't argue with them. In that way, my brother was a lot like Pops.

Russ hadn't landed his dream job yet, but he was getting close. As youngsters, we pledged to open up a restaurant together someday. He'd be the front man, the personality, the face of the operation. I'd be the brains behind the menu, decor, and overall vibe. By the time we turned ten though, he was a basketball prodigy, while life relegated me to the sideline. His talent tore him away from me, and he dropped our dream, picked it up again long after I was gone, when his hopes of playing pro hoops disintegrated. Now, four years into life as a working man, my brother kept our childhood goal on life support. But was it worth achieving alone?

He hadn't slept well the previous night—headaches were back again—and the day's monotony had sapped his energy supply. He went behind the bar, made himself a double espresso, and washed down three Advil; his shift wouldn't end for another few hours, and he doubted he'd stay upright and clear-eyed till then without reinforcements. His phone lit up, a text from his girlfriend.

Izzy: *Need to leave soon. Can you come home?*

A busboy dropped a platter of dishes. Food and drink spilled and splattered. Plates and glasses rattled and shattered. Six Wall Street brokers at a table in the corner stood up, cheered, and applauded. One guy yelled, "Just put those anywhere, dude!" His friends laughed. Several patrons got up and left, including the man in the cardigan and his Yeezy-hating wife.

My brother rushed over to help the busboy clean up, and two servers joined the effort. Another staffer, the newest member of the team, an NYU student named Sam, tapped Russell on the shoulder. "Hey, man. I got a customer on the phone who wants to reserve a table for fifteen tonight at six. What should I say?"

"We don't take reservations." Russell didn't look up from the sweet potato fries he was scooping off the floor.

"But she says it's for a baby shower."

"Tell her they can show up and we'll do our best to make it work."

"Is six a good time, or should I tell her to come earlier?"

Russell dropped the fries onto the tray, stood, and faced Sam. "Yo, I don't care, just handle it, please." His voice, calm but direct. "Be honest, say you'll try to make it happen, but don't promise anything." My brother never gave advice he wouldn't take himself.

A shout, loud and angry, rang out from the kitchen.

Then another, louder and angrier. Russ scooted behind the bar and snaked his way to the grill area, where two cooks screamed in a standoff. As my brother moved between the combatants and held his hands up, flames sizzled and flew off the grill. "Hector, drop the knife," he called out to the bigger of the two men.

"Fuck that! Marcus better drop the cleaver first." Hector raised his blade.

"I ain't dropping shit!" Marcus puffed out his scrawny chest, adjusted his glasses.

Hector glared down at my brother. "I told you, Russ, I can't work with this *maldito* no more." The giant man's eyes were wider and wilder now. His lip twitched behind his heavy black beard, sweat poured off his bald head. The flames grew.

"You both need to relax," Russell said. "We got fifty people out there waiting for their goddamn food."

Marcus ripped off his grease-stained apron and flung it toward my brother. "You motherfuckers can make it yourselves. I'm out!" He tossed the cleaver onto the grill and left.

Another text appeared on Russell's phone.

Izzy: *Call me!*

When Russell dashed out onto the sidewalk, wind and cold shocked his system. His body trembled as if he were running a jackhammer, and he could hardly hold his phone. Rush hour commuters, wrapped in heavy coats, toasty under warm hats, whizzed around the intersection of Twenty-Sixth and Sixth. Before calling Izzy, my brother debated what to say. *How can I get her to stay?* He chided himself for not supporting her dream while making her wait for his.

A voice from behind: "Hey, Rusty, can you please come inside?" Blue Moose's most experienced server, a twenty-nine-year-old aspiring actress named Alisha, leaned her pretty face halfway out of the doorway and snapped her gum. "Someone, other than me, wants you."

Russell stowed his phone in the back pocket of his jeans and huffed hot breath onto his hands. "Who is it, Ali?"

"Bad news, dude. Health inspector."

"You kidding? Now?" He followed Alisha inside.

Unannounced health inspections occurred once a year for all city restaurants, but in his eighteen months on the job, Russell hadn't handled an inspection alone. He wished his boss, Slate Hetan, were there. With twenty-five years in the business, Blue Moose's owner knew all the inspectors by name and welcomed their cursory checkups and solid grades. My brother would never forget the sage and simple five-word instructional Slate gave him should he ever need to oversee an inspection: "Don't shit the bed, Jacoby."

Alisha pointed Russell toward the inspector, an older white woman holding a notebook and wearing gaudy makeup. She was short and slight, appearing to be in her early seventies. He approached her with slow steps. "Hello, ma'am. I'm Russell, the general manager." As he extended his hand, his phone vibrated in his pocket.

The woman glanced up at Russell and down her nose. "Elena Reichstein. Let's get this over with, shall we?"

Sweat beaded up on his forehead. "Um, I was actually wondering if we could do this some other time." He laughed a timid laugh. "Not sure if that's possible."

"It's not."

Russell phonied a smile, heart pounding like a frightened pony in a burning barn. He worried about the temperature in the fridge, the expiration date on the meat, the rats in the trash heap outside, and whether bald Hector should've been wearing a hairnet. Above all, he worried about his future employment at the Blue Moose.

"We'll begin in the kitchen." The woman opened her notebook, and when she clicked her pen, the tiny sound boomed in my brother's brain.

His phone vibrated again, and he touched the inspector's elbow. "Sorry," he said. "Can you excuse me for one second?" He stepped away and read the text.

Izzy: *Goodbye. I love you!*

The words were hot needles jabbing into his heart. He put a hand over his eyes, hung his head, tried to slow his breathing. He hit Slate on speed dial and waited. "C'mon, answer already."

"What's up, Jacoby?"

"Hey, man, there's a health inspector here." Russell's voice lost a race with his thoughts. "I got an emergency at home with Izzy. I really can't stay for this. Sorry."

"What the fuck, dude?" Slate said. "You flakin' out on me?"

My brother would never flake out on Slate. The grizzled restauranteur took a flyer on Russ after they met in Vegas two summers ago, convinced him to leave his bartending gig and move to New York, promised him the GM job based on intuition alone. Now they were like brothers, and if anyone could save Russ in a time of need, his brother would.

"Please, Slate. Can you cover for me?"

"Won't need to."

Russell shook his head, and blood pumped into his cheeks. "Are you firing me?"

"I would," Slate said, "if I didn't love messing with you so much. That inspector's my mom, you gullible dipshit."

When Russell turned toward the bar, Elena and Alisha offered sympathetic smiles. And in that humiliating second, my brother wished the health inspection had been real and Izzy's leaving was the joke.

"Go home," Slate said.

∽

Izzy Dominguez crammed the last of her clothing into a large suitcase and scurried across the apartment that she and Russell shared. The simple, comfortable third-floor one-bedroom had been good to the couple, as much as they'd been to each other, but the future was iffy for both units. Their time together would live on, it seemed, only in memories.

My brother and Izzy were breaking up; it was almost mutual. She was moving upstate for a job as an assistant editor at the *Poughkeepsie Journal*, a gig that wasn't supposed to begin until early February, but her new boss had called three weeks earlier and said he needed her a month sooner. Talented folks like Izzy were too valuable to keep waiting, he'd told her.

She locked her suitcase, steered it through a maze of boxes in the living room. "I'm sorry about all this stuff," she said. "The moving company will be here first thing tomorrow. You'll be awake by seven, right?"

Russell stared at a box marked *Fragile*. "Guess I don't have a choice." His comment burned his face, while Izzy's silence spread across her lips.

They met in June 2021 when the magazine she worked for sent her on an assignment in Las Vegas, where he worked tending bar. My brother fell hard the minute he saw her, a junior reporter from the Bronx with an inferno in her eyes, someone who might change the world, beginning with him. From the start, Russell saw his future with Izzy: marriage, three kids, an old colonial in New Jersey, a yellow Lab. But he wasn't ready to quit the Big Apple and his dream of being a restaurant owner in the apex of the culinary world.

And what of Izzy's dream? Her goal was to be a novelist, but my brother didn't know why she couldn't write a book in New York. Or why she insisted on hanging a painting of the Venezuelan national tree above their bed. Or why she always took the stairs up to their apartment instead of waiting five minutes for the lazy elevator. Or why she never talked about her father.

She flipped through a mound of papers on the kitchen table. "Have you seen the printout of my new lease agreement?" When a small purple envelope peeked out from under the pile, Izzy picked it up and flashed it close to my brother's face. "You saw this, right? The wedding is tomorrow."

Russell had ignored the invitation when it arrived, and left it buried under the junk mail. He received a text from Mom about the wedding a week back but still hadn't decided if he'd go. My twin almost never felt only one way. Should he attend and make amends with Gia? Should he share with Pops what I'd begged him to share for ten years? About the recurring dream that haunted him: me and my dad stuck on the side of the road, me fighting for air, Pops pounding on the steering wheel and weeping. Should Russ lay it all out there? Should he tell our parents about the vision he saw the night I died? When I appeared beside him in the dark while he was sleeping at a friend's house, woke him and whispered, *Tell them I'm okay.*

Would they lock him in a rubber room if he said any of that?

I had to connect with my twin, get him to share our secret with Pops, but Russell worried about our family being together in Wickford, the havoc it would create, the horrific memories it would conjure. With his headaches more intolerable of late, he'd be a mess at the wedding without Izzy, the person who believed in him the most. She was the backbone of the relationship, the one who said what she meant and advocated for the truth. My brother, diplomatic and thoughtful, never confronted anyone, especially in our family. But Izzy Dominguez had a surplus of moxie, and a strong enough voice for them both.

As she zipped through the apartment, from bathroom to kitchen to bedroom, Russell followed then stopped beside their unmade double bed. "Please, come to the wedding with me," he said, slouching.

She moved around to her side of the bed. "My bus leaves in an hour. My job starts in three days. The journal helped me get into a new condo. I need a minute to get settled."

My brother grabbed at an invisible straw. "What about our rent? How can I afford this place on my own?"

"We talked about this." Izzy shook her head. "You knew this day was coming. Break the lease and find a studio. Or get a new roommate. Or ask your mom for a loan and stay here till you move into a new place. You have options, Russ, but you have to do something."

Her words stunk of a familiar appeal, common as dirt in our family. My brother closed his eyes, lowered his chin. "I know." He'd told Pops that same thing: *You have to do something.* Bowled over by trauma, our father hadn't picked himself up in the years since my death. Now Russ was taking a turn as the toppled statue.

Izzy walked around the bed and took my brother's hand. "Hey, look at me."

He picked at the black rubber band around his wrist, the one that held my stack of Pokémon cards together when I was young. He'd found the cards before he left for college and wore the rubber band ever since. By now though, it was loose and cracking, deteriorated, had lost almost all elasticity.

"We got something special, baby," Izzy said, her voice rising and falling. "You know I want you to come with me. I've told you I want to make this work."

Her declaration shot into his ears, jammed up in his throat, was hard for him to swallow. He locked in on his boots. "I just need time to think."

She shielded her face from him, and Russell knew she was crying, but where were his tears hiding? She placed her apartment key on the purple envelope on the kitchen table. "If you're staying, promise me you'll go to Gia's wedding." Izzy had blind faith in him, thought he could help unite our family, always told him he owed it to me to keep trying.

Stonelike in the bedroom doorway, my brother couldn't find the energy to reply and ended his search while the woman he loved retrieved her suitcase and backpack. His inertia surprised me. He was always the passionate twin; I was passive. He would spring when I froze. He didn't stand for what I tolerated. He swung back when life threw haymakers at me. He had a destiny; I had half-formed dreams—ones about happy families and growing up and endless summers at the beach, dreams I'd never fulfill.

Russell followed Izzy out of the apartment but stayed at the top of the staircase. She walked down the first flight and looked up. He should've said something, anything, and maybe he would've if she hadn't beaten him to it. "Call me when you're ready to talk," she said, then turned the corner and disappeared.

As he pressed his palms against his eye sockets, I called to him: *You need to go!* He tried to ignore me, fought the impulse to respond, and he knew I wasn't talking about Poughkeepsie.

❧

The City That Never Sleeps kept one eye open for the snow-storm a meteorologist on Channel 9 dubbed the "Thanos of blizzards."

Under bright streetlamps, pedestrians swerved down Manhattan sidewalks, eager to grab trains home to their families or drinks with friends. Russell pulled the frosted door handle of a bar called the Limbo, on Lafayette, around the corner from his apartment, about to escape the harsh winter air, but not the ruthless despair that gnawed at him since Izzy left for Port Authority twenty minutes earlier.

My brother ducked into the dark room, shed his flannel jacket, and sidled up to the bar, his hands sticking to the century-old oak. The usuals sat in their usual spots: Tommy the dispatcher near the door, Vincent the cobbler by the pool table, Clive the actuary closest to the restroom. The place smelled of stale popcorn and whiskey, while a Nat King Cole song warbled out of a jukebox.

Plopping onto a corner stool next to a wooden beam wrapped in white Christmas lights, Russell caught the bartender's eye. "All good, Hatch?"

The old man replied in his familiar rasp. "Same as always, kid. Not a care in the world, not a dime in my pocket."

My brother threw his eyes toward a bottle of Hiatus tequila and nodded at the barkeep. "I'll trade you all of my dimes for your zero cares."

Hatch grinned, reached for the liquor, and filled a

glass. As he pivoted to put the bottle away, he grabbed at his lower back. "Jesus."

Russell leaned forward. "You okay?"

"Yup." The man winced. "Just Father Time announcing my two-minute warning."

Hatch had never told Russell his actual age, only that he snuck into Ebbets Field for Jackie Robinson's first game in 1947 and helped build the Verrazano Bridge in 1959. Whenever my brother visited the Limbo, his friend recounted how the bridge was the longest suspension bridge in the world upon completion in '64. Tonight was no different.

Hatch examined a framed photo of the Verrazano displayed on the wall, got lost in his thoughts, then came back. "You know the secret to a sturdy bridge, kid?" Hatch savored his favorite question. "Each girder and—"

"—each cable has to do its job." Russell piggybacked onto the answer.

"Ay, you been listening." Hatch flashed a toothless smile.

My brother pulled out a bottle of Advil from his coat pocket, popped two pills with a swig of tequila, and peered at the row of glossy bottles on the shelf above the bar.

"Somethin' bothering you?" asked Hatch.

Russell couldn't bring himself to talk about Izzy, not yet anyway, and he'd already told his therapist-with-a-liquor-license all about the random asthma attack that killed me ten years back; not that my death bothered Russ anymore. But my brother valued Hatch's wisdom and unspooled a recent concern. "Nothing wrong," my twin said, "except some potential family drama at my sister's wedding this weekend."

"You want family drama?" Hatch said, scratching at his gray scruff. "My daddy was a truck driver his whole life, had a regular route from New York to Carolina. At his funeral, my mama and me discovered that man had a whole secret family down in Greensboro. People just came out of nowhere, saying they're my brothers and sisters. You believe that?"

Russell didn't have the heart to say he'd heard the story before. "Damn, how do you forgive something like that?"

"Shit." Hatch filled my brother's glass. "Forgiveness always sounds like the right thing to do till you got someone to forgive," he said. "Fact that my daddy was dead made it easier though."

Despite my brother's respect for the old man's openness, Russ wouldn't divulge his own dark secrets; my badgering him from beyond the grave was off limits, so too his recurring dream that revealed untold facts about my death—that Pops knew his car was low on gas, left his phone at home, turned a ten-minute ride to the hospital into an hour, and concealed the entire story. But Hatch deserved more than silence.

"I don't talk to my family much anymore," Russ admitted. "And I have weird dreams, man, get bad headaches, like there's a time bomb in my brain and I better start pulling wires before it explodes."

"Family can send us over the edge," Hatch said. "But

we ain't gonna be here forever, kid. Gotta do what we gotta do while we still got breath to do it." The old bartender drained the rest of the Hiatus into Russell's tumbler. "Cuz what happens after we're gone is anyone's guess."

My brother gazed into the glass, at the glimmer of Christmas lights swimming in the alcohol. "Wish my pops could hear you say that."

"Why don't you tell him yourself?"

"Maybe I will," Russell said. "I got a good enough buzz right now." He slid off his stool, made his way over to the pool table, and dialed our father. While the phone rang, my brother rolled the eight ball down the length of the table and awaited its return.

Pops answered. "Hey, son, got my hands full, can't really talk right now."

"Yeah, okay," Russ said. "Just wondering if you're going to Gia's wedding."

"Not sure, gotta see how your grandmother feels in the morning. You?"

"Don't know yet. Might be weird, you know, after all this time."

"Well, your sister would appreciate the effort, but it's up to you."

"All right, I'll let you know. Maybe we can—"

"Listen, son, sorry, I gotta go. Text me later, okay?"

"Yeah, of course. See ya, Pops." Russell stuffed the eight ball into the side pocket and shuffled back to the bar.

After Hatch persuaded Clive to head home to his

wife and gave Vincent coins for the jukebox, he faced my brother. "How's the old man, kid?"

"Busy, apparently, doesn't know if he's going to the wedding. Said he couldn't talk now, but I'm not sure it was the truth." Russ drummed his fingers on the sticky bar. "The guy never changes, always forces me to keep the connection."

"Like old bridges," Hatch said. "You can try to fix 'em, or you can let 'em fall."

Russell passed his empty tumbler from left hand to right, and back again. Should he go to Rhode Island or not? Would he survive the grueling gauntlet of meeting up with our family, hearing Mom's complaints, facing Gia again, watching Pops mope around, and waiting for the arguments to end? "What should I do, Hatch?"

"If you decide to go, what's the worst that happens?"

"We don't mop up our bad blood, the weekend is a fuckin' disaster, and the decision haunts me for the rest of my life."

"And what's the best?"

"By some miracle, we all get along and I regain my sanity."

"Shoot for the miracle, kid." Hatch winked. "Just be careful where you aim."

Russell texted Gia: *Congrats, see ya tmrw.*

FIVE

Jake, or clocks

SITTING ON COLD kitchen tiles, my father twisted his creaky body and wrestled with a wrench under his next-door neighbor's farmhouse sink, trusty toolbox at his feet.

For a former college professor, and master problem solver, fixing a leaky pipe should've been a cinch, but he'd been under that sink for a full hour. Though he had to get home and make dinner for his mother, finishing this favor for Anna Sikorsky would come first—Pops spent twice as much time maintaining Anna's beach house in Old Saybrook than Nana's, and the Sikorsky place was twenty years younger. If the other residents on Plum Bank Road paid closer attention, they'd say my dad and Anna were involved in a tryst. But they'd be wrong.

Pops ran calloused fingers through a thatch of gray on his head, stroked his unruly beard, grunted and grimaced. "This should do it," he said, turning the wrench. The pipe cracked and sprayed, soaked his corduroy pants and denim shirt. Renegade puddles collected on the Spanish porcelain tiles, seeped under the oven and fridge.

Anna laughed and flashed a clever smile. "Now you've done it, Jake."

"Sorry." Pops didn't mind making a mess of his own, but he hated disrupting other people's lives.

"Don't be silly," she said, placing a firm hand on his back. "How can I complain when you've done all the work?" She grabbed a mop from the closet while my father wrapped the pipe with electrical tape and sealed it with hose clamps.

He pushed himself upright, staggered to his feet, and leaned on the countertop. "That'll hold for a while," he said. "Give Paradis Plumbing a call later, ask for Mike, he's the best." My father eyed his cane across the room, in the corner by the sliding door that led to the back deck.

Anna put the mop down. "Can I get that for you?"

"No, thanks." Pops glanced at his neighbor, appreciated her looking out for him, though it often felt like pity.

He'd helped her out a lot over the past three years, ever since her husband, Greg, died of a massive heart attack, which his doctor called the "widow-maker." Pops sometimes wondered if Greg would care—assuming the dead cared about anything—if Anna remarried. My father found her attractive, in the same way all objects of a particular shape and size pleased his mathematical brain. The angular cut of her cropped auburn hair, her symmetrical facial features, her proportional build. But he hadn't asked her out; when Mom cut him loose, she severed his confidence too.

Anna's positive outlook, which had brightened over her sixty years, couldn't reach my father, who turned away from the light long ago. But he enjoyed her company, made himself available for any odd job: thawing frozen pipes, changing AC filters, hanging wall art and mirrors. In return, she helped him shovel in the winter and rake in the fall. And twice a week, Tuesday and Thursday mornings, Anna and Jake strolled the beach with his dog. She walked Dewey alone, more often of late, whenever my dad needed to drive Nana to her cardiologist appointments.

After Anna dried the floor, Pops took the bucket and mop from her, hobbled to the closet and placed them inside. Then he grabbed his jacket and cane.

She wiped her hands on a cloth towel and peered at him, as if through slats in a confessional. "You know, I saw that strange glow in your upstairs window again last night."

My father shook his head, almost tired of Anna's odd claims. "Should I tell the sheriff we've got a peeper here on this street?"

"Don't get fresh, Mr. Jacoby, I'm serious." She touched her neck. "This time the glow moved from window to window."

Pops pushed one arm into his jacket sleeve. "Told you before, Anna, probably just the lighthouse, or some headlamps coming around the curve."

"I've lived here longer than you, Jake. It wasn't the beacon or any car lights."

He rested his cane against the wall and reached behind

his back, searching for his other sleeve. "It's almost seven," he said. "Gotta put the chops on."

She smiled, took his hand, and guided it into the sleeve. "When will you take me up on my offer and make *me* dinner one of these nights?"

He had never cooked for any woman not named Iris or Joan, but Anna didn't know that. She knew little about my father, in fact, though not for lack of curiosity.

She buttoned the bottom two buttons of his jacket. "You must've made some fabulous dinners back in Hopedale, with that big family, all those kids, all that life in the house."

"A few, I guess."

He neglected to say that he cooked a full meal for us every night. We sat down together all the time, no matter how busy my siblings were with sports, or how much homework I had, or how late Mom had to stay after school. Anna and Greg couldn't have children, and Pops shared little about his own family, out of courtesy and guilt. She only knew the basics about my death, the divorce, and where Gia and Russell stood in their lives. He hadn't elaborated on the strain, the dysfunction, the monthlong silences. The way he saw it: what Anna didn't know couldn't hurt him.

Pops limped back to the sink, got down on a knee, and checked the pipe again. He loaded his toolbox and, as he struggled to his feet, a firecracker popped in his patella, and he winced. *Jesus!* My dad was weaker that day than all his days prior, though he'd been in agony for fifteen years, starting when he developed rheumatoid arthritis. Soon after, hip replacement surgery left him with a staph infection, a thirty-day hospital stay, and an unwillingness to go back under the knife. When I died five springs later, a greater pain coursed through his body. He retired from his job as a community college math professor, filled each subsequent day caring for Nana Joan, and spent each night avoiding memories that had become his mortal enemies.

My father headed toward the door, paused, and looked back. "Almost forgot, Anna, can you take care of Dewey till Sunday afternoon?"

"Of course." The soft wrinkles around her eyes melted with the kindness of her voice. "Where are you headed?"

"Gia's wedding in Rhode Island, depends on how Joan feels though."

"Oh, Jake! How wonderful." Anna rubbed my father's arm. "I have so many questions, but I know you have to go. Promise you'll tell me all about it on Sunday."

"Thanks," he said. "If we go, I'll leave the key in your mailbox." He nodded and tried to smile, walked through the back door and down the steps. He felt better when he got outside—as good as he could feel. The pain of losing me hadn't eased, like so many claimed it would. To his credit, Pops hadn't numbed it with alcohol, hadn't beaten it back with anger or ignored it with cheery smiles. He just asked the anguish to settle in, allowed it to stay, and let it rot. And with every step he took, self-resentment became more a part of him, till even the ground beneath his feet felt pathetic to his boots.

On a quick path between houses, he stopped and

looked past the perfect darkness as a river of stars flowed above and salt air streamed into his chest. Tints of blues and purples beamed off the moonlit ocean, but then a cloud drifted by and veiled the colors. Now the moon itself was a dull rivet beaten into the sky. In front of his face, a snowflake sailed and sank to the ground, followed by many others. Until alone in the quiet, Pops fell into a frequent fantasy where he vanished from all he knew and loved.

He felt like me then, like he was dead, but he wasn't; he was just a man who'd stepped away from life, a lost soul stuck in time, searching for what he'd never find, fettered and unsettled. Like *he* was the ghost.

Unnoticed in my grandmother's kitchen, I watched my father clean a serrated knife. He stabbed at three seared pork chops and transferred them, one after another, from frying pan to cutting board then sawed through the chops and sliced half the meat off the bones. Praying for scraps, Dewey sat up straight at his master's feet. While trays of roasted potatoes and broccoli kept warm on the stove, Pops fixed two plates and tossed the bones into a ceramic bowl on the floor.

Around a spacious table for six, Nana Joan waited in a small wicker chair, hands folded on her lap. A wooden chandelier teetered above; one of its five bulbs dead. In the dim light, the outdated kitchen—linoleum floor, laminate countertop, lace curtains—aged by the second. Three oil paintings, beach scenes Gia made ages ago, before she left for art school, hung in a line along the wall that divided the kitchen from the living room. In the first painting, a flock of gulls glided over a crashing wave. In the second, a lighthouse shined bright in a storm. And in the third, an elderly man and a young boy held hands while admiring a setting sun.

When Pops put Nana Joan's plate close to her, she drew in the warm smell and said, "Mmm, Dewey having chops too?"

My father sat beside her. "You know it's his favorite."

"My goodness, Jake, you spoil that dog like no one's business." My grandmother felt for her knife and fork. "Getting him to eat kibble now would be like trying to put legs on a snake."

"Probably right." He poured a can of Bud Light into a glass and slid it toward her.

"How'd it go with Anna's sink?" she asked.

"Not bad." He smoothed his beard.

Nana poked around for a potato wedge. "Who are the Celtics playing tonight?"

"Clippers," he said.

"Storm coming tomorrow, I hear." The wedge fell off her fork, and she chuckled.

"Yep." Pops took a long sip of beer. The apprehension linked to Gia's wedding and the unknowns awaiting him in Wickford combined to seal his lips.

As I looked on from the corner, imagining the room smelling like goodness and comfort on that frosty night, Dewey lay next to my father, mauling a bone and slobbering with delight. The dog's wise eyes, carved in devotion, softened when Nana Joan reached for the pepper shaker and grabbed it on the first try.

Pops picked at his broccoli. "You listen to any podcasts today?"

"Sure did." Nana Joan manipulated her fork and knife like puppets. "Heard an interview with an interesting young lady who developed a drug that extends the life of dogs."

Pops looked into his mother's empty gaze. "I'd never put Dewey through that."

The mutt nuzzled my dad's shin as Nana savored her last bite. For my father, the meal tasted as bland as it would've to me, same as every night.

Since he moved in with my grandmother, my dad kept a daily routine: coffee at six, a walk down the beach with Dewey, errands and shopping, lunch with Nana at noon, some tinkering around the house, a nap at three, another walk with Dewey, dinner at seven, kitchen cleanup, then the Celtics or Red Sox on TV till bedtime at ten thirty.

"Mmm, delicious." Nana Joan wiped her mouth with a paper napkin. "Thank you for cooking, honey."

"Of course, Ma."

"You don't always have to make such a fuss though."

"Don't get used to it," he said. "We'll be eating Hamburger Helper if the butcher keeps raising his prices."

Pops paid the bills with his meager pension and Nana's social security checks. His alimony payment had siphoned his savings, but he qualified for Medicare recently, which helped. His shrinking bank account didn't bother him much; my grandmother had taught my father to find joy in having nothing, referring to material things, not people.

Nana Joan placed her utensils on her plate and faced her son with wide eyes, which grew greener and more alive when she was serious. "I felt him again this afternoon."

She was talking about me, which she did every few weeks, and I was glad she sensed me in the house. But Pops didn't respond to her claims, never wanted to humor her senility. "Guess that kind of stuff happens at eighty-four, feeling things that aren't there." And in that moment, as he stared at his mother, my father forgot she couldn't see him.

Sometimes, as she listened to the radio or knitted or daydreamed about the past, she'd acknowledge me with a smile or a gesture or a quiet hello. Oddly, she was the only member of the family who accepted my absence, and who believed I was still present.

"Oh, and I heard him too," she said. "Just little whispers and coos, like he used to make when he was reading at bedtime."

"It's an old house, Ma, and old houses make noises." My father carried their dirty plates to the sink. "Probably the radiator or the wind."

"I'm really looking forward to tomorrow." My grandmother blinked twice, and her green eyes darkened. "What time's the ceremony, Jake?"

"Um, six thirty, I think." He sat and gulped down the rest of his beer, wishing he hadn't mentioned the wedding news to his mother. "Think you'll be okay to go?" he said. "We don't have to, you know."

"Don't be silly. I wouldn't miss it."

"Then we should get on the road first thing."

"Agreed," she said. "Can't wait to be with my Gia again and finally meet the man who ended up with that philandering ex-wife of yours."

"You should know all about cheating," Pops mumbled, low enough that she couldn't hear. His father had abandoned him when my dad was a child because of Nana's infidelity, though initially Pops thought it was his fault.

My grandmother reclined in her chair. "When's the last time you saw Iris, anyway?"

"I don't know," he said. "Four, five months maybe. Ran into her and Tom at a wake for an old friend in Hopedale, Frank Hutchinson. Pancreatic cancer." He stood and collected the empty cans, limped to a corner in the kitchen and dropped them into the recycling bin.

My father was beside me now, though unaware and preoccupied, mourning another loss: his marriage. Mom had been the one who left, but she held him responsible, used his lack of energy after his surgery and anguish after my death against him, convinced Pops that the divorce was his fault. Instead of fighting his ex-wife's reasoning, my dad accepted it.

He had loved my mother once, threw all he had into their marriage. But that was another time, before she changed—or before she claimed *he* did. Now, as he revisited the past in his mind, fond memories of Iris were patchy, bright images long since faded. Recalling their best days together was like trying to find his way back into a dream.

"Have you spoken to your son lately?" my grand-mother asked.

Pops flinched and turned toward her. His mouth hung open, but no words came out, until he realized she was talking about Russell. "Yeah, he called earlier today."

"And?"

"Wanted to know if I was going to the wedding." My father gazed out the window into the starless sky. "I was busy and couldn't talk," he said. "Wish I told him why I had to leave."

Dewey looked up from his bowl.

I was getting what I wanted, and what my family needed. Soon they'd be together in Wickford, where they could be honest and seize the opportunity to be happy again. Then I'd complete my purpose in the ghost world, transition to a higher realm, and move on.

The clock on the microwave read 9:05.

My father washed the last dish and placed it on the drying rack, draped the wet cloth over the faucet. He limped around the kitchen, wiped the table, and swept the floor. While cleaning the counter, he spotted Gia's invitation next to his *Soup for Every Season* cookbook. He dropped the purple envelope into a wire basket with his wallet and keys.

When Pops stepped into the living room, Dewey followed. Against the back wall, under the broken ship's wheel clock, a thirty-inch flat-screen rested on a sixty-dollar entertainment stand, the enthusiastic play-by-play call of Boston Celtics broadcaster Mike Gorman blasting out of the TV speakers. Nana Joan pushed up from her easy chair. "Morning's a blink away," she declared over the blare. "I'm calling it a night."

My father rescued the remote from between the chair cushions, lowered the volume, and took his mother's hand. "It's okay, Ma, I've got you."

"I know we're winning, Jake, but how much time is left?"

He squinted at the television. "Less than a minute, up by eight."

"They should hold on," she said. "Suppose anything can happen though."

As they started down the hall, Pops said, "If I could've seen the future ten years ago, I might've named Dewey after Jayson Tatum instead of Dwight Evans."

Nana Joan laughed and turned back toward the living room. "What do you think, Dewey? Should we call you Tate from now on?"

Dewey growled.

My father pushed open the door to the bedroom, retrieved her nightgown from the top dresser drawer, and handed it to her. "It's the blue one," he said.

She stroked the fabric. "I can tell."

After she changed, he guided her into the bathroom, squeezed toothpaste onto her brush, and ran the water. While he waited he peered into the mirror, at an old woman who'd aged rapidly in the past few years. He handed her a comb, and she raked it through her thin gray hair. When he was a child, she combed his hair every day before school, and took care of everything else for him too. Now, as he studied his own reflection in the glass, he still saw that little boy.

He helped her to bed and pecked her on the forehead. "See you tomorrow, Ma." Then he turned out the light and shut the door.

"See you then, son," Nana whispered.

Pops went upstairs and washed up. While taking his bathrobe out of the closet, he eyed the brown shoebox on the top shelf, where he kept the gun. He'd bought the pistol fifteen years earlier, after a rash of neighborhood robberies in Hopedale, kept it loaded but never used it in self-defense. Last time he held the thing was the one time he visited the range.

Then my dad took a bigger box down from the same shelf. He recalled the first time he opened it, twenty-five years before, when Iris gave him a sweat suit for Valentine's Day—after she insisted he lose a few pounds. He placed the box on the bed, lifted the lid, and a million memories fluttered out. With a slight smile he filed through a stack of papers he'd saved from when Gia, Russell, and I were young: poems, drawings, letters to Santa and the tooth fairy, apology notes for tantrums we threw, anything Pops thought we'd look back on and laugh about someday. When he found sonogram images of his four children, he set them aside.

From the moment I passed, I wondered if I'd ever meet my dead sister, if her soul wandered freely, or if it was stuck somewhere like mine. But she had never lived, never took a breath, and I doubted whether she had a soul at all.

My father opened a plastic shopping bag and removed a large leather scrapbook, tan with gold trim. Inscribed on the book's cover: *Cherish Yesterday. Dream Tomorrow. Live Today.*

From the bag, Pops took out a bottle of glue, a roll of tape, and a book of colorful stickers—rainbows, butterflies, balloons. When Gia was little, he used to help her put stickers on her schoolbooks, when my sister was his best friend, when they were both happy and innocent.

My father read the notes and keepsakes, then put Russell's things and mine back in the box. He smoothed Gia's wrinkled childhood drawings and taped them in the scrapbook, as if restoring pictures of the past might hold the present in place. The smell of fresh paper mingled with the scent of nostalgia, and my father lost himself for a minute.

He found a poem—penned on pretty pink stationery—that Gia wrote when she was eleven, back when she followed her imagination's lead and trusted wherever it might take her. He glued the poem onto the middle page of the book.

"This I Know"

I'll never figure out my hair,
But this I know: Mommy's care.

I may not run the fastest mile,
But this I know: Daddy's smile.

My singing may cause many shrugs,
But this I know: Nana's hugs.

I may get lost in science class,
But this I know: Russell's laugh.

I may not find the end or start,
But this I know: Devan's heart.

I may not sail the skies above,
But this I know: Family love.

In the living room, the Wheel of Time sang its evening song. One by one, the chimes climbed the stairs until all eleven reached the top, and Pops knew it was midnight.

He jotted a quick note to Gia, stuck it onto the first page of the scrapbook, and wrapped his gift in glimmering red paper. He looked forward to seeing his daughter, glad that she invited him to the wedding, but wasn't sure he deserved to be there. In his mind he was a culprit, responsible for my death and exacerbating my sister's drug problem. But his little girl wanted him back in her life. Shouldn't that matter more than anything?

My father changed into sweatpants, slipped into bed, and waited for sleep to arrive on the wings of forgotten days. He looked through the window, stared at a single star shimmering in the coal black sky, and knew that our family—as he wished to remember us—would never be together again.

PART II

THE DAY OF THE WEDDING

∽

A word is dead when it is said, some say.
I say it just begins to live that day.

—Emily Dickinson

SIX

Realms, or me

As my father and grandmother prepared to leave for Rhode Island, I roamed the Old Saybrook house, wandering from room to room. We were all uneasy about the weekend, each in our own way. Pops laid his corduroy sport coat over a kitchen chair. "Almost ready, Ma?"

"Just about," Nana called from her bedroom.

The house was cold; it was always cold, though I felt nothing. My grandmother pulled a sweater tight around her shoulders and touched her way down the hall. After my father scribbled a note to Anna and positioned it prominently on the kitchen counter, he reached down and mussed Dewey's scruffy neck. "Be a good boy till I get back, okay?"

Dewey angled his boxy head upward, maximized the loving scratch.

My soul usher, Simone, appeared. "This is what you've waited for, Devan, isn't it?"

"Yes," I said. "They're on their way."

When we first met, Simone said I ought to relinquish everything—my friends, my school, my home, my family, my body. She told me I should accept my death and follow the light, but I couldn't detach from what I had on earth, refused to release my ego and fell back to a restricted world where my soul remained unsettled. Why did I stay? Unfinished business.

As always, Simone knew my thoughts and questioned my plan. "And when your family reunites, you'll let go of your attachments?"

"Of course," I said. "But I have to help them somehow."

"The most meaningful journeys are traveled alone."

"But they've been alone for so long. They've suffered enough."

"All of life is learning, and all of life is suffering. Everyone in your family needs to discover that, in their own way, in their own time."

"You don't understand, Simone. I need to know they'll be okay, but I have to be *with* them. It's not enough just watching."

"You've always had the ability to leave this house and visit your parents and siblings. But earthbound souls have low energy levels, and if you get too close to your family, if you stay too long, your level will deplete."

"I don't care."

"You're free to decide how frequently, and for how long, you want to be with them. But your visits will weigh you down, endangering your ability to cross over when it's time to move on into the heavenly realm."

"I'll be ready to move on after we're all together," I said.

"Oh, Devan." Simone's aura brightened. "You don't decide when you're ready."

"Who does?"

"The light."

"What?"

She was gone.

After Pops and Nana Joan walked out the front door, I went to the living room window and glimpsed them in the driveway. Then I thought of my sister, and she appeared in the stained and scratched-up glass.

SEVEN

Gia, or lies

WHEN A FRISKY strand of hair tickled Gia's nose, she stirred and woke next to Mara, whose tangly tangerine locks had crept onto my sister's pillow like vines.

The friends had spent the night together, alone, while Gia recovered from what Mara had dubbed "Iris-itis." Outside the bedroom window, a steady snowfall filtered the morning light, which poured through the glass, doused the walls, and splashed onto the well-worn furniture. The old room—a cozy haven, comfy and quiet, filled with books—smelled new.

Gia blinked and groaned, stifled a yawn. "You don't look like my fiancé."

"But I bet my breath stinks like his." She blew into Gia's face.

The bride-to-be didn't laugh, heavy thoughts of her wedding day pounding hard inside her head; the drama, like the storm, was well on its way. She pulled the comforter over her head. "Ugh, tell me when it's tomorrow."

Mara joined her under the covers. "Can you at least brush your teeth before you start wallowing?" she said.

"It's my party," Gia said in the toasty darkness. "I can wallow if I want to."

Mara slithered out of bed, ripped the blankets off, and threw them onto the floor. "Let's get moving, girl!"

Gia flipped onto her stomach and buried her face in a pillow. "You can't make me!" Her muffled words lost their oomph in the cotton.

Mara slipped into a yellow terry cloth bathrobe, with *Cozy Cove* stitched onto the front. She folded her arms, stared at her bestie, and smiled. "Get the fuck up, G."

My sister stumbled out of bed. "Grrrr." She tossed her silk headscarf onto the nightstand and trudged into the bathroom, peeled off her underwear and baggy T-shirt. She turned on the shower and dialed up the heat, needed to ditch the chill in her bones if she hoped to warm up to the challenges of the day. She wasn't worried about the wedding though; getting married would be easy. Dealing with our family? Not so much.

Mara peeked into the bathroom. "I still don't understand why Luke had to spend the night in Brodie's room."

Gia pulled on her plastic shower cap and ducked in under the stream. "He's traditional," she said amid the spray.

"Want me to sneak him in here for a quickie?" Mara held up her phone and pretended to send a text. "Or is that against tradition?"

Gia spit out a mouthful of water and laughed. "The quickest quickie in the history of sex won't be quick enough. He and I have breakfast plans with his parents, and my father should be here soon."

"You know that Bill Potter is kinda hot for an old guy." Mara wrote the initials BP on the steamy mirror and drew a heart around the letters.

My sister turned off the water. "You really are unbelievable." She stepped onto the bath mat and wrapped a towel around her soaked torso.

"What?" Mara said. "You're not the only girl with daddy issues."

⚜

Dressed in black leggings, a denim collared shirt, and an auburn sweater, Gia spun and looked over her shoulder into a full-length mirror. "What do you think, Mar?" she said. "Be honest."

Mara leaned on the wall and stared, her eyes sticking to my sister like leeches. "Okay, honestly," she said, "I would literally kill you for your body."

"Stop it."

"I am so totally serious, G." Mara tightened her bathrobe belt. "When I look at my ass in the mirror, I wanna stick my head in an oven."

The friends laughed and, without a prompt, made the bed together. Gia chuckled as she faced the woman across the mattress. They'd joined forces like this ever since freshman orientation at RISD, when they hit it off and promised to always stay in each other's corner.

Stevie Wonder's "Superstition," the ring tone on my sister's phone, sang out. "Oh God, it's my father," Gia said. She put him on speaker. "Hi, Dad."

"Hey G, we're stuck in some traffic, should be there soon enough."

"Oh wow, okay, that's great. I mean, not the traffic but that you're on the way. I wasn't sure you were coming. I hoped you would, just wasn't sure."

"Sorry," Pops said, "couldn't quite hear you, spotty connection. Say hi to your grandmother."

"Oh, hey, hi, Nana."

"Hi there, sweetie," our grandmother yelled. "See you in six shakes of a snail's—"

The conversation cut off, and my sister stared at the phone for a second.

Mara fluffed the comforter and propped up the pillows. "Wait. Snails have tails?"

"He's really coming," Gia said as she placed the cell down. "I kinda don't believe it."

"Of course he's coming. He's your father. Your whole family will be here because you invited them, G. Remember? As fucked up as you say they are, they obviously still love you. I mean, how could they not?"

"It's just been so long, and we've all been through so much," Gia said. "But I can't wait for you to meet Nana Joan." My sister teased out her hair with her fingers. "Damn, I really need to visit her more often. It's been a minute. She and I used to be really tight, but nothing's been the same since Devan died." Gia wouldn't admit that her bond with our grandmother changed while I was still alive, when my sister threw herself into painkillers and tossed everyone who loved her aside.

"Where were you again the night your brother passed?" Mara asked for the tenth time in ten years, steady in her spirited search of a straight answer.

"The story keeps changing in my head, but pretty sure I went to a house party in Cranston, and a bunch of us took Molly, and I kind of remember fighting off some creep who was trying to get in my pants. Anyway, my dad called me the next morning and told me about Dev." Gia squeezed her eyes shut. "And the first thing I did, before I even shed a fucking tear, was score some pills."

Sin-spinning spiders crept up my sister's spine as she revived the echo of my death and her relationship with Pops, how close they used to be and how he'd despise her if he knew the whole truth about her drug use. She itched to tell him exactly why and when she fell prey to her demons, vowed to spill the story when he got to Wickford, blamed herself for the divide between them. In the bleary decade since my death, she'd visited him once a year, either Thanksgiving or Christmas—depending on if she had enough concealer to hide her sunken cheeks and the blotches encircling her eyes. Tired of playing the part of pariah, Gia wanted to *come* clean now more than she ever wanted to *get* clean.

She sat in front of a vanity, motionless for a second, then opened a makeup case and applied foundation to her forehead. "But I'm not the same person I was ten years ago, Mar. That's not who I am now."

"You know I believe that."

"At Brightstar," Gia said, "they say if you don't tell people you've changed, you can't expect anyone to accept it."

Mara nodded.

My sister twisted a tube of lipstick. "I texted Iris earlier, asked if she'd please eat breakfast somewhere else today." Gia called our mother by her first name when she needed to create emotional distance between them, which was often. "I can't have her in that dining room with me and the Potters."

"I'll check in on her," Mara said, "and see if she wants me to bring her and Tom some bagels or something, though he'd probably prefer milk toast." Mara removed her bathrobe and squeezed into a pair of jeans. "It's still so weird to see those two as a married couple."

"I guess."

"Nothing like your mom and dad when I first met them."

"Because you only met them once." Gia puckered and smacked her ruby lips. "And that was before they imploded."

"Yeah." Mara fastened her bra. "But I always assumed they were, like, the perfect parents."

"They were perfect when I was little." Gia stood and checked the mirror again. "They had a great marriage, did everything together back then, treated the interracial thing like no big deal, even when assholes in Hopedale would go out of their way to tell Mom that she was 'articulate' or that they 'don't see color'"

"I think your parents just grew apart," Mara said slipping into a white blouse. "But at least they brought you into this fucked-up world before they split."

My sister straightened her collar, kept hold of the cloth. "It's just, you know, sometimes I wonder if they'd still be together if my brother were alive."

After buttoning her blouse, Mara undid the top three buttons and adjusted her fit for maximum cleavage. "Things happen for a reason, G."

"But my mom and dad are like brutal enemies now," Gia said. "Is it too much to ask that they don't murder each other? And what does that mean for me and Luke?"

Mara picked lint off of my sister's sweater, flicked it into the air. "Don't mean shit, girl."

Through a window in my nana's house, I watched Gia make soft steps in the foyer. When someone tickled her ribs from behind, she jumped. "Whoa!"

"Well, hello, Miss Jacoby," Bill Potter said, wearing a slippery smirk and a black turtleneck. Next to him, his wife, Beth, tilted her head, acting as if she'd never seen her husband embarrass a young woman before.

My sister took a step back, pretended to reshape her curls, and spit out a phony laugh. "Wow, um, sorry, guess I got some pregame jitters."

Bill's hearty hoot tumbled through the air as Beth kissed Gia on both cheeks. When the three of them walked into the dining room, my sister spread invisible light and blended with the sunny environment. She sat and silenced her phone, placed it face down on the table. And as Bill and Beth spoke to one another with the enthusiasm of new friends with fresh stories, Gia tried to decipher their relationship and interpret their body language. She guessed at the meaning beneath their banter, caught the spots where their gazes lingered.

Low music droned out of a portable speaker on an antique hutch—the beginning bars of a song, "A Better Place to Be" by Harry Chapin, our father's favorite musician, who Pops saw in concert sixteen times and would've seen a seventeenth had Harry not died in a car crash on his way to a free benefit on Long Island in the summer of '81. Forming a slanted smile, my sister remembered how her thirteen-year-old self would groan whenever Pops broke open his case of eight tracks and played Chapin's never-ending saga songs. But now, on a more positive note, she knew how to tolerate at least the next eight minutes with the Potters, and while Bill and Beth chatted, my sister nodded along, following a string of lyrics in her head: *And she tried to fight her empty nights by smilin' at the world.*

"Good morning," Helen Nielsen crooned as she pushed through a swinging door leading out of the kitchen. She sidled up to the table and explained the breakfast menu: spinach and onion quiche, a side of mixed fruit, and fresh cranberry juice. "It's straight from a bog, fifteen miles north in Coventry." When Helen tugged on her apron her wrists looked like fifty toothpicks bundled together. "All righty, now if you'll excuse me, I need to help Stan in the kitchen. He's handy and all, but you don't want him fussing too much with the cooking."

After the innkeeper left, Beth made small talk: banal inquiries about the weather, my sister's sweater, the tint of her eye shadow. At the start of every question, Gia cringed, a newly adopted, previously alien reflex. Years ago, she had a boldness about her, especially around adults, acted with verve and a willingness to be surprised, back when she was unafraid of the unknown. Then she grew up, took a wrong turn, and life's mysteries flipped from magical to maniacal, teaching Gia to fear dark roads with no signs.

Beth turned to my sister and said, "So, I think Luke's big brother dragged him out for a jog a couple of hours ago. I swear, I don't know where Brodie gets his energy."

"Beats me," Gia said, sitting on a rock-solid theory. "Not the best weather for a run though."

"Snow always excites Brodie," Bill said. "He's been obsessed since he was a kid. For whatever reason, the stuff flicks a pleasure switch in his brain and sends him into overdrive."

"Really? Wow." My sister didn't need a lesson in compulsive personalities and addictive behavior.

The minutes puttered, and Gia's heart sputtered when she glanced up at the grandfather clock in the corner; it was only a quarter past ten. In a little more than an average workday, she'd be Mrs. Luke Potter, and she flashed a Mona Lisa smile as the last line of Harry's song hit her ears: *'Cause you know I'm going nowhere, and anywhere's a better place to be.*

Helen brought coffee and juice to the table; her husband followed with the quiche. "Forgive us," she said.

"Stan forgot to buy onions yesterday, so this may not taste the way you expected."

"Don't worry about it one bit." Beth leaned over her plate and closed her eyes. "Mmm, smells delicious."

"You can apologize to me with a Bloody Mary," Bill said with a wink. "Double shot of vodka, please."

As they ate, Bill got personal with Gia: What was her first impression of Luke? Why the quick wedding? Did they have plans for a family in the future? Would she continue painting?

My sister fiddled with the cloth napkin on her lap, calmed the churn in her belly, and answered Bill's questions without revealing too much; only Mara and Luke had direct access to her feelings. Meanwhile, Helen and Stan filed in and out of the dining room, freshening up coffees, refilling water glasses, inquiring about the food. And as the Potters chuckled and joked, Gia got caught in the tangle of voices.

Beth laid a hand on my sister's shoulder. "So when do you expect your father and brother, dear?"

"My dad called this morning, said he's on his way and should be here soon." Then my sister's tone went gray. "And Russell texted last night, but I'm not really sure when he'll get here. You know, with the storm and all."

"Are you and your family close?" Bill babbled with a mouth full of quiche.

"As close as most families, I guess." The sentence scribbled off Gia's lips and couldn't be erased. *Covering shit up; crazy the effort it takes*, she thought.

Then the conversation slithered down a forbidden pathway. "You must be thrilled to have everyone here," Beth said. "I'm so happy for you considering the circumstances."

A shadow stole along the floor and mushroomed onto the walls while Gia nodded in slow motion, then she changed the subject back to the weather: the growing flurries yesterday, the storm intensifying over the Atlantic and slamming the coast overnight, the wild snow attacking the dining room windows.

"I'm calling bullshit on the forecast." Bill scoffed and fished an olive out of his Bloody Mary. "How often do these so-called catastrophes actually happen?"

My sister stutter-laughed, "Hardly ever." But what she wanted to say was, *It only takes one to destroy everything.*

Stan approached the table. "You can leave your dirty dishes here when you're finished." He arched a brow, rubbed the bridge of his bulbous nose, and looked at Gia. "The wife and I need to meet with the mother of the bride about something."

Hidden under her denim shirt, my sister's heart ticked ten times faster than the grandfather clock.

"Of course, Stanley." Beth put down her coffee cup and lifted her eyes. "When we're done, you won't even know we were here."

"And don't you worry that shriveled old head of yours," Bill added, "I'll fix my own drinks the rest of the morning."

Gia smiled under her breath and assumed she'd someday grow close with the Potters. Once she got more comfortable with them—and with herself—she'd become a beloved member of a family once again. She knew a lot about Bill and Beth already, though they knew nothing about her. Not the *real* her. Not the real *us*. If my sister's drug use was the "elephant in the room," the tragic story of my death was a crash of rhinos.

She peeked at her phone: three missed calls from our mother but no voice mail messages. Gia excused herself, abandoning her half-eaten breakfast, and left the room—while the rhinos snorted and scuffed and kicked up dust.

The library had bloomed into life, courtesy of a half dozen hip-high terra-cotta vases bursting with roses, peonies, hydrangea, orchids, and gardenias: a welcoming sight on a gray winter's day that grew colder and darker as the morning grew longer.

"This is unacceptable," Mom said. "There aren't enough flowers, the colors are all wrong, and half of them are dying. And who orders orchids for a wedding?"

"Mom, there's nothing wrong with these," Gia said.

"No, no, that's my fault." Helen hovered over one of the vases, shoulders slumped, as though someone had demanded she put down a cherished pet. "I'll go outside and see if the delivery truck hasn't left yet."

"Just fix this," our mother said, glaring at the old woman shuffling toward the door.

"Truck's gone." Stan intercepted his wife before she got five feet. "No time to place a new order. What we got here will have to do."

My sister stood between Mom and the Nielsens. "Really, it's fine."

Cemented to the floor, our mother leered at Gia. "This place needs to be ready by the time everyone gets here," she said. "Do you even know when your brother is showing up?"

"Probably like an hour before the ceremony." My sister picked at the Band-Aid on her finger. "I'm not sure."

Gia was certain of one thing: Russell knew exactly how long her addiction had plagued her. The second he opened the bathroom door at a mutual friend's high school party and saw that tiny tab of LSD on her tongue, the snitch ran home and told our parents, my sister was positive. Though she wanted to repair her rickety relationship with him, she didn't want my twin ridiculing her at the wedding, disparaging her, and making everything worse. *What if Russ calls me out in front of everyone? What if he blames me for everything?* Mouth dry, knees buckling, Gia felt an unwanted pull—the need for a drink or a pill—like the tide controlled by the moon.

Mara strolled into the library. "Holy shit! These flowers are frickin' gorgeous!" She squeezed in between the Nielsens, smirked, and cocked an eyebrow. "Stu and Karen, you've outdone yourselves."

"Thank you, dear," Helen said, forgiving Mara for the slipup, whether accidental or intentional. "Mind helping us for a bit?"

As the trio brought three vases into the sunroom, my mom and sister followed through the foyer and ran into Brodie hopping down the stairs. He'd showered and changed after his jog, wore tan chinos and a burgundy suit jacket.

"What's up, ladies?" he said as Mom brushed past.

Gia stopped. "Where's Luke?"

"Don't worry about him." Brodie pulled an envelope out of his jacket pocket. "Here's a little something from yours truly."

Gia took the unsealed envelope, peered inside, and discovered a plastic Ziploc baggie containing three pills that resembled candy: one red, one yellow, one blue. *Fentanyl.* She wanted to throw the bag in Brodie's smug mug and curse him out, but her words turned into barbwire and snagged in her throat—she couldn't spit them out.

Brodie rubbed his hands together. "You know you want it."

My sister had smoked weed for the first time as a Hopedale High sophomore and lapsed into a wake-and-bake habit. The marijuana transformed her into an imposter, and she felt safer wearing the mask. The following year, a soccer injury gave her a taste for painkillers, which led to a buffet of questions: Would our parents find out? Could she quit if she wanted? Had she made a mistake she couldn't undo? Caught in her own sticky web, she cut off longtime friends, watched her grades suffer, and got accepted into art school by the hair of a paintbrush.

After I died, Gia's drug use ramped up and barreled away at breakneck speed: first OxyContin, then Vicodin, then pills of any kind, whatever she scrounged up, nothing off limits, nothing too potent. On routine weekends in college, she scanned the online real estate section of the *Providence Journal*, attended open houses, and rifled through medicine cabinets to settle her shakes. When her funds got low and prescription suppliers dried up, she switched to heroin, blacked out for days on end. And each time she returned to reality, she recognized herself less and less. Now, as she gazed at the pills in the bag and considered her 766 days of sobriety, my sister deliberated which to flush down the drain.

"I think we both know how you can repay me," Brodie said. "Room 204." He smiled and headed back upstairs.

Gia poked her nose into the doorway of the sunroom, where our mother prowled and barked orders to the group. "No, no, not there," Mom exclaimed. "Do I need to do everything?"

My sister shoved the baggie into her pocket and followed Luke's brother upstairs as a rush of self-contempt flowed through her veins. She couldn't feel the steps beneath her feet, and for the first time in two years, Gia longed to be lost in the haze of a high, where anxiety died a quick death; she'd deal with its resurrection when she came down. *Fuck, it would feel so good right now.* Standing at the top of the staircase, she gazed down the hall as Brodie closed the door to his room. *What else does he have in there?* My sister knew this kind of temptation, the kind that made her resent every single piece of her life.

Breathe, Gia.

The kind that made her build barriers to hide her shame.

Just breathe.

The kind that lurked inside her brain while she prayed for help.

Breathe, dammit.

Silent whispers demanded she reverse course, to the opposite end of the hall, toward her own room. She obeyed and went inside, latched the door, leaned hard against the wall, and called her sponsor from Brightstar rehab facility. One ring. Then two. Then she hung up.

Seconds later, her phone rang. She didn't answer, paced the floor, wore a path like an agitated puma in a new cage at a zoo.

A sound from outside barged into the room: the crunch of wet snow under rolling tires. Gia moved past the bureau and peered out the window, into a sea of floating flakes, big as gull feathers. Down on the street, a silver Outback pulled up in front of the Cozy Cove. When the car stopped, our father rocked himself out and limped around to the passenger side. Nana Joan exited and craned her head upward, as if gazing into Gia's window.

My sister held the baggie tight in her fist, while the smooth plastic teased her fingers, and the tiny pills inside begged for release. She reconsidered then if she should tell Pops everything about her drug-addled past, the seriousness of her addiction, the suicidal thoughts—or her other secret, his unborn grandchild. *What does it matter?*

She turned from the window, yanked open a dresser drawer and stuffed the baggie into a half-empty box of tampons, which she'd mindlessly and needlessly packed for the weekend; Luke would never look in there. She spun and collapsed face down onto her bed, the cool fabric of the comforter softening her fall. Then Gia curled herself into a ball and cried.

In Old Saybrook, I left the living room and moved to the attic, where my siblings and I used to sleep all summer long. The space seemed smaller now, filled with crates and boxes, old patio furniture and broken beach toys. Three twin-sized mattresses still rested on the floor, busted and dirty and covered in mouse droppings. The smell of timelessness lingered, while the sound of eternity echoed.

I looked into the oval window—wedged under the slanted eaves and shaped like a ship's porthole—through which Russ and I would survey glimmery horizons, pretending distant sailboats were pirates on the attack. And then, through the scratches and stains of the charcoal glass, I saw my mother.

EIGHT

Iris, or stains

IN THE SUNROOM, Mom fussed with the Nielsens over the flowers—amazing how long she could drag out an argument, tenacious as a barnacle. The room was sunless, bitter, and cold, as if the heat from the basement furnace reached every inch of the inn but there. Tom was at his wife's side, as always, which kept my mother on her hammertoes—he often supported her during conflicts, but sometimes asked her to stand down. She never quite knew which way he'd lean, though it was usually the direction she wanted.

"Get me my coat," she said. "The Nielsens have work to do."

"Yes, dear," Tom replied.

Around the corner in the foyer, the main door creaked and closed. An invisible person stomped inside and knocked snow off his or her unseen boots. The first thought that came to Mom's mind: *Helen better clean that floor.* Then came a voice, familiar and meager, a sound that sped up my mother's pulse.

"Hello?"

My father and grandmother peeked into the sunroom, paused, and stepped over the threshold. His cane in one hand, Gia's scrapbook in the other, Pops kept his head down while Nana held his arm.

Mom focused hard, her memory dull, thought back to when she last saw him. *Was it a funeral or wake? April or May?* "Well, look who decided to show," she said.

Pops looked up at his ex, defeat smothered all over his face. My mother stared back, had him right where she wanted: trapped, with no way to escape.

"What kind of greeting is that?" Nana Joan asked, removing her crocheted purple hat.

Tom rushed over. "Hey there, Jake," he said, reaching out a hand. "Great to see you."

"Yeah, you too." Pops gripped and released the hand all at once.

"Hi, Joan," Tom said in a loud voice, implying he thought she was deaf and not blind. "I'm Tom Hyde. Very nice to meet you."

My mother steadied herself, inhaled, and held the breath captive. *What does Joan think of Tom? Does she know he's Black? Should I care?*

My parents' relationship was a wreck, and Nana surely had suspicions about Mom's affair, but my mother still respected my grandmother, appreciated her help when Gia, Russell, and I were little: the rides, the babysitting, the late-night talks and glasses of wine when the stress of those child-rearing days took a toll.

My grandmother peeled off her gloves and shook Tom's hand. "My pleasure," she said. "Now where's that wife of yours? I heard the bark but haven't felt the bite."

Mom glared at Pops and approached his mother. "Hello, Joan," she said. "So glad you could make it."

"Oh, I wouldn't miss it." Nana moved her head up and down, and side to side, as if she were admiring the atmosphere in the room. "How'd you find a nice place like this on New Year's Eve?"

"You know me," Mom said. "I pulled some strings and got exactly what I wanted."

Stan and Helen turned to each other, perplexed wrinkles squiggling on their foreheads, unaware of the recurring plot point in my mother's flawed fairy tales: spinning lies into truth.

"You always had a narrow focus," Nana Joan said, a small smile brightening her face. "Like someone poking around a dark room with a penlight."

"Well, we had a tough drive," Pops said to the Nielsens. "Mind if we check in and get settled?"

Helen scurried off to the front desk and returned with a key. "Here you go," she said and passed it to Pops. "You're in room 206, and you're a lucky duck because your bill has been taken care of already."

"Hope that's okay, Jake." Tom tucked in his already-tucked-in shirt. "I told Iris I wanted to pay for your room."

Nana turned to Tom. "Easier done than said, wasn't it?"

Tom chuckled, glanced at my mother, then back at Nana. "Oh well, you know."

My grandmother reached over and pried the room key from my father's hand. "Now Mr. Hyde, since you're so generous, would you be a dear and show me to my abode?"

Tom looked twice. "Oh, ah, sure."

Stan stole a peek at my father's cane. "Hey, mister, I'll go out and get your luggage," he said. "Car unlocked?"

"Appreciate that." Pops gave Stan the keys. "Awfully kind of you."

As Tom and Nana made their way to the door, my mother scowled. "Tom, I believe Jake is fully capable of taking his mother up to their room."

Tom stopped and turned. "It's not a problem, Iris."

Mom fumed, hid it well. "It's only one flight of stairs. They'll manage."

"Don't be so sure," Nana said. "Between my eyes and my son's hip, we'd have an easier time scratching our ears with our toes." She took Tom by the arm and walked out.

After Helen surveyed the emptying room, she scuttled off for something, anything, else to do and left my parents alone. When Pops started fidgeting, Mom fired an opening shot. "How's the limp?"

My dad looked down at his cane, shifted his weight. "It's fine." He tried to smile, but it came out as a wince, as if Mom had stitched his lips and plunged a dagger into his back.

She studied the gift in his hand wrapped up in red. "Wedding present, I suppose?"

"Oh, um, yeah, a scrapbook for Gia." His answer lagged behind her question, got lapped by her comment that followed.

"Wow," she said, "big spender." Her ex couldn't leave now even if he wanted to—and my mother knew he wanted to.

Pops glanced out the window and into the yard, at a hill of snow amassing around the old white oak. Behind the tree's naked branches, the clouds looked like leaves.

Mom set her sights on the oak as well, at a rope dangling from a low, sturdy limb. *What in the world?* Then she blinked, and the vision was gone, forgotten. "I made a lunch reservation for six people at noon," she said.

My father focused on the snow in the yard. "Okay, I'll drive."

"No, Tom will."

"Sounds good."

"Typical Jake," she said, her voice ratcheting up two octaves, "just going through the motions, lifeless as a stone." She stepped closer to him, comfortable in the clash. "Why don't you take a stand for once?"

Pops mumbled, turned, and hobbled toward the door, triggering a reaction in my mother, confirming that she wasn't a priority, a feeling her parents had driven deep into her psyche. In a gradual span of sixty-four years, Mom's destructive behavior rewired her nervous system and constant conflict became her lifeblood, supporting her hardened theory that everything in life was fucked up.

"There you go again," Mom chirped as he left, "scuttling away like you were never here." She ramped up her voice again, just shy of a shriek. "We all would've been better off if that were true, don't you think?"

My dad's only response: a fading thump of footsteps up the stairs.

჻

Noon in Wickford, twelve hours before a new year would deliver fresh resolutions. Mom sat alone at a corner table at the Harborview restaurant, a bayside seafood spot with an obstructed look at the water, a place specializing in fried fish and false advertising.

Gia, Tom, and my father hung up their coats and settled into their chairs; my mother had assigned everyone seats, made certain to stake a claim between her second husband and daughter, opposite Pops—keeping him in her crosshairs. Placing her napkin on her lap, she glared at my father. "Too bad Joan couldn't join us."

"Been getting tired earlier," he said, zeroing in on his menu, shifting in his seat. "I'll bring something back for her."

Mom repositioned her utensils. "And where is Luke, Gia?"

"With his family across the street at Tavern on the Ocean," my sister said.

Mom arched an eyebrow. "Hmm, fancy." She dabbed her cheeks with her napkin, though she'd eaten nothing yet.

"It's so weird not seeing Luke all day," Gia said. "Who started this stupid tradition of denying what we love on the most stressful day of our lives?"

Tom tweaked his glasses and looked at Pops. "Iris tells me your mom had a hospital stay recently. Everything okay?"

"Yeah, fine." My father nodded, rubbed his forehead, and glanced at Gia. "So, um, how are you feeling, kiddo?"

Gia touched his arm and smiled. "Good, Dad." Then her eyes lit up. "Now tell me, what've you been tinkering with lately back in Old Saybrook?"

He rolled up his shirtsleeves. "Well, you know, seems like I've been working on the house next door more than my own. You remember Anna Sikorsky, right?"

"From the beach?" Gia asked. "Not sure I ever met her."

"Yeah, well, since I moved in with your grandmother, Anna's kept me pretty busy." He showed a hint of a grin. "Probably good for me though, you know?"

Gia laughed. "That's my dad, always looking for something to fix."

The conversation sent Mom hurtling back through time. Lost in our Hopedale days, she recalled when Pops retired from teaching after I died, when he fell into a depression, when his descent ignited our family's demise. She criticized him a lot then, argued that he let his fear get the best of him. Her tirades and insults were just a ploy, according to her, a necessary evil to pull him out of his malaise. For his, and everyone's, own good.

When the bells above the restaurant door jingled, Mom refocused on the present. "You still keep that gun in your closet, Jake?"

Tom interjected. "What?"

My father shook his head, lowered his chin. "Not now, Iris."

A server approached, a pretty girl in her late teens, wearing a wide smile that reminded my mother of a younger version of Gia. Same gorgeous complexion, same dancing curls, same wistful glint in her eye. "Happy Almost-New Year, everyone! My name is Janae, and I am so sorry it took so long to check on you. Ready to order?"

While the others mulled over drinks and appetizers, Mom forgot her pointed effort to make Pops uncomfortable with the gun comment, cared only about retrieving warm memories of Gia as a little girl. Back when mother and daughter baked cupcakes together, finger-painted, made papier-mâché puppets, and braided each other's hair. Back when the future predicted they'd form an eternal bond, built with honesty, friendship, and mutual respect.

"Is that okay, honey?" Tom asked.

Mom heard nothing, staring at Janae, thinking of Gia.

"Iris?"

"What?"

"I got you a gin and tonic," Tom said. "Is that okay?"

"Yes, fine, sorry."

While Janae confirmed everyone's order, my father scratched at his beard. After she stopped speaking and clicked her pen, he raised his hand to his cheek. "Excuse me, but could I also get a BLT and a cup of chowder to go, please?"

"You sure can," the young server said. "Be right back."

But before the girl moved an inch, Mom grabbed

her wrist. "Dear, there are coffee stains all over this table. Please take care of it."

Janae narrowed her eyes. "Of course, let me get a towel."

My mother tracked the girl's movements as she bolted through the double doors leading into the kitchen. Once Janae was out of sight, Mom's facial features fossilized, and she turned to my father. "It really kills me when people make a mess of things."

Tom scanned the table. "I don't think it's that bad."

Training her eyes on my dad, my mother said, "You know the type, don't you, Jake, the people who leave stains wherever they go, and ruin whatever they touch?"

Pops squirmed and muttered, "Don't do this."

My mom looked at my sister and broke into a laugh. "Oh my goodness, Gia, remember how this man could never fix that ridiculous clock at the beach house?"

"Mom, please."

"Gosh," said Tom, eyes jumping from table to table, then to the double doors. "I'm starving, wonder what's taking our waitress so long."

"Maybe she's getting a new tool for Jake's old box," my mother said, folding her arms and sitting back.

Gia leaned in close to her and whispered, "For me. Please. Stop."

"Stop what? I'm just complimenting your father on his handy-dandy skills."

"That's enough, Iris," Tom said.

But his plea fell on apathetic ears. Mom wasn't running the show anymore; her demons were. "Oh, it's not nearly enough," she said.

Janae returned with a damp rag. "God, sorry, it's a little hectic in here right now." She dabbed tiny wet blots onto the faint stains.

"We forgive you, dear." My mother's voice was soft, almost honest. "Besides, you're not even close to the most incompetent person here today."

"Okay, that's it." Pops placed his napkin on the table, scooted back in his chair, and struggled to stand. "Gia, can you bring Nana's lunch to her later, please?"

"Wait, Dad, where are you going?"

"Back."

"No, wait, I'll go with you." Gia got out of her seat and reached for his arm.

Pops pulled away from her, snatched his cane and jacket from the nearby rack.

"Gia, sit down," Mom said, her hands flat on her lap. "If your father wants to leave, let him leave. It's too cold and too far for you to walk, baby."

My sister chewed her lip while our father limped away.

Mom bobbed her head and sighed. "That man will never change."

⁓

In my mother's bedroom, a hair stylist named Monk, dressed in leopard-print pants and a blue leather jacket, bopped behind her while sculpting her curls. "There you go," he said with a finishing flair. "All set, my darling."

Expressionless, Mom sat in front of the vanity and stared at her reflection. "Hmm."

Thelma Houston's "Don't Leave Me This Way" pulsed out of Tom's iPhone on the nightstand and pinged off the walls. The air around my mother was stagnant, the stench of her hair coloring lingering.

While Monk danced at Mom's side, a sliver of early-afternoon light slid through a crack in the drawn curtains. The stylist leaned over, put his cheek next to hers, and gazed into the mirror. "Fuckin' fabulous," he gushed.

Monk was a friend of Gia's from RISD, half Filipino and half Italian—on the six-year college program back then, in his early thirties now. Platonic as their relationship had been, my sister spent dozens of wasted nights with him in Providence. Monk always knew where the popular parties were, and the right people who sold the right drugs for said parties. Funny that Gia never knew his last name, or his real first name.

Out of the corner of her eye, my mother snuck a glance at the gloating stylist and raised her chin. "Tom," she called, "turn off the music."

Monk frowned. "Ooh, bummer." He ran a hand over his short blond mohawk. "That jam was my shit."

"Sorry," Tom said.

Monk pulled open the curtains. "Let's get some life up in here," he sang before a wave of light cascaded into the room. "Oh Lord!" He craned his head and gazed out the window, shielding his eyes from the whiteness. "Looks like a Klan meeting in Crackerville, not no wedding in Wickford."

Mom stood and tightened her robe, grabbed another glimpse in the mirror. "Seems like we concealed most of the gray. You can go now, thank you." Even if she were unhappy with Monk's work, she wouldn't ask him to make any corrections, had no tolerance for his "type." But she kept such judgments to herself and hid her hostility well. The way the man moved, spoke, dressed, and danced especially, told my mother all she needed to know about him. And the sooner Monk left, the better.

"Well, I am off like a prom dress," the stylist said, preening. "Gotta take care of your girl and that firecracker friend of hers." He packed his things and strutted toward the door. "Tight as those two were in college, I still can't believe Gia be marrying a dude."

"What was that?" Mom asked, hoping she misheard.

Monk turned. "Said I gotta do your daughter's hair now."

Satisfied with his answer, my mother said, "Yes, just make her look beautiful."

"Shit, I been taming that wild, Black-girl hair for a decade." Monk cracked the door open, kept a grip on the handle, faced my mom. "G's curls get kinky as fuck, and when she wears it short, I keep that kitchen of hers real clean, don't let her use no relaxer." He took a step into the hall. "She ain't tryin' to be white on my watch."

After Monk left, my mother thought back to how Pops managed Gia's "wild, Black-girl hair," and how much patience he showed. How he specialized in pigtails. Then, lowering her eyes, Mom recollected the man who soothed her after she delivered their stillborn infant, four years prior to Gia. The man who held their dead daughter for an hour, said goodbye to her when his wife couldn't. That event devastated my mother, left her with a constellation of questions. Was it her fault? Had she wished the baby away? Would it happen again? And if it did, would her marriage survive? Blaming herself for her daughter's lost life, she loathed every February first thereafter, when guilt settled in her heart, kicked off its shoes, and stayed for months. It scared her to have more children, and she struggled to get pregnant again. But while they tried, her husband held her up with one arm and held hope with the other. Now, she wondered where that brave man went. Why had he vanished? Or why was he banished?

As Tom belted out a Springsteen song in the bathroom, my mother touched up her makeup then stood by the window. She sensed eerie eyes following her then, an unseen presence, a product of her imagination, nothing but a dream. Out in the cove, a thin layer of ice surrounded a lonely, inert buoy, and a quilt of snow covered the small beach. Tiny waves—like those that trickled with life the previous day—had frozen over and were dusted in white. The shore now blending with the ocean, Mom could detect no line of delineation. She missed the beach, remembered the sand under her shoes in Old Saybrook, when she and the rest of the family dumped my ashes into Long Island Sound. *Oh, Devan.*

In the bedroom, Mom opened a pine armoire and sifted through a truckload of hanging clothes, crammed in and dangling like giant bats in a cave. "I need more space." She traipsed to the locked closet, tried to pry it open again, jiggled and yanked at the handle. "Why can't Stanley just kick this in?" she said, appalled at the door's disobedience.

Tom plucked a bobby pin from his wife's purse. "Here, let me try." He picked and poked at the stubborn lock, and in a fit of frustration, he dropped the pin. As he crouched, he inspected the lower portion of the timeworn wooden door. Then he paused and noticed a small etching, carved with a jackknife perhaps, just above the floor: *E.H.*

My mother put her hands on her hips and huffed. "Stay down there any longer and you won't be able to get up."

"Got some initials engraved here." Tom stood, shook out a crick in his knee, and laughed. "Maybe Ed Helms is locked inside."

"Whatever." Mom returned to the armoire, removed three dresses and laid them on the bed. "Should I wear the black, the gray, or the white?"

Tom stared at the door with his arms folded. "Or Emmylou Harris."

"I asked you a question."

"Imagine if it was Engelbert Humperdinck." Tom smiled and nodded, satisfied with his self-amusement. "That would be cool."

"Which dress?"

Tom spun away from the door and glanced at his wife. "You really want my opinion?"

"Forget it," my mother said. "Doesn't matter."

He removed his glasses, wiped them off with a handkerchief, and placed them back on. "The gray dress would bring out your bedazzling blue eyes."

"I'll go with the black one." Mom faced the mirror and held up the dress, obscuring her body. "Not sure about jewelry though," she said.

Tom opened the top drawer of the bureau and fished out a long red velvet box, presented it to my mother, and bowed his head. "For you, my love."

Mom lifted the lid, gasped, and cupped her mouth. "You bought it," she said. "But how? When?"

"I moseyed back to the Silver Lady early this morning." Tom removed the gold necklace from the box, moved behind my mother, and strung it tenderly around her neck. "Told Raymond that this was made for you, had him fix it up."

She held the double-heart pendant in her hand as if it were a wounded bird. Then, after letting it fall against her chest, she kissed her husband softly on the lips. "Tom Hyde," she said, "you always did know how to put things back together."

NINE

Russell, or signals

WITH NINE MINUTES to catch the 2:08 Acela, Russell slalomed through a crowd at Penn Station, dodging hundreds of bundled up New Year's Eve partiers—most from New Jersey and Long Island, all of them already drunk—on their way to Times Square, where they'd attempt to stay sober long enough to count down from ten in ten hours.

When he got stuck behind a pack of giddy high school girls, he slowed down. "Excuse me, ladies," he said, wedging between them.

A brunette wearing glittery plastic glasses, with *2023* frames, tugged at the cuff of his brown leather bomber jacket. "Got plans tonight, stud?"

He turned and flashed a smile. "Afraid so."

He found an open ticket window and requested a round trip to Wickford, with a transfer in Providence. While the teller processed his credit card, Russell checked the pockets of his black jeans then unzipped his turtle green backpack, stared at the contents. *What did I forget?* With plans to stay in Rhode Island less than twenty-four hours, he'd only brought an extra T-shirt, an extra pair of underwear, and socks. He always carried a spare toothbrush and stick of deodorant in his bag. *I know I left something behind*, he thought.

"Here you go," the teller said.

Russell lifted his eyes. "What?"

"Your card and ticket."

"Oh, thanks." He shoved both into a small pouch in the front of his backpack and kept searching for the unknown forgotten item.

"Hey, kid." The teller jutted his jaw and waved his hand. "Move it."

"Oh, sorry." Russ moved over and fiddled with the elastic band on his wrist, a reminder for him to focus, then he remembered. "Shit, my charger." Anxiety seeped into his psyche, which occurred whenever he forgot anything, and a subconscious fear surfaced—the inability to make a phone call.

As my brother squirmed, I took advantage of his vulnerability and sent him a thought message: *It wasn't his fault.* He'd received my formless note before through his dreams, understood what it meant, had filled in the blanks.

His temples throbbing, Russ ran tensed fingers through loose dark curls, palmed his skull like a basketball. *I'm going fuckin' crazy.* Negative thoughts excavated his mind, hollowed him out. My voice tormented him, a psychological manipulation, a ghostly gaslighting, telling him he'd lost his grip on reality, let it slide through his hands, like what happened with Izzy, like what happened with everything he ever wanted.

An announcement crackled over the intercom: "Due to the upcoming winter storm warning, customers may experience detours, delays, or cancelations for all rail services."

My twin distrusted his decision. *Why risk going to this wedding with a nor'easter about to hit?* The four-hour journey would surely take longer, and he'd get to Wickford late, if at all. An uprising of second thoughts threw his self-assurance off its wobbly throne. Doubting himself was a new concept for Russell. When we were growing up, our mother blindly supported his words, actions, instincts, and entire worldview. It never occurred to him that his thoughts had to be based on anything.

If he was going to Rhode Island though, he'd need a charger; his phone battery was more than half dead and wouldn't last the trip. He bet on his train being late and rushed into a nearby Duane Reade, scanned the impulse-buy bins at the checkout counter. No dice, except for the fuzzy ones that hang on rearview mirrors in cars. He asked the clerk, "Do you sell phone chargers?"

The guy swept a greasy lock of hair away from his eye and assaulted Russell with disdain. "Not sure, maybe aisle four."

My brother followed the unreliable lead, speed-browsed the shelves of household items in aisle four and came up empty. Lathered in sweat, he bolted out of the store and hurried toward the gate, checked the display board for departure info. His train now scheduled to leave at 2:17, he leaned against a steel pillar decorated with silver garland and texted Gia: *ETA around 6:30, don't say "I do" without me.*

He wondered if she had a sense of humor anymore. It'd been more than a year since they'd seen each other— the previous October at a two-hour birthday brunch for Mom in West Hartford. While Russ waited for an ellipsis on his phone, an elderly man with stringy white hair approached. He wore frayed jeans, a camouflage windbreaker, a Baltimore Ravens winter hat, and suede moccasins. Fingers and face were filthy. "Hey, brother, spare a buck for coffee?"

Russell opened his wallet, sifted through the bills, and took out a five. "It's all I got."

"Bless you," the dirty man said, hand out. "That'll get me a good hot meal."

My brother forked over the cash, glanced at his phone: no reply text from Gia. He imagined the awkwardness of seeing our sister again, felt responsible for pushing her away. Eleven years earlier, almost exactly, when he stumbled into that bathroom at that high school house party and caught Gia dropping acid with a friend, she swore him to secrecy. He agreed, but she was never the same. Later that week, when he tried to speak to her about it, she blew him off and crawled into a shell. Stayed there till she left for college.

After I died and Russ went to Texas Tech, he and Gia didn't talk for four years. During that time, he clung to his dream of playing pro hoops, while she refused to let go of her grudge. When his dream didn't pan out, he put his energy into *our* dream: a career in the restaurant business, a manifestation of his survivor's guilt. Without me, Russell was missing a piece of himself, listened to my "crazy" voice in his head more than the honest one in his heart. He wanted our family to reconcile but didn't know how he could help.

The old guy with stringy hair walked past my brother with a bottle wrapped in a brown paper bag, flaunted a yellow-toothed smile and threw up a peace sign. Then he shoved his hand into his pants pocket, pulled it out again, and spilled some loose change. Two nickels landed face up by my brother's feet. Russell didn't notice and checked his phone; it was 2:16. No way he'd make it to Wickford in time.

❦

On the Acela, after my brother chose a seat in a quiet car with few passengers, a young Asian woman sat across from him. She had long, straight hair and wore a puffy white coat, black tights, and white earmuffs. Her lipstick the color of an apple blossom. As the train chugged, the woman's seductive smile overtook Russ. If he weren't still with Izzy, he'd hit on the beauty. Then he thought: *Am I still with Izzy?*

Leaving its underground station, the train picked up speed and charged through a tunnel of blackness. When a conductor asked Russell and the woman for their tickets, my brother dug into the empty pockets of his coat and checked his wallet. He stretched out in his seat, legs long and stiff, and patted down his pants. "God, it's here somewhere, sorry." He examined his pockets again, blood rushing to his face. He glanced at the woman, and she pointed to his backpack. He unzipped the small pouch in front, peeked inside, and found the ticket.

From Old Saybrook, I watched the scene unfold, marveling at the woman's intuition, and questioning her abilities. *What's her secret?* I could only read the thoughts and feelings of my family members, not those of strangers. But how did she know where Russell's ticket was? A good guess? My conclusion: she was either a psychic or an empath, sensitive to the emotions of others and able to take on their suffering. *Maybe she can help me.*

I wanted to be with Russell on that train. He'd rejected my messages, and I needed to contact him differently. Had to shock his system and compel him to take my voice seriously, pressure him to tell Pops that I forgave him for the mistakes he made the night of my death. Since my passing, I'd thought about "visiting" my parents and siblings but never followed through, lacked the daring and resolve, my efforts derailed by Simone's warnings. Though I had the freedom and ability to leave Nana's house, my soul usher had cautioned me about decreasing my energy level and risking my chances of "moving on" when I was ready. But now my family would soon be together, and I didn't care about ascending into the heavenly realm. The spirit world couldn't offer me more than this; what I wanted was right in front of me. Focusing hard on my brother, remembering our connection, I broke through.

The striking woman with empathetic powers under-stood my desperation, felt me there, and knew I wanted to communicate with my twin. She let me tune into her, like finding a station on a radio dial, and suddenly I was inside both of their minds.

Russell smiled at her and held up his phone, assumed she didn't speak English, used hand gestures and con-torted his facial muscles while drawling the words: "Do you have a charger?" His query was slow and deliberate, as if he were speaking to a toddler.

Shaking her head and blushing, the woman drew out a pen and a little red notebook from her bag, wrote something and showed it to him: *Linh*.

"That's your name? Linh?" The word tasted strange on his tongue. "It's beautiful." My brother grinned and reached out his hand, took the pad and pen from her. "My name is Russell," he said, jotting down the seven letters, all in caps.

"Yes? Is you?" She said with a giggle as he offered her the pad.

When Linh began writing again, my brother got lost in the scratching sound of pen against paper, as rhyth-mic and precise as the clacking of tracks beneath them. "You're giving me your phone number?" he asked—more of a plea than a question.

With access to Linh's mind, I'd instructed her what to write, and she transcribed my thoughts with no knowl-edge of their meaning. But my exact words got lost in translation. After ripping out the page, she brushed the pen against her bottom lip. And as she handed Russ the note, their fingers touched.

Staring at the paper, he mouthed the sentence: *The boy is killed…*

When he looked up, Linh said, "Yes? Is true?"

He tilted his head and chuckled, tried to play it off. "I don't understand."

"I tell." She scribbled something else and tore out the page.

He took it from her: *The truth hides away…*

Linh looked at him with big, dark, alluring eyes.

Russell shook his head, wary of the direction her words pointed. "I need to go," he said.

"Please, no." Linh jotted another note and ripped it out, folded the paper in half and passed it to my brother.

He wanted to run and hide, but fear rooted him in place.

She nodded, encouraged him with her gaze.

He unfolded the note:…*in your father's heart.*

Reaching out with both hands, Linh emitted the full force of her empathy.

"No, no, no." My brother crumpled the paper, tossed it onto the floor. "You're insane."

"Russell, stay."

He grabbed his backpack and rushed through four cars toward the back of the train, skidded into a seat, and gulped down three Advil. Four rows in front of him, a middle-aged couple turned and stared. "This is not real," Russell whispered. "This can't be real."

It is, I told him, *and you know it.*

My words thundered in his skull, and he was certain the couple ahead heard them too. He was coming unglued; it wasn't the first time. "Stop! You're dead!"

I can't stop. And I'm still here.

Russ jerked the hood of his sweatshirt over his head and covered his face with his hands. "Why is this happening?" he said out loud. And he didn't care who heard.

ॐ

I was with him on the train when he opened his eyes.

An hour into the trip? Two? My brother didn't know. Had Linh been part of a dream? He wasn't sure of that either. He'd lost his grip on reality and didn't trust himself to grab it again, but he kept trying, as if following a path of trick questions to the edge of a cliff.

When he squinted out the window, and into a blizzard, the train tracks intersected with Route 95. He knew he was in Connecticut, near New Haven, close to Hopedale—a place he wasn't sure he'd recognize. Russ had been thankful when Pops sold our childhood home. If Nana hadn't gone blind and didn't need her son to move in with her, our father would've stayed in Hopedale, and our house would've sat on top of him like a shell, a suffocating trap of memories that he'd drag around the rest of his life.

My brother sat up tall and looked around. The old couple had gone, and he was alone. He leaned back and squeezed his eyes shut.

Since appearing to Russ in a vision the night of my death, I'd sent him indirect signals: left nickels for him to find, two at a time, face up, like twins; cast double rainbows in the sky, reminders of the ones we saw after sun showers in Hopedale; sent blue herons to visit him—the first arrived on the beach in Old Saybrook the day of my funeral, glided above my family as my ashes soaked into the sea. Russell didn't receive those signs though, wasn't open to them. By shutting me out, he gave me no other choice—I had to penetrate his thoughts, a strategy that would take a toll on us both. At stake for him: losing his mind. For me: losing all hope.

He'd gone to therapy a few times after I died, stretched himself out on a hard leather couch and spoke about the hurt of losing a twin, the guilt and the incompleteness, but not the voices in his head. The therapist prescribed antidepressants and tried to help my brother accept his loss. Tried to help him become one with it and learn to live with it. The meds helped, but the sessions failed, and I feared failing too.

The train rumbled on.

Tell him, I begged.

No, Russ thought, writhing in the throes of a migraine, defenseless against the agony strewing through his body. He dreaded my presence there less than he dreaded doing what I asked of him.

Tell him, please.

"Stop!" he whisper-screamed.

Please!

He slammed the back of his head against the seat cushion and took a shaky breath. "I swear if you don't go away," he said, "I'll do something we'll both regret."

No matter how much I needed Russ to speak with

our father, I couldn't bear causing irreparable pain. *I'm sorry*, I said.

As he clenched his fists, his knuckles turned hailstone white. "Promise you'll leave me alone, Dev."

I promise.

By ending my visit, I knew we'd never get closer than we were at that moment, but I'd always be a part of him. Holding on to that thought, I said goodbye with a reservoir of regret, and I left my twin for what I thought was the last time.

Again, at a darkened window back in Old Saybrook, I watched. Unappreciated. Unwanted. Unable to act. Was visiting my family pointless? Worthless for all of us?

On the train, Russell pulled his jacket tighter around him, trapping in the warmth. His muscles freed of tension; his brain freed of me. Now he needed someone else, the one person who could guide him when life got complicated and save him when panic held up his heart.

He dialed Izzy and thought, *What am I doing?*

She answered. "Hey."

"Hey, I, um, just wanted to, um." *Go on, tell her.*

"Yeah?"

"I've just been thinking." *And?*

"About what?"

"Sorry, I shouldn't have called." *Tell her!*

He wanted to apologize for how he behaved when she left, how he crumbled. Wanted to tell her about my voice in his head, that he thought he might need psychiatric help. But he couldn't say any of those things. Not because he didn't love her, but because he did. "I really have to go," he said.

"Wait, what's going on with you? Are you okay? Talk to me."

"My phone's dying." He checked the battery. Fourteen percent, enough to get by. "I need to hang up."

"I can't keep doing this, Russ."

He ended the call, slipped the phone into his pocket. "I know, Iz."

Eyes wet and vision blurred, he gazed out the window—Long Island Sound was a tundra, endlessly white, and he got lost in the view. Then as my brother considered what Izzy had said, and what he *should have* said, another voice haunted him: his own.

TEN

Jake, or scars

I HATED BEING alone.

As I drifted through my nana's abandoned house, the solitude dredged up memories of my last moments on the planet—when Pops got out of our car on that deserted road and left me by myself, those confusing and irrational feelings of neglect and disregard.

I went up the stairs and into my father's bedroom, past his closet and over to the window. From that spot, with that view—on long summer days in a brighter Old Saybrook—my dad would occasionally break out his binoculars and laugh to himself while watching his children play on the beach. Now, through the same glass, I was the watcher.

At the old Wickford inn, Pops was disheveled in blue sweats and a white T-shirt, shaving at the bathroom sink, trimming his unkempt beard. His nap an hour earlier hadn't put to sleep the sting of seeing his ex-wife again, nor had his shower washed away her words. He stared into the mirror, at his gray and straggly facial hair. *Might be time to cut it all off.*

He'd grown the beard while in the hospital recovering from an infection after hip surgery. That was fifteen years earlier, almost to the day, so long ago that Pops forgot what he felt like before arthritis infested his joints. And what he looked like before the beard.

When giggles and chatter floated in from the hall, my dad lumbered out of the bathroom, dollops of Barbasol dotting his neck. The door to his room had been left open, just a crack, and he pushed it closed without waking Nana Joan snoozing in her bed. My grandmother had been ill for a few weeks, needed extra rest before attending the ceremony and reception. After my father shut the door, it popped open again, wider than before. Out in the hall, the chatter grew as the family with three little girls skipped past my dad. The youngest two daughters wore heavy winter coats. The oldest, only a dress.

"I can't wait to play in all that snow!" one kid said.

Her dad laughed. "Me too!"

Enjoy it while it lasts, Pops thought while peeking through the crack. *Cuz it doesn't last long.* He banged the door shut, locked it, and returned to the sink. As he ran his razor roughshod over his saggy neck, he sliced the skin. "Dammit!"

Nana stirred and yelled, "What's all that racket?"

"Nothing." Pops folded a tissue and dabbed the blood. When the cut stopped oozing, he entered the dimly lit main room, took off his shirt and sweatpants. He stood naked for a moment then scrambled to pull on his sweats. His mother was blind, but the all-seeing Universe didn't deserve an eyeful of cellulite, lesions, and psoriasis. *Oh, how the mighty have fallen.* That was his go-to line when we kids poked fun at his paunch back in the day.

My grandmother rolled over in bed. "Nervous about the ceremony?"

Pops laughed. "Wouldn't be if Iris wasn't here."

"Everyone in this house might say the same."

My dad couldn't imagine being married to my mother now. But he wished he could restore his image of her, turn her into who she was when they first met, when she ticked every item on his list, when they flew into love. He didn't know why she changed, but he couldn't hold on to the past, couldn't unmake her. He'd unmake himself though, if possible, and become a better man, a husband who'd stand strong if his marriage ran off, a father who'd mourn the loss of his son and be done with it.

Pops had always linked the good with the bad. To him, happiness itself was a kind of grief. Each movie he watched or song he heard, each walk he took or town he visited, came with the feeling that he'd never experience that kind of pleasure again. My death reaffirmed that every joy ended in suffering, and his marriage had produced the same sorrow. Could he ever forgive Mom for not sticking around, for not realizing what she had, for not being the wife she should've been, for not loving him till the end?

Spinning away from Nana, my father buttoned his shirt and scanned the room for his tie. When my grandmother sat up in bed and propped a pillow behind her, Pops moved to her side and asked, "Want help getting ready?"

She grinned. "I certainly raised you right, didn't I?"

For a single second, my dad felt good about himself. Then his spirit dropped low, like the corner of his frown. As a child, he was strong, happy, and kind. Now, just one of those virtues remained. But his kindness had backfired, and the people who loved him disappeared. Only his mother hadn't left him, but she wasn't blameless.

"What are you gonna wear tonight, EJ?"

Pops did a double take; she hadn't used his nickname since he was in grade school. "Tan suit coat," he said, "blue pants."

"How 'bout Daddy's watch?"

How does she know I still have that? My father spied his tie on the floor, snatched it, and threw it around his neck. "I left the watch at home, Ma. It's busted anyway."

"A shame, really."

The real shame, Pops thought, *was that a guy deserted his family because his son made a mistake.* The cracked watch wasn't the reason his father left them, but my dad's inner child still assumed the blame. "He could've fixed that thing," Pops said. "Guess he didn't care enough about me to try."

"Shush up right now! You were the love of my Elliot's life." Nana swung her legs over the side of the bed. "I told you before, your daddy didn't leave you." She stood and softly said, "He left me."

ക

When my father entered the library it was 4:05. Luke was late.

In the back corner, next to the dusty bust of Canonchet, a man in his late thirties tucked his Hawaiian shirt into his khakis and arranged stereo equipment on a folding table. Hanging on the wall behind him, a large rose-colored acrylic sign with brilliant blue lettering: *Rock It with DJ Socket!*

Cane tap-tapping on the hardwood, Pops approached the man and asked, "Need some help?"

"Aw thanks, I'm good, bro." The DJ took an elastic band from his fanny pack and tied his weedy brown hair back in a ponytail. "Just got in from Woonsocket, took ninety friggin' minutes. Goddamn snow's a pisser." He wiped his fingers on his pants. "Oh, sorry, dude, I'm Dylan."

"Jake Jacoby, father of the bride." Pops shook Dylan's hand. "You a friend of Gia's?"

"Nah, I just know Mara, met her at a bar in Boston eons ago, hooked up a few times, haven't seen her in forever."

My father surveyed the DJ's setup. "Guess folks in your line of work don't play vinyl anymore, do they?"

"All digital these days, dude, and careening light-years into the future by the millisecond."

Pops sighed and asked, "So, what's on tonight's playlist?"

"You know, standard pop kinda stuff, some hip-hop

too." Dylan scrolled through his texts. "But Gia wants 'How Deep Is Your Love?' by the Bee Gees for her first dance. Super corny if you ask me."

"Except the part about living in a world of fools." Pops paused before asking, "Did she suggest a song for a father-daughter dance?"

"Lemme see." As the DJ scrolled, he smacked his lips, sounded like bubblegum popping. "She sent me something, but hell if I can find it now. Got Charlie Chaplin in my head for whatever reason. But he didn't even talk, never mind sing, right?"

"Don't worry about it, just curious." My father pulled out his wallet. "I'd like to settle up now, if you don't mind."

"Already got paid, older Black guy with glasses, looks like Al Green."

"His name is Tom."

"Love me some Reverend Al." Dylan snapped his fingers to an imaginary beat and sang, "Whether times are good or bad, happy or sad."

Luke strolled in. "Looks like the party started without me." He wore jeans, a black sweater, and a red New England Patriots hat. Held a bottle of bourbon in one hand, two tumblers in the other.

Pops checked his phone. "Hope you don't make Gia wait this long at the altar."

"No way, Mr. Jacoby." Luke stood up straight and lifted his chin. "I would've married your daughter the minute I met her, if I had your permission of course."

My father smirked. "Good catch."

"Gia's shown me so many pictures of you, I feel like I know you already," Luke said, crushing my dad's fingers as they shook hands. "Very nice to finally meet you, sir."

Pops winced. "You too."

The men moved into the sunroom, stood at a tall table by a wide window. Above the cove, a heron carved a path through the falling snow, its wingspan as long as the depth of a grave. In the backyard, the young family my dad saw earlier played ring-around-the-rosy under the craggy white oak. The eldest daughter, the one without a coat, stayed outside the circle near a gray picket fence and gazed up at the tree. Wore a frown, more angry than sad. *That girl will catch her death out there*, Pops thought.

After Luke filled the tumblers halfway, the men knocked glasses, and a medley of smells cruised in from the kitchen. The wedding feast—lobster risotto, cheesy flatbreads, and mixed vegetables—simmered in pots, baked in ovens, sautéed in skillets. The hints of celebration overloaded my dad's senses, numbing him to the moment. Soon he'd give his daughter away to a man who understood her better than he did. The light faded out in the yard.

Luke looked my father in the eye. "I need you to know, sir, that I love Gia more than anything. I want to be a better man because of her, and I will never let her down."

"You're the kind of guy who speaks his mind, huh?"

"Just what's in my heart, sir." Luke tugged on his hat, smoothed his nut-brown beard. "And I have to say that I totally respect your family and how you and Mrs. Jacoby raised Gia."

"Thank you," Pops said. "It wasn't always easy."

"I can't wait to meet your other children, I mean your other son, I mean Russell." Luke scuffed the floor. "God, I'm really sorry."

"It's okay, honest mistake." My father stared out at the snow. "So, what's the future look like for you two?"

"Well, we can't stay in my small apartment forever, gonna need more space soon." Luke shot back his bourbon. "My plan is to work hard, save up for a house in the suburbs, and make Gia happy along the way."

Pops nodded, a trace of a smile playing around his lips. He peeked at his phone. "Almost four thirty, Potter, better get ready."

"You're right, I'll leave you with this." Luke set the bottle down and gave my dad a quick, powerful hug. "Thank you for accepting me into your family."

You're a good man, Pops thought as Luke walked away. *I trust you with my daughter.* He wanted to say the words aloud, didn't know why he couldn't.

Alone now in the sunroom, my father felt a draft. The cold outside crying, pressing against the windows. In the backyard, the two younger girls lay in a pile of white, flailing their spindly limbs, forming angels. Anxious crows fluttered from tree to tree, while strings of snow tumbled off abandoned branches, twisted and drifted, dropped to the ground in ropes. And the evening grew darker.

᷍

Outside Gia's room, Pops tucked the leather-bound scrapbook under his arm. He waited, and waited, and finally tapped on the door with his cane's rubber tip. On the hallway walls, ornate sconces cast fractured shadows onto the floor.

His daughter answered in a yellow *Cozy Cove* bathrobe, her curls busting out from behind a blue bandana. "Hi, Dad."

"Hey, G." He limped in, set his cane against the wall, and offered my sister his gift. "I know it's not much."

Gia sat on the bed and opened the present, while our father leaned against the bureau and prayed he didn't look as uneasy as he felt. "Oh my God, Dad. I love it." She tossed the wrapping paper onto the floor, turned to the first page, and read the note he'd written.

Dear Gia Grace,

May your future take you further than you ever thought possible. And may your past remind you of how far you've already come.

Love always, Dad

He studied his loafers. "I'm not a poet like you."

Her eyes as wide as a painter's palette, Gia flipped page after page of the scrapbook, a million silent questions swirling in her mouth. She looked up and said, "I can't believe you saved these things."

"Nothing worth more than memories, right?"

Gia scooted over on the bed. "Dad, come sit."

He shifted his weight. "Listen, G, I want to apologize for—"

"Please, Dad." She patted the mattress and smiled like she used to, back when he was the person she loved most.

Pops sat beside her, and they pored over the scrapbook together, commented on every photo, drawing, and poem. Plus all seven love letters eleven-year-old Gia wrote to Taylor Lautner in 2005, after the release of *Sharkboy and Lavagirl*. They laughed, and when she turned another page, she found a note to the tooth fairy. On the next page, a list for Santa. Gia pressed a hand to her cheek. "God, I used to believe in everything."

"All you kids did." Our father smirked and turned to a newspaper clipping with the headline: "Freshman Jacoby Crowned Conference Player-of-the-Year." The article included Gia's position, her season stats, and a picture of her slide-tackling an unlucky opponent on the soccer pitch. "Aah, there's the fighter I remember," Pops said.

She shut the book.

Our dad asked, "What's wrong, G?"

"There's something I need to tell you." Gia exhaled and closed her eyes, searched for courage in the self-imposed darkness. "Remember when I tore my ACL junior year? Final minute of our first game in the—"

"—state tourney," Pops said. "Of course I remember. You guys lost in OT."

"Sudden death." She pulled up the hem of her bathrobe, exposed her right knee, and traced over a four-inch scar. "Funny, sometimes I imagine I kept playing, and we won."

"You could hardly walk." Staring at her kneecap, my father was amazed at how much bigger and uglier the scar had grown since her surgery, and how so much else had gotten worse in those twelve years.

Gia nibbled on her lip and covered up her leg. "I also imagine a world where I never got hurt that day and never started taking those pain pills." She tried to meet his eyes but turned away. "I'm so sorry, Daddy, I let you down, and I know you probably hated me. Maybe you still do, but I just couldn't stop. I wanted to for so long, but I just couldn't."

He didn't know how to respond, but her tears bought him time. He waited for her sniffles to fade and said, "Hey, listen, you didn't let me down, and I could never hate you. Whatever it was you went through, it's over now." He placed a hesitant hand on her back, and her weight fell against it. "You're so strong, Gia," he whispered. "You've always been so strong."

My sister reached for a tissue. "God," she said, voice quivering, "talking to you like this actually feels okay." She wiped her nose, shoved the crumpled tissue into her bathrobe pocket, and faced our father. "I can't undo anything, Dad, but I'm going to make up for the time I wasted. And I hope you can forgive me."

I should be the one pleading, our father thought as shame scribbled across his face. "Of course I forgive you." He paused for a moment, lowered his chin, then waded into deeper waters. "How bad did it get after Devan died?"

From Nana's house, I watched Gia squirm and stare at the ground, like she'd lost something she could never find. I watched our father consider saying what happened the night I passed. Saw the argument form in his head

while he debated admitting how he really felt—that he'd
die if he thought her addiction had worsened because he
couldn't save me.

She didn't tell him that she sank into a depression
after my death. Didn't say that drugs had taken ahold of
her by then, or that she thought she could regain control.
He didn't tell her that he let his past overthrow his future.
Didn't say that he was terrified of the man he'd become,
or that he was more afraid of the hopeless years ahead.

Gia sensed our dad had more to say but didn't press;
Pops uttered a couple of words but cut them off. Then my
sister cleared her throat of everything she hadn't revealed.
"The best thing I ever did was find someone to talk to."
She laid her head on his shoulder and looked out the
window. "Rehab got me clean, but therapy reminds me
that my life now is worth something, and worth saving."

Pops reached over and put his hand on hers, squeezed
it tight. And their quiet conversation continued, unit-
ing them further, moments of understanding stringing
together, one after the other.

"I still have demons," Gia said. "But I won't let them
beat me." She ran a finger across the cover of the scrapbook. "I don't know what really happened with all of us,
but whatever it was, and however you feel at fault, I want
you to know that I never blamed you."

"That means a lot, G." More than that, it was all he
needed to hear. "Wish your mother felt the same."

In less than two hours, Gia would be a married
woman. Not a little girl any longer, but still a big sister,
still a daughter. Someone who made him proud, and

someone who forgave them both. He closed his eyes, kept his hand on hers, and had no intention of letting her go.

"I got a text from Russell earlier," Gia said. "He's on his way." She pulled her fingers out from our father's grip. "And you've got to go now, Dad, unless you wanna brush off your skills and style my hair like you used to."

He took a long look at her. "Can't say I've seen a bride in pigtails."

They laughed, standing at the same time. He grabbed his cane while Gia put the scrapbook in her suitcase. "For safekeeping," she said.

Pops smiled. "Yeah, that's a priceless work of art." He kissed her on the forehead, and as he walked out, neither of them felt the hollow eyes of a little girl staring at them from a shadowy corner of the room.

"Love you, Dad." Gia closed the door.

In the musty hallway, almost too narrow for breathing, the sound of my father's steps sank into the carpeting, while a mazelike pattern of the black-and-white wallpaper created the disturbing illusion of an unsolvable labyrinth leading to unknown treasure. Halfway to his room, he stopped and leaned against the wall—next to a faded painting of five children, four boys and a little girl, playing under a tree in a yard full of flowers. Pops thought about the asthma attack that killed me, wished he had the guts to tell Gia the real story: that he forgot to fill the Ford with gas, that he left his cell phone on the desk at home, that if he hadn't made those two unforgivable mistakes, I'd still be alive, and our family would be happy.

Sadness pummeling his heart, he bowed his head. I

wanted to yell at him, tell him that I was okay, demand that he shake his courage loose and claw his way forward. But even if Pops could've heard me, he would've chosen not to, and I remembered what Simone once said: "Your father's journey has no end. He'll lose you every day for a lifetime."

PART III

THE NIGHT OF THE WEDDING

৵

Our mind thinks of death. Our heart thinks of life.
Our soul thinks of immortality.

—Sri Chinmoy

ELEVEN

Visits, or me

ON THE BEACH behind Nana's house, small waves rippled, and seagulls cried as they took cover from the night—or so I imagined.

Having lost my earthly senses long before, I couldn't feel the cool ocean breeze or smell the salty wind as it snuck through drafty windows. Couldn't look out over Long Island Sound and lose myself in the darkening colors of the horizon.

Then, a familiar voice: *A ghost misses being human, wants its body back, craves what it lost, and stays hungry for what it can never have.*

My parents and siblings would soon be together at the inn, our happiness awaiting in the reachable future. The second I visualized that scene, Simone arrived. "It's time to let go."

"But I want to be with my family still," I told her.

"How do you expect to help them?"

"I don't know, but I have to try. Maybe just having me there with them, all of us in the same place, will be enough."

"There's so much more waiting for you in the heavenly realm, Devan. You'll gain an extraordinary level of omniscience, reunite with souls from past lives, find true peace."

"I don't care about any of that."

"Your energy level is extremely low already," she said.

"But they need me."

"I can't stop you from going," Simone said. "Just know that your visits may cause your family more pain, serving only as a reminder of what they lost. And grief too long continued will delay the journey, for all of you."

"I have to do something," I said.

TWELVE

Gia, or secrets

GIA'S STYLIST HELD up a mirror. "Bitch, take a good look," Monk said, "cuz the girl in that glass ain't coming back." He moved a delicate hand around her head without touching her hair. "Only thing we gonna recognize are these curls."

My sister sat tall in her chair and tugged at the purple nylon salon cape around her neck. "Think marriage will change me that much?"

Mara stood in the bedroom's corner. "Hope not."

Gia picked at her nails under the cape. "What if I don't like the new Gia Potter?"

"Then you change right back," Monk said, stealing a glance at Mara, then refocusing on Gia. "You got some bounce-back shit in you, G, some takes-a-licking-and-keeps-on-ticking Timex DNA. The *real* you is indestructible."

"I'm definitely stronger than I used to be," my sister

said. "Guess I just had to find an honest man like you did, Monk."

The stylist tipped his head back and roamed the room. "My Steven is a lot of things, but 'honest' ain't one of 'em." Monk flicked on a lamp switch, hit one on the wall too. "Why this old inn gotta be so dismal?"

"Because shining lots of light on it," Mara said, "shows every imperfection."

"Speaking of imperfections," Monk said, snipping the air around Gia's head, "badass Iris gave me strict instructions to make you beautiful tonight, G. You believe that? Like I could improve on flawlessness."

My sister dropped her chin. "Ugh."

Monk snickered. "Your mama be like the Cruella de Vil of buppies."

When Gia was young, our mother affirmed her beauty every day but loved her conditionally, only valued her physical features, didn't appreciate what she looked like on the inside. Mom brought my sister everywhere when she was small, parading her around like a pampered poodle in fancy clothes for Hopedale housewives to fawn over. As a result, Gia learned to use love as a tool to get what she wanted, preferred pretending over telling the truth, and contorted for others. Trading authenticity for attachment, she became a thoughtful but anxious anomaly, a giver who shielded herself from the world. And when our mother showed her ugly side, Gia did too.

Using the bed as a prep area, Mara arranged my sister's jewelry, veil, and shoes. She took Gia's lace wedding gown from the closet, laid it out on the bed's gray comforter. She walked by the mirror, stopped, and said, "Forever a bridesmaid." Then stroked her long tangerine locks, which fell in waves around her shoulders. "Hey, Monk, think if I became a bleach blonde, I'd find true love like G?"

"A woman's hair can only take her so far," he said.

"I'm not looking for a trip around the world," Mara said. "The end of the block will do."

My sister craned her neck, twisted her hair around her fingers. "I'm gonna go for a new look after the wedding," she said, "cut this real short, like Halle Berry."

Monk crossed his arms and stared, as if envisioning a different Gia. "Short like *Boomerang* Halle, or like *Monster's Ball* Halle?"

"I might experiment with a new style of painting too," my sister said, now in a conversation with herself. "I need more negative space in my art." She considered how the area surrounding a subject was as important as the subject itself, how a lack of detail simplified the image. There was artistry in what appeared before the eyes, but also in what did not. For Gia, true beauty lay in the invisible, in what didn't exist.

While Mara searched the room for Monk's boar bristle brush, the stylist attended to my sister's luscious curls. "So honestly, girl," he said, "you got butterflies somersaulting in your belly yet?"

"More like pterodactyls doing back handsprings," she said. "I can't help but think of everything that can go wrong at the ceremony."

"That's the existential terror of being alive, baby." He

swiped fresh clippings off of Gia's neck. "All that matters though is your daddy walking you down that aisle. After the shit you all been through, this is his day as much as it's yours." Monk held up the mirror behind Gia, showing the back of her hair.

"I can't really see it, but I trust you." She stared into the blackened window, saw nothing in the abyss. But she heard the wind and felt the storm.

Monk unsnapped the salon cape and dropped in onto the floor. "All right, up we go," he said. "Let me behold your essence."

My sister stood and brushed stray hairs off her gray Ricky Martin concert tee, the one she bought for me when we saw him at Mohegan Sun in 2011. The only item of mine she kept. She peered into the vanity mirror, then turned to Mara. "What do you think?"

Mara stared like a child regarding an unwrapped gift.

"Holy shit, you hate it," Gia said and looked into the mirror again. "It's too short, isn't it? We'll fix it. Monk, can you fix it?"

"No, stop, I don't hate it." Mara said. "I love it. I love—"

A phone buzzed.

"Oh, that's me." Gia took her cell from the nightstand. "It's a text from my dad. My nana wants to see me." She scrunched her face and released a sigh. "I should go."

Mara moved aside.

"You're not going anywhere yet." Monk got three plastic cups from the bathroom, uncorked a bottle of Dom Perignon, and poured bubbly for the group. "A toast," he said, "to friends, to love, and to our girl's dream wedding."

"Thank you," Gia said and smiled while Monk and Mara drained their champagne.

"I gotta break out too," Monk said, gathering a few of his things. "Need to fight this weather and meet Steven in South Kingstown."

Mara handed him the salon cape. "Don't tell me you're going to a URI frat party."

"Nope, a Cinderella-themed bash at an old friend's place," Monk said. "Got my fairy godmother costume in the Wrangler." He smooched Gia's cheek. "At the stroke of midnight, everything will be different, baby."

Eyeing Gia's fuzzy white slippers on the floor by the bed, Mara said, "Remember that New Year's Eve we all spent together in Providence in 2018?"

"Remember it?" Monk laughed. "The bartender I got with that night still slides up on my Insta every month."

My sister turned back the calendar to that foggy evening, the cocaine and the ecstasy and the forty-eight hours of darkness that followed. She closed her eyes and shivered, mortified by her old life, feeling cold beside the memory. Haunted by the days when she wanted to forget herself. Frightened by the nights when she wanted to erase her entire world. Now she couldn't help but think, *Are those nights gone for good?*

"We had some good times, huh?" Mara said, her gaze dead set on Gia.

When a sudden chill seeped into the room, my sister puffed on her hands and rubbed away the prickles on her arms. But no matter how much pressure and heat she applied, her track marks would never disappear.

~§~

Quiet as a feline, Gia took a half step into our father's room. "Hello?"

At the desk by the window, with his back facing the door, Pops pushed up from his chair, turned, and whispered, "Hey, honey." He had on the same suit jacket and pants he wore to my funeral. My sister couldn't believe they still fit, but she kept the comment to herself.

Gia said, "The door was open so I—"

"Yeah, come on in." He glanced at his mother, who lay in bed, above the covers, her eyes flickering open. He grabbed his cane and hobbled toward the door. "I'll leave you two alone. Might check downstairs and see if the Nielsens need a hand with anything."

Pops touched Gia's forearm, winked, and walked past her.

She waited for the door to close and sat on the bed. "Hi Nana," she said, surprised at the sight of our grandmother, so different and diminished from the image my sister held in her mind.

Nana Joan stirred and cooed, "Mmm, my Gia." She reached up with wrinkled hands, felt her granddaughter's satiny face, and flashed a knowing grin like she was reading her favorite poem in braille. "Darndest thing about losing your sight," she said, "people seem to get frozen in your mind."

"Well, you haven't changed a bit," Gia said.

"That's not exactly a compliment." Nana laughed. "I'm afraid I'm a bit green at the gills tonight, dear. I won't make it down for the ceremony."

"That's okay," Gia said, a needle of disappointment poking at her heart. "I know you'll be there in spirit."

"How are you fixed for a dress?" Our grandmother ran her fingers up my sister's arm and tugged at the hem of her T-shirt. "This doesn't feel like Vera Wang."

Gia giggled. "No, it's not." She stopped her smile, remembering it went unseen. "Mom gave me the dress she wore when she married Dad, and I altered it."

"Oh, I loved that dress, simple and sleeveless, lace with a flower and leaf motif."

"Yes," Gia said. "Excellent memory, Nana."

"You bet I remember it," our grandmother said. "I *made* it."

My sister pulled back a gasp. "Oh my God, I had no idea. That makes it so much more special." She leaned over and gave the old woman a light hug, like she'd crack her in half if she were too rough.

"After all you've been through, dear, you deserve the most special things life can offer." Our grandmother propped her head up higher on her pillow. "Hope that dress brings you better luck than it brought your mother."

"It already has," Gia said.

"Now, tell me about this Luke Potter. Is he deserving of you?"

"He's amazing. I think we're really compatible."

"Compatibility isn't a requirement *for* love," Nana said in a wistful voice. "It's an accomplishment *of* love."

Gia smiled. "Hmm."

"Your betrothed will need some help dealing with Iris, you know. She's got a knack for prying and meddling and tucking away the truth." Nana sighed. "Like a fish covered in feathers, trying to convince the world she can fly."

"Maybe she'll change."

"Oh, sweetie," our grandmother said, "quenching our thirst with turpentine would be considerably more feasible."

"You might have a point," my sister said, twisting her modest engagement ring around her finger in nervous circles.

"While I'm lavishing my infinite wisdom," Nana continued, "you should set things right with Russell. Your father tells me you two don't talk much anymore, but you're going to need each other one of these days."

"I don't know," Gia said. "We've got trust issues, and I think we're both too emotional."

"Show me a heart that won't melt, and I'll show you one that'll break in a breeze."

My sister couldn't help but laugh. "Okay, I'll speak with him."

"Good," Nana said. "We're not on this random rock in this remote galaxy for long, so we need to make the most of it."

At that instant, as if life had granted our grandmother more time, the wrinkles, age spots, and blotches on her face vanished. When Gia peered into the old woman's alert eyes, she was certain they could see. From my sister's perspective, Nana's thin gray hair became fuller and darker, similar to the way it appeared when we kids were little, when our grandmother covered her long, blonde, windblown locks with a silly straw hat, the one with a plastic red rose, while collecting shells with us at the shore in Old Saybrook.

"I'll try to fix things with Russ," Gia said. "But getting married is scary enough."

"Marriage is not for fraidy-cats, my love. It can damage the toughest folks, and having a family of your own will put your heart to the test, day after day. Lord knows my marriage tested me, and when my Elliot left, it crushed your daddy."

Gia rubbed Nana's leg. "Dad said it was because you cheated."

"But that's not the actual reason." Our grandmother filled her old lungs with as much air as they could hold. "I made up that story, so he'd stop blaming himself. Your father never knew the truth." She slipped deep into the past, and as she told Gia the tale, her eyes darted through the years. "My husband was a sweet man, but he was also a sick man, had an illness the doctors couldn't diagnose, not at first. He lived in a nightmare of hallucinations and delusions, couldn't tell what was real, saw and heard things that weren't there, said people were trying to hurt him. Your father, EJ, as we called him, was only six when the doctors told me my husband was schizophrenic. They said they could treat him, said there were new drugs that would ease his symptoms. But my Elliot was stubborn and didn't want to take the medication." Nana paused and faced the ceiling as gravity pulled water from her eyes. "Well, one infernal summer night, around two a.m., I found him sitting on your father's bed brandishing a long, sharp fishing knife. He was shaking and crying, saying he was going to take our son away, someplace where no one could hurt them. I had no choice, Gia. I called the authorities, and they arrested my husband. Your father, bless his soul, slept through the whole ordeal. And my Elliot? They committed him to an asylum outside of Boston. He got better, somewhat, after a year or so, and told me he wanted to come live with us again."

"And?"

"Oh, honey, I was still so worried. Hardest thing I ever had to do was make him promise to never contact me or your daddy again. And he never did. He was such a sweet man."

A shiver slid across the nape of my sister's neck.

"Jake idolized his father," Nana said, "so I lied to him about what happened, told him I kissed another man, and that's why Elliot left. I took the blame and buried the truth, and the longer it stayed in the dirt, the tougher it was to dig up. I didn't want Jake to know the sick person his father really was, or that I thought the man might kill all three of us. What good would that have done? Maybe I should've handled it differently, but I did what I thought best."

"Oh my God." My sister took in a long breath and

peered out the window, at the storm turning the night into nothingness.

"I'm concerned about your father," Nana said. "Please look after him for me."

"I don't understand." Invisible strings entwined Gia's conscience, and the more she wriggled, the more they tangled. "Why are you telling me this?"

"I had to tell someone, and I knew you could handle it. For this family to patch itself up, we need to help your father first."

My sister's breath quickened, and she couldn't keep back her tears. "Why'd you keep this to yourself for so long, Nana?"

"People are driven by one of two things, Gia, either love or fear." Our grandmother took my sister's hand. "But I've always been driven by both."

"Why don't you tell Dad the truth?"

"It's been so very long, and I don't want to hurt him again."

After Gia wiped her eyes and hugged Nana, a warm calm washed over my sister, relaxing her muscles and mind. "I'm sorry, I have to go," she said with a sniffle. "But I promise to come up and visit after the ceremony."

"Oh, sweetie, you're going to be a beautiful bride, and you deserve all the happiness the world has to give."

"I am happy." My sister lowered her head. "But I've got this guilty feeling, you know, because Devan's not here. Like he'd want me to be more upset."

"You listen up." Nana gathered Gia close. "Guilt is a

useless emotion, and your brother doesn't get to decide when you're done being sad about him."

"But the pain is still scary sometimes."

"No need to be afraid, dear. Our pain isn't here to hurt us. It only wants to be seen."

My sister texted Pops and let him know she was leaving. She rose from the bed and placed a hand on our grandmother's bony shoulder. "Will you be okay till Dad gets back?"

"Of course, dear."

"I love you," Gia said.

"I know you do." Then with the same wishful eyes, the older woman turned to the younger and said, "Now go out into the world and love some more."

My sister went to the door, which hadn't closed entirely, left open wide enough for a conversation to creep out. She pulled the handle, looked up, and met our father's blank stare in the hall. Her heart slipped, and she stepped back. "Dad? How long have you been out here?"

∽

Gia was twenty-five when she hit rock bottom, posing for a mug shot at the Providence police station after stealing Amazon packages from her landlord.

She was a zombie at the precinct that night, strung out, incoherent. Her fingerprints, the only evidence of her original self. When the officer on duty allowed her one phone call, she didn't contact Mom or Pops, she called her one true friend, said she wanted to kill herself. The next morning, after her landlord dropped the charges,

Mara picked Gia up from the station, took her home and talked her down.

Our parents never found out about the arrest. If they had, what would they think? That their daughter was a joke? That the screwup had shamed our family and dirtied an already soiled reputation? How could anyone think any less of her? My sister withdrew even further then, stayed high to block out her embarrassment, while redemption remained a pipe dream.

At the Cozy Cove, camera clicks and flashes bounced around Gia's room. While perched on the bed, Chrysalis focused her lens and snapped shots of the pre-wedding scene. She crouched in the corner as my sister put in her earrings. Lay prone on the floor as Mara twirled in her bathrobe. Teetered on a chair as Gia touched up her hair. *Click. Click. Click. Click.*

"Time for the moment of truth," Mara said.

My sister slipped into her gown.

Mara shook her head and smiled. "Stunning, G. Totally stunning."

As Gia ran her fingers over the lace, across the flower and leaf pattern, she reflected on our grandmother's secret and the reality our father never knew. My sister drew a deep breath, and every muscle in her body constricted, every cell ached. How much of Nana's story had Pops heard outside the door? Then came a slew of unrelated questions: Did Brodie tell Luke about the pills? Would Mom make trouble at the ceremony? Would Russell show up?

Mara fastened the backside of my sister's gown and

said, "These bad-boy buttons are dainty as shit. They don't like it rough. You sure I'm the right girl for this job?"

Gia laughed. "There are only six of them," she said. "You can handle it."

"Yep, just one more left to—" Then the top button popped off.

"One more what?"

"Oh, crap!"

"What happened?"

"Nothing."

"Mar?"

"I might've been *too* rough." Mara dropped to her hands and knees. "A button fell off, but it's right here, somewhere."

Gia spun around and looked down. "Do you have it?"

Chrysalis snapped a photo.

"Not yet," Mara said.

My sister's face went pale, and she started trembling. She hiked up her gown and crouched, scanning the hardwood. "The ceremony's in thirty minutes," she said. "I'm gonna be sick."

"We'll find it," Mara said and crawled toward the nightstand. "I hope."

In an instinctual act of self-preservation, my sister's mind skipped from the lost button to a game we used to play when we were kids. Her eyes lit up at the thought, and her lips curved into a smile. *Click. Click.*

On cloudy days at the beach house, when we were bored or fighting over the last waffle or arguing about what DVD to watch, our mother would dump a giant bowl of sea glass onto the kitchen table. My siblings and I would select thirty of the shiniest, most colorful pieces. Then, we'd lie face down on the living room rug while Mom and Nana Joan went out back, drew an enormous circle in the sand, and buried the pieces. A few minutes later, they'd call us outside and set us loose to dig up our treasure. "Okay, ten each," Mom would yell, but Gia and Russell found all the sea glass, all the time, pushed me out of the circle, kept me away. Once, after they went back inside, Nana hid the glass again and played the game with just me.

Through a window in Old Saybrook, I watched Gia and the others searching for the button, scrambling on their hands and knees in her room. I had to visit my sister, felt like she wanted me there. I concentrated and focused, invested my whole being into the effort, hoped and wished to be there, harder than I'd wished for anything over birthday candles or shooting stars. Then—at the speed of thought—I traveled to the inn and found myself in the library. The atmosphere surrounding me was thick, heavier and darker than the veil that covered the beach house. And as I passed through the narrow halls looking for Gia, I felt the strange aura of another being, something ominous, overflowing with energy and power. I couldn't pinpoint its location, but I knew it wanted me to leave.

I arrived in my sister's room just as Gia was drawing a picture with her recollections: the two of us on the shoreline, searching for snail shells in tide pools. I stayed near to the bedroom door at first, then moved into the far corner. My sister sensed my presence; I was certain. She allowed me in closer, let my spirit filter through her, and didn't push me away. I hoped my visit meant something to her, more than my visit with Russell meant to him. Would Gia create a bigger place for me in her life? Should she paint a lasting portrait of us on the canvas in her mind? Could she be brave and keep her memory of me alive?

Flat on her stomach, Mara swept her arm under the bed like a fleshy windshield wiper. "How can that button just vanish?"

Chrysalis stood above Mara. "I thought it rolled over near the headboard," the photographer said, aiming her camera lens. *Click.*

Gia had lost more than a delicate, fabric-covered button; now she couldn't find her breath either. She linked her fingers behind her neck. "What am I going to do?"

The button was half-hidden under the baseboard, and I wanted to point my sister in the right direction. From the back of the room, I tried to get her attention. When I made the radiator steam up and spit water, a puddle formed near the lost item. Gia looked up and around, like she knew I wanted her to find something that had been needlessly lost, a small yet necessary part of an intricate design, out of sight and missing now, but maybe not forever.

"Hang on!" Mara got up off the floor, ran into the

bathroom, and came out with a safety pin. "Okay, G, just pretend you're Kim Cattrall."

"What?" My sister turned her back. "From *Sex and the City*?"

"No, *Mannequin*."

"Oh God." Gia stiffened and squeezed her eyes. "Please don't ruin this."

"I can't promise anything," Mara said. "But I'll try not to draw blood." Then she smiled and secured the back of the dress without ripping the lace.

My sister bit her lip and opened her eyes. "Do you think it'll hold?"

Mara swept Gia's hair aside, inspected all the buttons. "I do."

In a chair by the vanity, Chrysalis scrolled through the digital photos on her camera.

"Bet you got some keepers, huh?" Gia asked before releasing an anxious laugh.

Staring at the display screen, Chrysalis wore a dazed expression. "Um, yeah," she said. "They look great." In each of the wide-angle pictures of the bedroom, in the corner near the ceiling, the photographer had captured a shadowy image, my humanlike silhouette, vapory and disfigured, like a thundercloud sculpted with wires.

THIRTEEN

Iris, or arrows

NEEDING TO STAY at the inn with my family, I moved through the hallways until I reached my mother's room. The ceremony was less than a half hour away, and she was ready, decked out in a black dress and black heels, double-heart diamond necklace dangling from her neck.

Tom emerged from the bathroom in a classic Brooks Brothers tuxedo, no standout accessories, no splashes of color. "Debonair, no?" he said.

"Hmm."

Tracing the subtle strains of classical music, the couple walked downstairs, while I followed, and headed into the library. A roaring fire threw crackles at the walls, packing the room with warmth, in a showdown with drafty windows. The place looked "satisfactory," according to my mother: chairs and flowers tastefully arranged; DJ tucked away in the back near the entrance, Mendelssohn's "Wedding March" filling the space. *Not terrible,*

Mom thought—except that Stanley had gone against her wishes and removed the rug, exposing the engraving of the gruesome Ouroboros.

Before she and Tom sat, the Potter family greeted them. "Oh, Iris, you look dazzling," Beth said with out-stretched arms.

My mother eyed Beth's simple blue dress and Bill's run-of-the-mill slacks-and-jacket ensemble, a Men's Wearhouse special. She scanned Brodie and Luke's attire, plain gray suits with pink ties. Mom sighed and said, "You too."

From the corner of the room, I spied the group as they took their spots up front. My mother and Tom sat in the first row, Bill across the aisle, while Luke, Brodie, and Beth stood by the fireplace. Clicking his tongue toward Tom, Bill leaned over and said, "Hey, I hear your boy's taking a train here from the city."

Tom glanced at my mother, who hadn't acknowl-edged the comment. "Yes," he said, "Russell should be here soon."

"I love your optimism, Tommy boy." Bill tossed his head back and laughed. "If I were a betting man, which I am, I'd throw a bundle down on the storm winning that battle."

DJ Socket played a song by Vanessa Carlton, which my mother once sang with Gia at a karaoke party in 2003. Mom lost herself in the memory of that night when Nana Joan surprised her and Pops for their fifteenth wedding anniversary at the American Legion hall in Hopedale. Staring into the fire, my mother saw her and nine-year-old

Gia sharing a microphone, belting out the song together. Mom leaned back in her chair and whispered to herself: "'Cause you know I'd walk a thousand miles if I could just see you tonight."

After I died, she never uttered those words about me. Not aloud, not even to herself. The sentiment stayed locked in her throat, and in her heart. She was supposed to say she missed me, that she'd travel the universe for one more day with me. She was supposed to feel something, but she chose not to.

Tom squinted at the wedding program. "Oh, for crying out loud," he said, "I forgot my glasses up in the room."

Mom pierced him with a sideways glance. "Shocking."

As Tom bounded up the stairs, he passed Pops inching down. I wanted to stay, hoped my father would sense me there. I had felt so alive and loved with Gia earlier, but Simone's warning came back to me: *You'll need energy to cross over.* Despite my love for my family, and despite my claims that I didn't care about ascending into the heavenly realm, something had changed.

Protecting my chances of moving on in the afterlife, I returned to the dismal ache of being alone in Old Saybrook. But going back there was different this time—more permanent, more distinct—a longer stride taking me a measured distance away from my parents and siblings. The spool of string had turned again, and the connection between us had lengthened. Soon, I feared it would unravel and separate.

Back in my nana's house, I strained to look through the sliding glass door and begged for a view of the beach.

But I only saw the old inn in Wickford and the Nielsens' last-minute preparations in the library: Helen straightening shelves and lighting candles, each flame shimmering and white; Stanley stoking the fire and tying back curtains, offering a disconcerting view of the blizzard.

Uneasy in her chair, my mother noticed two black blemishes on the plaster wall near the fireplace and motioned for Stanley to come over. "Those weren't there yesterday," she said with crass candor, as if reprimanding one of her students.

The innkeeper locked his wiry thumbs behind red suspenders and explained that two young girls had been playing with a broom handle in the room earlier and scuffed the paint. "Kids will be kids," he said. "You remember those days, don't you?"

"No, I don't," my mother said, tugging at her sleeve and covering up a thumbprint-sized cigarette burn on her shoulder, six decades old. Mom's abusive childhood had left permanent marks on her body and holes in the walls of her memory. She never forgave her parents for beating her, for stealing her childhood, for dying without telling her they were sorry. Swore she never would.

Escorted by his cane, Pops limped down the aisle and scuttled next to his ex. "Hey, Iris, can we talk in private?"

The old-fashioned scent of his Brut cologne filled her face, and she remembered that he started using the brand—a name contradictory to his character—when they began dating. More disinterested in his question than her recollection, Mom faced forward and replied, "Do I have a choice?"

Her cold shoulder dragged down the temperature in the room, and Pops shuddered. "Please, Iris."

My parents left the library and entered the sunroom as Ben E. King's "Stand by Me" slinked between them, keeping the peace for the moment. At 6:20 in the evening, in the dead of winter, with a snowstorm whipping outside, the word "sunroom" would've won a ribbon for misnomers.

Posturing beside a high-top table, my mother flicked a crumb off the white cloth and folded her arms, while an orchid in a crystal vase leaned away from her. In the dank room, Mom was only an apparition, her dark dress becoming one with the shadows. The shifting light caught and released the brilliance of her necklace, the sheen of her hair, illuminating the impatient glare on her face as she confronted my father. "Is this little chit-chat about Russell?" she asked. "Don't tell me he's not coming."

"No, he'll be here." Pops kept the table between them and his chin on his chest. "I wanted to talk to you about Joan," he said. "She can't make it down for the ceremony, but I overheard her talking to Gia about my dad."

"You must be joking."

His shoulders slumped in a silent sigh. "I didn't catch the whole thing but—"

"Unbelievable," Mom snickered. "The woman travels all this way then skips her granddaughter's wedding vows."

My father lifted his head like a tentative sunflower at dawn. "She's been under the—"

"I wish Luke would skip it too," she said, blue flames in her eyes. "I could do without the Potter family in my life."

Pops dared to meet my mother's stare. "Do you hear yourself?"

"Loud and clear."

I hated it when my parents fought. They got along great when I was young, and I loved their love, the way they laughed and teased, like all of us did. But after his hip surgery, my father got quiet, which was fine with Mom, who'd been spending less and less time at home. And it was fine with me too; I kept to myself then, didn't fit in with any one group, had a hard time connecting, didn't know who I wanted to be. I was happiest reading and studying, playing video games, and watching TV. When I turned sixteen, I got braver though, closer with a couple of classmates in Hopedale, wandered up to the edge of the scary forest called "life." Didn't matter, it was too late, the last ring had already formed around my tree, and Death had an axe in its grip.

"I have an idea, Jake." My mother scoffed at the orchid, and at Pops. "Why don't you join Joan upstairs and stay there for the ceremony?"

"Please, can you stop with the act?" My father had lost the last of his patience, like the final molecule of helium escaping a leaky gas balloon. "Our daughter is getting married," he said. "We should be happy for her, and for ourselves, God forbid, at least for one night."

My mother gaped.

Just then Mara stormed into the sunroom. "Mrs. Hyde, Gia needs you!"

"Ugh. What now?" Mom said, and she left my father again.

❧

"G, let's go, baby. You need to be down there in ten minutes." Our mother leaned on the bathroom door and
knocked again. "You're just nervous, I get it." Mom couldn't
fathom what could've paralyzed her daughter, causing the
girl to lock herself away and create such a major inconvenience. The pitfalls of marriage? The sanctity of trust? The
unknowable future? *Grow up already, will you?*

On the other side of the door, Gia sniffled.

"I know what you're going through," Mom said, loud
and direct. "I felt the same way before I married your
father. Didn't know if I was doing the right thing, or if he
was the right man for me."

Sniff.

My mother waited for the silence to end, but the
silence didn't cooperate either. "Gia, baby, people are
waiting downstairs. Everything's ready. It's time to go."

Foiled plans never brought out our mother's good
side, and the other side of her screamed: *Do not embarrass
me, Gia Grace!*

"I don't want to end up in a marriage like yours," my
sister blurted. "Dad doesn't deserve to be lied to, it's not
fair to him, he's been lied to enough."

"What's this really about?"

"The truth."

"Well then, let me tell you."

For a split second, my mother considered coming
clean and admitting her affair. But the pebble of honesty
got stuck in her throat. Since she was little, she had

survived the world trying not to get hurt, and nothing had changed. The thought of telling Gia the truth now stung what remained of Mom's conscience, so she fell back on the easier, more reliable choice. "Before Devan died, while your father was recovering from surgery and spent a month in the hospital, he pulled away from me," she said. "That's when our marriage dissolved."

"And you never cheated on him?"

"Never!" Mom started sneaking around with Tom after my dad's hip replacement, but she'd never disclose that to anyone, even if they already knew. "Your father couldn't take care of me emotionally," she said. "Either he didn't know how, or he was just selfish." Mom had pushed against the actual story for so long, she became estranged from the truth. In her version of reality, she had no choice but to divorce Pops; he didn't love her, didn't satisfy her, didn't care anymore. In her mind, my mother had nothing to do with her own infidelity. The worst part: in her catalog of complaints against life, my death didn't call for a page, but I'd never been a priority.

When a bottle rattled in the bathroom, Mom considered telling Gia that she knew about Brightstar, that Chrysalis had told her, that going to rehab took guts. *Is she totally clean? Is the strain of the wedding pushing her over the edge?* But my mother pocketed her concern and took a different tact. "Baby, you're lucky," she called from the other side of the threshold. "I won't ever worry about your marriage. Know why? Because on his worst day, Luke is ten times the man your father was on his best day."

Sniff.

Mom fingered the interlocking hearts on her necklace, shifted her weight from one side to the other. As she rubbed a wood stain on the doorframe with her thumb, more crucial questions struck: Were the hors d'oeuvres getting cold? Had Russell arrived yet? Was Gia as naïve as she used to be?

The bathroom door opened, and my sister came out, mascara running, eyes bloodshot, cradling a box of Kleenex like a newborn.

Mom extended her arms, and Gia fell right in. "Your dad has a hard time loving people," our mother said, "even people as lovable as you and me." She caressed my sister's back. "I think it's because he never learned to love himself."

"I don't know what's wrong with me," Gia said, and held on tight.

"Take your time coming downstairs." Our mother stared at the wall. "I'll cover for you."

"Thank you, Mommy."

After peeling Gia off, our mother gazed into her daughter's swollen eyes and scrutinized her puffy cheeks. "I don't know how you're going to do it," Mom said, "but you better fix that face."

᷾

Careful in her heels and dress, my mother stepped down the stairs.

When the Potters rushed over, all except Brodie, Luke was the first to reach her. "What's going on with Gia? Is she okay?"

With a pasted-on smile, Mom blinked away the fib behind her eyes. "Oh, she's fine."

"Like, totally fine?" Luke scraped his hands through his hair. "Should I check?"

"Of course not," my mother said. "She'll be down in a minute."

Beth touched Mom's arm. "Nerves?"

"Not even that serious, just can't decide if she should wear a veil or not. Silly, really. I told her I like a bride in a veil. I think it's smart for a woman to hide something from her husband before she has to bare it all."

Pops pulled my mother aside. "Is everything okay?"

"You really want to know?" Enchanted by hubris, she smirked and aimed her words like arrows. "My daughter asked why it didn't work out between you and me, and I had to be honest, said you weren't a real man and didn't care about her or me, only yourself." She laughed and threw her shoulders back. "The poor girl has no idea how weak you are."

Mom waited for Pops to fall, to break, to shatter again. When he didn't, her heart numbed, and her soul fell slack. What did she see in him then? A man who'd lost count of the compromises he made with himself, a man who after a long sleep now realized he was awake, a man who'd simply had enough.

His nose wrinkled and eyes narrowed. "I'm tired, Iris," he said. "Tired of you turning the kids against me, tired of your lies, just tired."

"Old men tire easily."

Pops tapped his cane on the hardwood, raised his

chin, and stepped closer to my mother. His breath was hot, and blood rushed to his ears. "You know," he said, steely-eyed, "you're not the only one who cheated before our divorce."

"Excuse me." She coughed and hoisted an eyebrow. "You would *never*."

"I would, and I did."

"With whom?"

"Someone from the beach."

"What's her name?"

"Doesn't matter."

"Because it's not true."

"Anna Sikorsky."

As the name soaked in, Mom felt a sea change, and then a tidal wave swept her up and threw her down. "Your neighbor?" She swayed and her voice cracked. "Are you, um, still sleeping with her?"

"Isn't it something, Iris?" Pops stared at his cane, took another step closer, and shook his head. "You live your whole life certain of so many things, then in a flash, the truth is anyone's guess."

My mother sucked in her cheeks, huffed, and swallowed hard. Her spine a crumbly wooden beam infested with termites. "Well, you know," she stuttered and stopped, searched her memory for the perfect comeback, stumbled on a dull cliché: "Our family would still be together if it weren't for you."

He chuckled. "You wanna keep playing games, then let's play." He walked away, approached the Potters, and draped his arm around Luke.

Thoughts muddying, telltale heart pounding, Mom scratched the back of her shoulder and gritted her teeth, eyes darting. *What's happening? Where's Tom?*

Chrysalis roamed around, documenting the scene, capturing the conflict, pointing and flashing her camera. When the photographer strolled by my mother, Mom grabbed her arm and said, "Show me those pictures right now."

"Yo, chill." Chrysalis pulled away, then presented a dozen images of the argument between my parents. "Looks like you had yourself a little dustup, huh?"

Shadows pressed against my mother's temples. "Delete those now."

"Thanks for the suggestion." Chrysalis looked Mom square in the face. "But I'll let Gia make the final cuts."

FOURTEEN

Russell, or storms

AT NANA'S SEASIDE house, the Wheel of Time ticked away as I waited for my family to reunite. On the couch in the living room, Anna petted Dewey's patchwork coat and watched *The Twilight Zone* on Syfy. I moved past them, went to the kitchen window, and beheld a blinding blizzard in the blackness.

Wickford Junction, 6:29. Wandering into unexplored territory, my brother stepped off the train and pulled up the collar of his jacket. *Gia's about to walk down the aisle*, he thought. He sucked in the gritty New England air, like breathing into a pillow stuffed with ice chips. The snow came down hard, and soft, an avalanche of shred-ded angel wings. The streets: buried, undrivable. With no taxis or Ubers available, Russell had a three-mile walk ahead of him, an hour-long trip in perfect weather. He texted Pops: *On my way.*

After punching up directions to the Cozy Cove on

Google Maps, my brother tried to memorize the route—his phone on life support, battery at two percent. He hoped to catch the end of the ceremony, arrive in time to give Gia an awkward hug, tease her with a clever quip, congratulate Luke and wish him luck with our moody and vengeful sister. But what would Russ say to Mom? Or to Pops? He covered his head with his hoodie. *Why am I even here?*

The wailing wind slithered under my brother's clothes, burning his skin. As he trudged down the road, thuggish gusts threw him off balance as the sky choked on heavy flakes. Houses and power lines, layered in muffled white. He hadn't thought to bring gloves, and his pocketed fingers were freeze pops. With each high step he took, the snow deepened until it reached his knees. The trip was slow going, torturous, and ironic for my twin, who lived every day of his life waiting for the other boot to drop.

Ten minutes into the trek, he considered the best-case scenario: someone would find his body in the spring.

Twenty minutes in, the worst case: Mom would scold him for being late.

Thirty, a grim circumstance: an intersection and a dead phone. *Wait, turn onto Tower Hill or keep straight on Phillips?*

The way ahead was a mystery; Russell only knew the way back.

From behind, headlights marred the night and swept the edge of another reality, and my brother's recurring dream—me and Pops stranded on a lonely road, me dying, our father wishing for the same fate. When Russ stumbled sideways, a drift hemmed his knees. He turned, and a beam of light stung his eyes; he tried waving it away, couldn't. A clanking silver pickup truck, with a rusted snowplow connected, stopped beside him. The driver lowered his window and sneered. He was thin and gruff, wore a puffy orange vest, no hat, spoke like he gargled with gravel. "Thought only folks in cartoons shivered like that."

The wind stopped in its tracks, and Russ froze.

"Get in," the thin man said.

Blackness tightened in my brother's gut, and he climbed into the cab while the night held its breath. Somewhere, far away, a new day glittered. My brother removed his snowy hood. "Hey, thanks," he said.

The driver stared ahead. "Buckle up." His limbs, gnarled pine branches. His hair, wisps of smoke swirling on a breeze. The man coughed and said, "Cozy Cove?"

"Please." *Don't know how he knows, but I'm not asking questions.*

The five-minute drive felt like five years. At road's end, they reached the inn, and Russell hopped out of the truck. "Really appreciate that."

The driver nodded.

My brother slammed the creaky door and slung his backpack over his shoulder. While the man drove off, the old oak moaned in the bawling wind. Anchored in the harbor, two boats rocked in place, their sails frozen stiff in the storm, snowfall piling onto their canvas coverings, a suffocating mound of white, like volcanic ash. Then Russ detected a sorrowful sound, meek and distressed, like that of a little girl crying, coming from inside the inn. *Maybe just the wind.*

I couldn't stay away.

❧

While waiting for my twin in the lobby, I felt peculiar, unlike the way I felt on my other visits, almost human. On her way to the dining room, Helen scuttled past me, a vase of scarlet orchids in her withered hands. She paused and spun, as if spotting me, as if recognizing me. She scratched her forearm, raked the skin till it reddened.

At ten past seven, the main door opened. The roar of the wind rolled in first, then the wind itself, then my brother, a Trojan horse of stashed emotion. He swept the wetness off his shoulders and removed his hood. When a rush of warm air brushed the back of his neck, he turned but saw no one.

Pops shuffled in from the library and greeted Russ with a grin, a handshake, and an embrace. "Got your text," our father said. "Told your sister to stall a bit."

"Thanks." My brother noted the old man's beard. "Getting grayer, huh?"

"Yeah, it's been a while." Our dad nodded and set his hands on Russell's broad shoulders. "God, you look just like Dev."

The sight of my brother had always reminded Pops of his loss, which was why Russell didn't come home much after he left for college. Along with avoiding his strained relations with Gia and Mom, Russ couldn't bear stirring up the old man's PTSD. After my twin moved to

Manhattan eighteen months ago, only one hundred miles separated him and our dad. But neither man wished to travel the long, lonely highway of regret.

"Gia's waiting for us." Pops motioned toward the echo of music coming from the next room. "You ready?"

"Why not?" Russ gripped his wrist and twisted. "Let's do it."

When father and son stepped into the library, time sputtered, and heads spun. In the front by the fire, Mom and Gia gawked, while in the back corner, Ed Sheeran's "Thinking Out Loud" slow danced out of DJ Socket's speakers. My brother straightened his jacket, and his scalp tightened, as if being yanked from the inside. Then his eyes linked with Gia's for a sliver of a second, and his thumping heart stilled. He drank in the silence. "Sorry, did I interrupt something?" Russell said, a grin lighting up his face, zest behind his eyes.

Our sister released Luke's hand and stomped through the gathering, the lace-trimmed hem of her gown sweeping over the snake scales engraved into the worn floorboards. As she approached the back of the room, my twin teetered in his Timberlands, and our father stepped aside. Gia gnawed on her lip and breathed heavy, tears welling up in her big brown eyes, her grudge against Russell still biting at her. "I don't know whether to hug you or hit you," she said, voice quavering.

My brother's arms tingled. "I'll take the hug."

As my siblings embraced, Pops beamed, while Mom loomed across the room. She eyeballed her son, daughter, and ex-husband like they were unwelcome strangers and strutted toward them. Eclipsed by our mother's shadow, Tom followed. She turned and glared, and he sat down.

When she reached Russ, he extended his anxious arms. "Hi, Mom."

She stopped a few feet away and droned, "Russell."

Up front, Luke smiled, and my brother gave him a salute, along with his approval, not that anyone asked him for it. Then Russ turned to Gia. "So that's your man, huh?"

"He's a lot like you," she said.

"Oh yeah?"

"The old you, at least. I don't really know you now."

My brother cut off his laugh, looked over his shoulder. He sensed me there, and I drew him into my thoughts, so far that he couldn't tell if he was me, or if he was him. Though he tried to fight it, a powerful love for each other, and for our family, seized us both—a longing, a togetherness. We felt identical then, our twin magic at work again. At once our minds rushed back, in fragments of memories, to the last time we used our power.

Our family. Summertime. Saybrook Marina Resort & Restaurant. Our dad's forty-eighth birthday. All of us, eating lunch at a table by the water. Dozens of boats lined up in rows, tied to the docks. A tall gate with narrow metal slats guarding the marina. Unsupervised kids weren't allowed on the docks. Boat owners needed a special code to unlock the gate. Russell and Gia wanted to look at the swimming pool by the hotel. I didn't want to go with them, and they asked why not. Our father said I wasn't an explorer like them, and he was right. Pops told them they could go, and they ran out of sight. I stayed with my parents, but I was still "with" Russell somehow. Saw what he saw, felt what he felt, heard what he heard, more than ever before. A handsome man at the pool invited my brother and sister to see his boat. It was a yacht, he said, and my siblings were excited, especially Gia. They went with him to the marina entrance. He entered the code, opened the gate, and they walked down the dock. Something was wrong though, I could tell, heard Russell's thoughts, knew he was nervous. Told my parents what was happening. Tried to explain. I was "being ridiculous," Mom said, but my father believed me. We went to the railing, looked out at the marina, couldn't see Gia or Russell or the man I described. Too many rows, too many boats, a hundred maybe, big ones and small ones with names on the back. "Where are they, Devan?" Pops yelled. "What row? What name?" I heard my twin in my head, shut my eyes. "Seventh row," I shouted. "The name is, the name is, the name—*Third Act*!" We ran to the marina entrance. I read the code Russell had memorized: *5-8-6-8-5*. My father pushed open the gate, flew onto the docks. Saw his kids, seventh row. About to board the boat.

Pops called to them. They ran to him.

And just like that, it was over.

None of us spoke of the incident again, too afraid of the power Russ and I possessed, too frightened of losing each other.

In the warm library, as the ceremony began, DJ Socket played a string quartet version of Journey's "Don't Stop Believin'," and everyone took their places. While my father and Gia waited together in the rear, ready to walk down the aisle, Russell sat next to our mother. Like always, I read his thoughts. My brother wanted me gone, but I had other plans.

It's time to tell him.

"Get out of here," he whispered. "You promised."

Mom turned to him. "What?"

Russ plucked at the black band on his wrist. "Nothing."

"Hmm." She stared at the elastic band and shook her head. "I don't know why I thought you'd make something of yourself."

My twin didn't reply. Gia and Pops paraded past him. The fire roared.

The music stopped.

✍

As if laced with strands of gold, Gia's gown glimmered in the glow of burning birch.

She unfolded a slip of paper and cleared her throat. "Luke William Potter," she began, "three years ago I was lost, alone in the dark, like I was on a raft in the middle of the ocean. And you were waiting for me on the shore. When I finally got the courage to make my way toward you, I stepped off the raft and realized I could walk on water." Gia paused, accepted her quaking voice, and looked at Luke with thankful eyes. "I was so scared, Luke, and if I wanted to drown I could have, but I didn't. Because after all the struggle, and all the pain, I didn't want to drown anymore. I wanted to live, and I wanted

197

to love. And I will walk across any ocean, in any darkness, no matter how dangerous, to take your hand. The one I know belongs in mine."

Russ couldn't help but think of Izzy.

"That was beautiful," Beth said and turned to Luke. "Tough act to follow, son."

Luke swallowed hard, wiped his forehead, and breathed deep. "Gia Grace Jacoby," he began, "I love you with everything I have and will give you all that I am, because I believe we were made for each other." He smiled at her and let out a little laugh, if only to keep from crying. "And I am honored, G, with the privilege of being seen by you *and* of seeing you." Now Luke couldn't keep from crying anymore, and he let it all out. "I promise to walk with you, and believe in you, and stay by your side for whatever amount of time we have together. I am so, so blessed to have you with me, Gia, on this amazing journey that's impossible for any of us to travel alone."

As the couple joined hands, candlelight caught in my sister's hair and clung to the edges of her gown. "Gia and Luke," Beth said with watery eyes and a wide smile, "may you reflect on the events of your lives as they pass, but also move forward with them. May you walk together, hand in hand, yet remain still. Live with laughter, joy, and levity, for it's been said, 'Angels can fly only because they take themselves lightly.'"

With Mom and Pops sitting on either side of him, my brother's joy for Gia and Luke drained away. The tension between our parents was palpable, worse than when they first got divorced. There was more discomfort now, more animosity, more mistrust. In the library's calm, their negativity tore at Russell from both sides, fighting over him, pushing and shoving. While he absorbed their invisible roundhouses like a bystander caught up in a bar fight—wrong place, wrong time. No stranger to emotional strain, my battle-tested brother had staved off my mental demands for years, wrestled his own conscience, and had his heart ripped out by Izzy. But none of that made this easier.

While the glow from the candles and chandelier harmonized, Beth moved on with the ceremony. "It's a formality, hopefully," she said, "but I'm obligated to ask if anyone here opposes this union."

Like someone had upholstered her chair with caterpillars, Mom squirmed, and Russell got ready to pin her down. He figured she hadn't accepted Luke, his nofrills occupation, his simple manner, or his family. Our mother didn't accept anyone for who they truly were, concerned herself only with how those people—and their real selves—reflected on her. If they didn't adhere to her standards, she altered them. If they didn't convert, she disowned them. I had witnessed Mom's insensitive actions firsthand, felt her silent sting more than anyone, hid my real self away, knew she never wanted that person to come out.

When no dissenters stopped the proceedings, Beth exhaled and chuckled. "Well, that's a relief." She looked at her son, regarding him with love. "Luke, you may kiss your bride."

I hovered in the library's corner, and with each lingering moment, I risked my ascension in the afterlife, gambling away my chances of joining the spirit world, gaining supreme knowledge, and finding true peace. But I had to impress my will on my family, grab their attention, show them that we were all together again. And I had to tell my father that I forgave him, but I couldn't do it alone.

A book fell from the shelf and thumped to the ground, landing close to my sister. The crowd jumped and gasped. Another book crashed to the floor, violent and loud, and Gia pulled away from Luke. The spirit I sensed earlier was present—nowhere but everywhere—wielding supreme energy, an intense vibration, and the power to cloak itself. Whatever or whoever it was, it controlled the entire house. Then a deep whisper, like a cottony clap of reverberating thunder, echoed around the room: *Get out!*

"What's going on?" Mom whipped around and fixated on the Nielsens, who stood stiff as fence posts in the back by the door. Another book fell, and another, and another. Flying from the shelves in a flutter of pages, like a flock of panicked birds. Then a chill encased the room, and a grunting gust killed the candles, snuffing out the raging fire, sending curls of smoke slithering toward the ceiling like serpents.

Standing and spinning, Russ looked from corner to corner, eyes darting, limbs shaking. He knew I was there and whispered, "Stop doing this." He scanned the space again, yelling under his breath: "You need to go!"

The room went silent, and my brother waited for a

sign, for a thought, for my voice. He buckled when he received my message: *It's not me.*

The windows flew open, and a torrent of snow poured in, wild and unbridled. A powerful wind careened around the library, knocked over chairs and vases and candelabras. The extreme force pushed Russell backward, moving through him like a devilish wave. The chandelier swayed and spun on its chain. Its crystals rattled, fell, and shattered on the wood floor. Shards of glass spraying onto the Ouroboros like shrapnel.

"What's happening?" my sister screamed.

Then the lights died, and the library went black.

"Gia, I'm here!" Luke shouted.

At once, the group turned on their phone flashlights, and bright beams bounced off their frightened faces.

Beth raised her hand and stepped forward. "Is everyone okay?"

"No, no." Brodie cowered in a corner. "I'm not okay."

Luke pulled Gia close.

"Let's all settle down." Stan shut the windows, and the chill backed off. "I hadn't planned on telling you all this," he said in a stern, saddened rasp, "but there's a history to Hayle House."

The room got quiet.

"Hold up." Tom forced out a low laugh. "You mean this place is haunted?"

Helen stood with Stan, the candlelight quivering in her dilated pupils, synchronizing with her flickering voice. "There was a girl named Emma," she said.

Brodie fidgeted, his complexion now a few shades paler. "What the hell?"

Stan shuffled to the mantel, lit another candle, and held it near his fatigued face. "In 1670, a colonist named Lazarus Hayle built this house for his young family." The old innkeeper threw a bundle of kindling into the cold fireplace, then faced his guests. "Five years later, Lazarus fought alongside the Narragansett tribe to defend their land against the New England militia in the Great Swamp Massacre. He was captured and hanged for treason from the old white oak out back, along with his wife, Mary, his four teenaged sons, and his ten-year-old daughter, Emma." Stan lowered his head, gathered his thoughts. "The um, the story, um…"

Helen took her husband's hand. "As the story goes," she continued, "the lynch mob did more than just hang Mary and her little girl that day." Her words trailed off.

Gia wrapped her arms around her belly. "And she's still here? Why?"

"Some say revenge," Stan said, "against any family that stays in her house."

A tree branch crashed onto the roof, rattling the chandelier.

Brodie jumped and let loose a squeal. "So she's trying to k-kill us?"

Stan placed two fresh logs onto the kindling and struck a match. "No, I don't believe so." He crouched and lit the fire. "I think she's just lost."

My parents faced each other. Did they believe the story? Did they think children could return from the dead? They couldn't feel my essence in the room, but I felt Emma's. I tried to read her thoughts, but they didn't come through. She kept quiet, waiting for me to speak first, giving me an opening.

Russell stood behind Pops, hiding in our father's shadow after evading mine for ten years. But my twin couldn't escape me now, and I cleared a pathway into his mind. *Tell him I'm here. Tell him I forgive him. Tell him now.*

My brother froze, couldn't speak.

"Anyway," Stan said, "I think the little girl's gone for now." He moved into the center of the room. "I'll try to get the old generator up and running. Hope there's gas in the tank."

Pops flinched at the sound of those final four words.

I drove deeper into my brother's consciousness. *Tell him, please!*

It wasn't enough for our family to be together. They had to purge their ill will and make peace with each other. But more than that, Pops had to absolve himself for contributing, however much, to my accidental death. For us to move on, he had to discover a path ahead, and I had to stop looking back.

The fire crackled, the room warmed, and Russell released his corked-up courage. He understood the moment, the urgency, and stepped closer to our parents. Gia joined and completed the circle. My brother's eyes brightened. "I need to tell you all something," he said, and his shoulders loosened. "I don't know if Emma Hayle is here—"

"Pfft." Mom crossed her arms. "Of course she's not."

Russell looked at our father. "—but Devan is."

Pops cocked his head then turned away. "C'mon, son."

"Seriously," our mother said, and winced. "What's gotten into you?"

As the dark room pressed in, my brother slipped his hands into his pockets and tried to sink into the floor-boards. When he looked toward the door, he caught Gia's gaze, her tender eyes telling him she believed him—and demanding that he believe in himself.

Russell took his hands out of his pockets and tight-ened his fists. "Devan needs me to tell you something, Pops."

Our father shivered and slouched, rubbed his ear. "Yeah, okay," he muttered, "he needs to tell me some-thing, right." He tapped his cane on the floor, banging out a disjointed rhythm.

My brother and I were eleven when Pops came home post-surgery with his hospital-issued aluminum cane. Russ used it as a weapon, loved to hide behind the couch and hook my ankle with the gooseneck grip, while I used it as an accessory for tap dance routines, loved to adjust the length and twirl it, pretending I was Savion Glover. Our father hated it when we played with his cane. "It's not a toy!" he'd yell. "I need that."

Russell wanted to deliver my message to Pops but crumbled. *Why am I such a coward?* He answered his question with another: *What difference does it make?* He always ran away from conflict, ignored his problems without trying to fix them. Why fail and ruin a perfect reputation? At stake now though: so much more than his precious ego.

"Dad, please listen." My brother raked his scalp with twitchy fingers, and his voice jittered as he spoke. "Devan didn't die because of you. I have dreams about that night. I've seen what happened. He needs me to talk to you."

My father tugged at his shirt collar, a tremoring chin beneath his beard. "And I need to check on your grandmother." He turned to leave.

"Pops, wait!"

Mom barred Russell with her arm. "Let him go."

The old man disappeared through the doorway while, in the center of the library, Helen swept broken chandelier crystals into a dustpan and picked glass shards off the twisted Ouroboros. She carried the pan to the fireplace, lingered a beat, and hurled the pieces into the flames.

FIFTEEN

Jake, or shadows

I WAS WITH him when my father entered the bedroom.

The door closed behind him, and he couldn't see a thing. He felt his way around with his cane, scanned the darkness with the flashlight on his cell phone. The barbershop scent of his shaving cream still hung in the air. The echo of Russell's claim, that my death was no one's fault, still lingered in my dad's head. He flashed to the day at the marina seventeen years earlier, when his sons' twin magic was on full display. *Russ might be telling the truth*, he thought.

He made his way to the bed, pawed for Nana's leg, and gave it a soft squeeze. "You okay, Mom?" He squeezed again. "Hey, the power went out."

He leaned over her body and shined the light onto her face. She was asleep, her breathing a faint whisper. In the glow of the iPhone, her body was like a hologram projected onto the sheets. Whenever she awoke, Pops would have questions for her, but should he confront her about the secret she kept about his dad? Should he ask if the man was still alive? No, he'd wait till they were back in Old Saybrook before bringing it up. After he cooled off, maybe in a week.

I sensed that Nana's soul was ready to leave, her time on earth nearly over, but Pops denied the notion. Though he understood, more than most, that death keeps coming and doesn't care who it leaves behind. That it takes everything eventually, and despair always fills the hole. He first met despair after his father left. Then despair reintroduced itself the day Pops held his stillborn baby girl in his tired arms. When he cradled her for an hour in the hospital room, praying for a cry, a coo, a breath, while his wife lay curled up lifeless in bed. Yes, my dad and despair were old friends.

"Mom?" He tapped Nana's wrist, gave it a shake. "You hear me?" He took her pulse, wasn't sure he felt anything, his heart pumping like mad for them both.

His body unable to support its own weight, invisible hands pushing down on his shoulders, my dad fell to his knees and rested his forearms on the mattress. Not panicky, resigned to the moment, he called 911. The dispatcher said an ambulance would come "as soon as possible," but the storm would slow its arrival. Again, time wasn't a friend.

The previous spring, my grandmother's doctor had informed her and Pops that she only had months to live, and expected she wouldn't survive through Christmas.

Her parents and grandparents had all died from heart disease; Nana never kept *that* a secret.

My father found a box of wooden matches and three candlesticks in the nightstand drawer, lit the wicks, and spread the sticks around the room. The glimmering flames enlivened the space, but my dad's dead eyes deflected the brightness. He sat at his mother's bedside in a stiff antique chair. On the windowpane, reflections cast by candlelight blinked like distant stars.

Pops whispered, "You still with me, Ma?"

She didn't respond.

He wondered if she heard him.

She did.

In a one-way conversation, Pops thanked my nana for who she was, for how she raised him to be curious and resourceful, to think for himself. He apologized for letting her down, sorry he wasn't as strong and positive as she was, that he didn't see the world, and himself, like she did. He lowered his head. What should he do now with the truth about his father, a man made only of one woman's words? He breathed deeply. Could he ever forgive his mother? He began to cry. Should he even try?

For once, Joan Jacoby had no advice.

And her son was alone. More than ever.

At Nana's house in Old Saybrook, Dewey lifted his nose from a ceramic bowl. Abandoning a half-eaten pork chop, he flew into the living room, scratched and barked at the door.

"Hey, Dew!" Anna sprung out of the kitchen, dish towel in hand. "What is it, boy?"

The dog ignored the sweet lady's calls, cried and clawed at the walls. Until one last, wild howl shot through the roof and pierced the icy air on Plum Bank Road.

I followed Pops downstairs, into the doleful library, where candles and phones provided poor light. The brightest spot was by the fireplace, and when Stan threw another log onto the flames, the glow grew.

As my father stood at the base of the stairs, far from the fire, Mom made a beeline toward him. "What's going on, Jake?"

Before he answered, Gia approached. "Dad, is everything all right?"

Russell joined. "Pops?"

"I think your grandmother may be dying," my dad said.

"Wait, she can't be," my sister said. "What do you mean?"

"Have you called an ambulance?" my brother added.

"It's on its way."

Mom clenched her fists. "Is she conscious?"

My family rushed upstairs, entered the room, and gathered around Nana Joan's bed. Mara, Luke, and Tom followed them up but stayed in the hall. The candles that Pops lit earlier had dimmed, and my grandmother lay still—dreaming but not—in the weakening light. Gia stood with Russell, my mother with my father, their faces drawn, their hearts heavy.

And I was with them too.

In front of Tom and Mara in the doorway, Luke caught Gia's eye. She pursed her lips and put a shaky hand to her chin, wedding ring glimmering. Her husband gave her a half smile, turned to Tom and said, "Hey, let's see if Stan needs help with the generator."

"Sure thing," Tom said.

Luke looked back at my sister. "Helen put some food out in the dining room," he said. "Mara and I will bring a few plates up."

"Thank you, baby," Gia whispered, her lips dry and trembly.

"Yeah," our father added. "Thanks, son."

"Of course," said Luke before he and the others walked away.

Then, our family was as one. Together again. Parents, siblings, and me.

We belonged to each other for a second time. United in grief, for a soul other than mine, we were more than the sum of our damaged parts. More than frayed strings, woven through space and time, pulled from opposite ends of the universe. Still though, as I scanned their four weary faces, their eyes cried out, *We're not alone.* Secrets stirred among us. Fear pressed down. Guilt closed in. Like my family, I felt those beastly forces, heard them in the air, smelled them in their breath, saw them beyond my father's faraway gaze.

Simone once told me, "The physical world is the

illusion." But as I mourned with my family and felt what they felt, I wondered, *Could their lives and my existence be both illusory and real at the same time?*

On bright spring mornings in Western Massachusetts, my dad and his father would fish for trout on the Housatonic River. On warm summer afternoons, they'd listen to Red Sox games on the radio and play catch in the backyard. And every night, Elliot Sr. told his boy about the story of a man who hid from evil monsters by escaping into a dream world. Now armed with the truth, Pops knew that dream world had been real.

Along the edges of the bedroom, I watched as the candlelight embraced the walls and my grandmother's breathing softened to a rhythmic hush. While my family waited for the paramedics, they spoke in subdued tones, conjuring memories of Nana. Gia brought up the sea glass game. Mom recalled Joan's "simple wisdom." Russ mentioned my aquarium at the Old Saybrook house, the pet snails I had, and how long they lived.

In that moment, a crushing density surrounded us, a powerful presence, the one I'd sensed before—a stranger in the room, not part of our family. The air was colder now, even I was aware. Then I saw her, a sullen shadow. Hungry, morose. Faded green dress. Hovering in the corner, as though suspended in water. It was her, the little girl, Emma Hayle, with a rope burn around her tiny neck. Thick, bright, and red, as if etched with a blade made of fire.

"What do you want?" I said, unsure of the response I hoped to get.

She communicated her thoughts, assured me she meant no harm. Revealed that she was lost and expected her family to return. When she died, her soul usher had told her to follow the light, but she refused and never saw it again. She'd searched the house for so long, she explained, that she almost couldn't remember who she was waiting for. She hoped her parents would come back with her brothers, thought if she left the house they wouldn't know where to look. They wouldn't leave her alone, not forever. They wouldn't forget her, she was sure. Emma said she wanted to find her family, like I found mine.

I told her she didn't have to worry, that her parents and brothers had crossed over, and she didn't need to stay in the house any longer. Her family was waiting for her, I said, beyond this life, in the most beautiful place she could imagine.

Like where we used to play, in a field full of flowers, under a great big tree?

Yes, you'll find them there, Emma, I'm sure.

She was confused. *How do you know?*

I don't know, not really, but I've seen the place where I'll meet my family, and you must have one too.

Her aura darkened, and she faded into the wall, disappeared like tepid breath on a chilly day. Emma had never accepted her death, I understood that. How could she, after dying at such a young age, and watching her family die too? That was why she stayed behind, and why I tried to help her leave. But like with my family, Emma's fate was out of my hands. She needed to release her desires, needed to wait for the light.

I called out to Nana Joan, to her spirit, not her useless body that lay there in bed. I couldn't wait to be with her. She wanted to answer me more than anything, I sensed, but she was still clinging to life, and I didn't understand her knotted thoughts.

"Wish I got here sooner," Russell said, wiping his eyes. "Wish I got to talk to her."

"Your nana helped me a lot when you kids were little." Mom's cough couldn't cover up her cracking voice. "I struggled sometimes as a mother, but Joan guided me through it, like she understood what I was going through, though I never opened up to her."

Pops glanced at Mom, thinking, *Guess there's a heart in there somewhere.*

Gia put her arm around our mother and stared at Nana. "She told me earlier today that we needed to help each other." My sister caressed the lace of her gown, appreciating every flower and leaf the old woman had sewn. "She always told the truth, and you always knew where you stood with her."

My father winced. *Did she always tell the truth? Did I really know where I stood?* A roiling ache surged in his stomach, and tension tugged at his bones. Something demanded that he relinquish his pain, commanding him to reveal what happened the night I died, to tell his own truth: that my death was his fault, that his stupidity and negligence killed me.

Russell held a candle up to our father's face. "What are you thinking about, Pops?"

That was all it took, one simple question, the tidal shift that washed Jake Jacoby away.

"I don't know why I let him do it," Pops said, "but Devan asked me if he could sleep with the kitten I bought for Gia, and yeah, I let him. Thought nothing of it. He said he'd be fine, told me not to worry. His inhaler was right there on the nightstand. I saw it for Christ's sake, I saw the thing. Then in the middle of the night he had an attack, ran into my room, couldn't breathe. We drove to the hospital, but on the way, we stalled out. I know you told me to fill up the Ford, Iris. I know, but I didn't do it. We weren't going anywhere that night. It didn't matter. Then I pulled over, and I was going to call for help but I left my phone at home, left it on the table. Left it fuckin' home. Devan was having a really hard time, and I didn't want to leave him alone, but I had to get out and try to flag someone down, but it was so late, no one was around. It was, I don't know, fifteen minutes, twenty, before someone stopped, a guy in an SUV. When we got to Milford, Dev was in bad shape, could barely speak, his breath was so low. He was so weak. Jesus. I'm sorry. When they said he was dead, I didn't know what to do, didn't think it was real. I don't know why, but I had a nurse call a cab, and I had the guy take me to a gas station, the all-night one on Broad, and I filled up a five-gallon drum. I had the driver take me to my car, and then I went home and waited, knew I had to call you all, but I didn't know what to say. I didn't know what to tell you, how to tell all of you. He was gone. He was gone! But I called, I called, I called. Oh, God. He's gone."

My father stared at the dripping candle wax, half-dead, half-numb to the moment. He rocked side to side, the light in the room finding only the margins of his shape, accenting the creases of his suit coat and the collar of his shirt, glinting in the hollowness of his eyes.

Russell's voice was faint at first, then grew louder. "Hey, Pops? What's going on? You still with us?"

The old man blinked three times and raised his head, returned from within a dark vision. "Sorry, what'd you say?"

Russ rested a hand on our dad's shoulder. "Where'd you go?"

"Where'd I what?" Pops said, and he went cold, as if every drop of blood had drained from his body. *My God*, he thought, *I didn't tell them*.

Two paramedics rushed into the room, moving so quickly the candle flames shivered with the motion of the air. The responders checked Nana's vitals just as the last spark of life left her body, and a beam of light streamed down onto the bed. When she drew her last breath, I expected her spirit to join me there—I looked forward to greeting her—but she rose out of my reach, toward the distant silhouette of a slender man in the golden light, his arms out wide.

Nana! No!

Just then, the beam split into two and shined onto the wall opposite me, where the ghost of Emma Hayle had reappeared. Her parents and brothers called out to her, waiting to greet her at the end of what looked like a long, bright hallway. As she drifted toward them, she reached out to me, begging me to join her, and I tried to go into her light.

But it wasn't my path to follow.

A buzz then a flicker, and the power returned. One medic dropped Nana's wrist and shook his head, gave the other a shrewd look. "She's gone," he said in a heartless tone. "Time of death, nine thirty-three." The medics counted to three and lifted my grandmother onto a gurney. I watched as Gia let loose a wail that had built in her chest. Mom turned away and wiped her eyes with a handkerchief. Russell hung his head and chewed on his lip, letting the tears he'd been holding back fall. Then Pops touched his mother's hand one last time.

❧

At midnight, my father and I were alone in his room. *Happy New Year, Pops.*

Would a flip of the calendar matter for my family? Make any difference? Bring togetherness, forgiveness at last? Force them to face their demons, and each other, in the days ahead? What did my grandmother say when I was five, after my pet snails died, and I couldn't stop sobbing? "Grief is just love with nowhere to go."

I'm ready to leave, Simone.

PART IV

THE DAY AFTER THE WEDDING

⤫

There are far, far better things ahead
than any we leave behind.

—C. S. Lewis

SIXTEEN

Spirits, or me

IN THE OLD Saybrook house, the gray veil hadn't lifted.

My family had come together, and I should've crossed into the spirit world, but nothing had changed. *What's happening? Why haven't I transitioned? Why are they making me stay?*

I should've been with Nana Joan, and I was desperate to see her. I didn't have to be alone any longer, didn't have to keep seeking what I'd never find. Maybe she was waiting for me somewhere. *The beach!* I rushed to the sliding door but still couldn't see outside—not the sun or the sea, not the gulls or the shells.

Simone appeared. "You can leave this realm when you're ready."

"I am ready."

"When you're truly ready, the light will return."

"Where is it?" I went to all the windows in every

room but only saw dark scenes from Wickford. "It's not out there. Nothing's out there!"

"Have you ever wondered why you can't see outside, Devan?"

"Because you won't let me."

"No," Simone said, her golden aura glowing. "Because all you ever wanted, your only wish in death, was to see your family. Because there's something else you're not ready to see, somewhere you're not ready to go."

"No, you're wrong. I *am* ready."

"And how do you know?"

"Because I wanted my family to reunite, and now that's happened. I stayed in this realm for them, stayed trapped inside this house for them, and now they need to let me go."

"But none of you can move on," Simone said, "until you let *them* go."

"What?"

"Tell the truth, Devan," she said. "Did you remain earthbound for them, or for you?"

I didn't answer.

Simone's thoughts flowed into me. *You could do nothing to help them. They needed to make mistakes, reconcile their failures and regrets, learn and grow, deal with their struggles and heartbreak on their own, without you.*

"Then why did I stay?"

"Only you know the reason."

But like everyone else, Simone lied. She and I both knew why I stayed; there were no secrets in the afterlife.

Did I think I could fool her? Sure, I did. Why not? I'd fooled my family for sixteen years.

From my first moments in death, I understood the difference between loving spirits, who safeguarded the living, and selfish ghosts, useless to those they abandoned on earth. I may have been a bit of both, always in between. True, I blamed my passing, in part, for splitting up my family, and I wanted them nearby, hoped to encourage their reconnection. I missed them and loved them, honestly. But the greater truth was, when I was alive, they loved me too little.

Gia and Russell had everything. I had nothing. I *was* nothing. Felt unimportant and unseen, trapped in a body I hated, torn and conflicted, and judged by others. I was invisible, better off dead, never fit in, never knew myself, never got the chance. When I died, I could finally breathe, felt comfortable out of my skin, felt wanted, remembered, and loved. Felt like somebody, for a while. But I wanted more.

I hoped that, in my absence, my family would accept me for who I was, for who I might've been, for all my faults and weaknesses, for all the reasons I was "different." Maybe I was the fool, but I couldn't let go. I wanted to stir their memories and feel their love, but not for any of us to heal. No, I stayed in the earthly realm, in the ghost world, to watch my parents and siblings mourn me, grieve for me, and regret how they treated me. I wanted to watch them grapple with the pain of losing me. But their own lives were so troubled and broken, they never cried for mine. Not as much as they should have.

Moving on meant nothing to me then; I knew I could never help them.

What have I done?

≪

In Wickford, the New Year had birthed a new day.

The storm over, my family trudged through heart-high grief which, like the fallen snow, had settled everywhere and touched everything. The cause of Nana Joan's death: the nature of life, not its unfairness, like the cause of mine. Her passing brought my parents and siblings closer together, while mine helped tear them apart. Her death would inspire their futures, while mine corrupted their pasts. Time for all of us to move on now. But which direction would we go? And how would we grow?

SEVENTEEN

Gia, or wishes

OUTSIDE MY SISTER'S window, a goldfinch sang in the old white oak and hopped along a high branch. Flanking the glossy pane, two equal parts of an open curtain greeted the silver morning, and the sun let itself into the room.

Gia lay in bed, studying the cracks in the ceiling with cried-out eyes, while soft sheets coated her skin. The warmth of Luke's body bathing her in comfort, she thought of Nana Joan and shivered, weakened by another death, in a different way. The night before: a bizarre blur, a morbid chain of events that thumbed its nose at the seminal significance of her wedding.

Maybe it's all I deserve, Gia thought.

You deserve so much more, I wanted to tell her.

She found Luke's hand under the covers, and her palm curled in his. As a faint light shined on her husband's face, my sister looked out onto a new horizon, as near and as welcoming as anything she'd ever seen. Her eyes flitting closed, amid all the grief and vanishing, Gia was now a bride to possibility, a woman married to hope.

Luke rolled over and smiled. "Happy New Year, Mrs. Potter." He brushed a stray curl from her face, tucked it into her silk headscarf, and stroked her eyebrows with his fingertips.

Gia arched her neck and kissed him. "Hey, you." She rested her head on the pillow again and continued to examine the ceiling.

"Hmm," he said, "guess married sex wasn't the thrill you imagined."

"Sorry." My sister wriggled her hand in his. "Still thinking about Nana."

"I know," he said. "She was a great person."

"But she had secrets, stuff my dad didn't even know." What should Gia do with our grandmother's truth? Should she come clean with Pops? The questions threw her off balance, her thoughts swaying with uncertainty. Luke's eyes kept her steady, would catch her if she fell.

She pinched herself, but it didn't hurt enough to confirm her new reality—wedded to a man she loved, and who loved her. She sunk into a part of herself she didn't understand, a delight she didn't think she earned, a depth she didn't feel she could swim. What right did she have to hold the gift that lay in her arms?

"What's rumbling around in that gorgeous head of yours?"

"I've got a lot of shit in my past, Luke, my whole family does," she said. "I'm not over it yet, and I may never be. There's still a lot to work through."

"Hey," he said. "You're not alone."

"Are you sure about me? About us?"

"You know how I feel, Gia. I'm a wide-open book."

My sister had revised the horror story she'd written, but half of her was still stuck in the nightmare she created ten years ago, one filled with vile characters she used to call friends, her dealers and fellow junkies who would always see her as who she *was*. Those dark figures wanted to lock her in their shadowy world and reinforce the old *Story of Gia*. They didn't want her to change, but my sister changed anyway.

"Isn't it crazy?" She rolled onto her side, removed her headscarf, and let her hair fall. "There's so much we don't get to know while we're alive. Then, just like that, we're gone."

"Okay, can we continue our metaphysical breakdown of death later?" Luke said. "Let's talk about *life*." He pulled the covers down and kissed her belly, ran his hand over her waist and down to her thigh, traced the outline of her tattoo—the oyster shell, ribbed and plumed like the tail feathers of a bird. Our grandmother used to say the world's greatest secrets hid within the prettiest shells.

"We're sixteen weeks in," Gia said. "When should we tell everyone the news?"

"Let's give her a name first."

My sister stroked Luke's beard, outlined his jaw with her fingertips, and whispered, "Joan? Johanna? Juanita?"

He looked down at her tattoo. "How about Pearl?"

᪥

The subtle scent of coffee and pancakes meshed with low chatter and the clatter of dishes.

Outside the dining room, Gia and Russell embraced, then faced each other with solemn eyes. My sister tensed, hesitating to speak, weighing every word. She didn't tell Russ what our grandmother revealed before her death—that Nana had her husband committed and kept it from Pops. And Gia didn't question what Russell had claimed minutes after the ceremony—that my spirit had been there in the library. She'd processed none of that information yet.

"So?" Our brother hooked his hands onto the neckline of his hoodie and raised his thick eyebrows. "How's married life treating you?"

"The first fourteen hours have been, um, interesting."

"Word."

My sister sighed. "I still can't believe Nana's gone." In her mind, Gia flashed through scenes of our childhood in Old Saybrook and paused on our grandmother's compassionate smile. "But thank you for showing up," she said and looked up at Russell. "I wasn't sure you would."

"Had to." He released his collar, then searched for something else to do with his hands.

"You know," Gia said, "I have to admit something." She wanted to wipe the slate clean, or mend fences, or bury the hatchet—or whatever idiom best described her need to trash the grudge she held. "When you ratted me out in high school, you were dead to me." She was so angry when Russ caught her dropping acid at that party, sure that the backstabber would tell our parents, positive his blood was thinner than water. He had exposed her secret, of course he had, and our family would disown her, she was certain back then. So she struck first, pushed everyone away, got high every weekend, ignoring the consequences. And she never looked back to consider her miscalculation.

Russell offered a small smile. "I never told a soul."

"Wait. What?" Gia drew her head back. "You're lying." A tiny wrinkle appeared on the bridge of her nose, the one that always surfaced when something surprised her. "Why not?"

His eyes reached out to hers. "Because you're my sister."

As she hugged him again, the strands of a new connection formed, expanding outward, quiet and slow, like ink being poured into water. My sister turned down the volume on her self-critic and tuned out the fraud who considered "self-sabotage" and "self-protection" synonyms. With my twin there by her side—in all his virtue and loyalty—Gia's hang-ups over their relationship began to run off, and she weakened her grip on the karma she'd clung to. Her love for him, and for me, existed outside of distance, outside of time, outside of ourselves, outside of death. Silently then, she and Russ agreed to hide past mistakes, share future secrets, and stay in the present together, an unspoken promise that couldn't erase ten years of estrangement. But it was a start.

"Hey." Gia peeked into the dining room then turned back to our brother using a softer voice. "Do you really think Devan's ghost, or his spirit or something, was with us last night?"

Russell nodded. "I know he was."

"Hmm." My sister didn't admit that she had felt me there as well, that she sensed me in her bedroom before the ceremony; she needed more time to process that too. "You know, someday we should talk about what you saw the night he died."

"Someday." Russ placed a feathery hand on her back. "Wanna head in? It's almost nine."

When they entered the dining room, Tom, Luke, Mom, and Pops were engaged in a semi-civil conversation at a table by the windows. With two hours till checkout, Beth, Bill, and Brodie had gotten a jump on their drives to Vermont and Pittsburgh. Mara was still sleeping, though my sister wasn't sure with whom.

After Luke pulled out a chair for Gia, she sat and examined the grandfather clock tucked away in the corner, quiet and unmoving. Its glossy mahogany frame, sturdy and narrow, was imposing at seven feet tall, and its harmonic pendulum swung dead behind the glass. Crowning the top: a double swan-neck pediment, like wooden waves carved into a perpetual collision course. The cream-colored face, illustrated with cherubs and birds on thin branches, glared from inside the hood. Dainty hands and ornate numerals pointed toward the future, while acknowledging the immortal past. The old timekeeper was gorgeous and perfect, except—

Gia untied her lips then said, "That clock says it's nine thirty-three." She tapped her husband on the elbow. "Why would it be a half hour ahead?"

Luke turned to investigate. "That's when the power came back on last night."

My sister scratched her cheek. "But why didn't it stop when the power went *out*?"

Pops cleared his throat. "Actually, it shouldn't have stopped at all," he said. "It's a spring-driven mechanism, needs winding with a key."

Mom shook her head. "You have no idea what you're talking about, Jake."

"Oh my God, I am begging you." Gia's words were like iron bars. "Please, stop."

"No, I won't stop. I'm sorry, baby." Our mother lifted her chin. "Because when it comes to things that are tightly wound, I'm the expert here."

Everyone at the table waited three seconds before laughing, except our father, who waited four. Then, adding to the good feeling, Stan and Helen arrived with mimosas in fancy flutes, yogurt parfaits, and apple pancakes. As they placed the items on the table, the sun streamed through the window, spreading its warmth.

"I'd like to make a toast." Luke stood and raised his flute. "To family."

"To family," the group replied together.

My sister tickled the back of Luke's thigh, lifted her glass, and set it down.

"Good thing you're here, Luke," Tom said, a wry gleam behind his spectacles. "Because the Nielsens didn't make any toast."

Nobody laughed, even after three seconds; they just waved away the bad joke, shared smiles and pancakes.

Russell tapped his fork on his coffee mug. "I'd like to say something about Nana, if I could for a second." His voice cracked like it did when we were in middle school, and he nodded at Pops across the table. "Our grandmother was a beautiful soul, and may she rest in peace." My brother stalled then, took a breath. "Um, and Dad, I want to say I'm sorry. I know how much she meant to you and how much you did for her, especially the last five years. I know she appreciated you and, um, that she was proud of you. And I know she's looking down now, and she's really happy."

Pops stared into his coffee, and his lip twitched. "She tried to convince me to visit you all more often," he mumbled, "said it was like trying to blow away the wind."

Gia sniffled. "I'm never going to forget being with her at the beach," she said. "I loved digging up the sea glass she and Mom buried in the sand. Remember? And the nights when Nana made gigantic ice cream sundaes for me, Dev, and Russ, and let us stay up till midnight to see if Dad's broken clock would ring twelve times, or just eleven."

Russell laughed and said, "Always eleven, never twelve."

Mom chimed in. "Joan once told me, oh, what was it now?" She clasped her hands in front of her lips. "Oh, shoot, something like, waiting for your father to fix that clock was like waiting for the sun to sing."

Gia swore our mother was hiding a smile, saw a semi-grin on our dad's face. And as my sister looked around the table, she glimpsed flickers of the past, when our family was happiest. But where were all of our extra pieces of time, those memories we didn't tape into scrapbooks or hang in frames?

"Don't listen to them, Mr. Jacoby." Luke patted our father's shoulder. "I believe in you, but if you ever want help, we can try to repair the clock together."

Gia smiled at her husband and recollected his proposal, at the WaterFire display on the Providence River. Inviting our whole family to their wedding was a risk, but her fiancé loved her, followed her lead and hoped for the best. When my sister was young, a fire burned inside her, used to keep her warm. Then it smoldered and died, but Gia refused to flame out. She dug through the ashes, spotted an ember, fanned it, and rebuilt the fire. In gathering our family together—in the same way she had transformed her life—my sister was extraordinary in her simple wish to find a way.

Mom stood and smoothed a crease in her pants. "I also have a brief announcement." She faced my sister. "Gia, my little girl, I know that spa gift card wasn't much of a wedding present, so I'd like to offer you something else." Our mother reached into her purse and pulled out her gold necklace with the interlocking diamond hearts. "When I saw this, I thought of the love you have for your family and how your heart links us all to each other."

Gia gasped, cupped her hands around her mouth. "Oh my God."

"Wow, how about that?" Tom said, boasting a proud smile. "Let's see how it looks on you, Mrs. Potter."

The two women stood, and our mother strung the

chain around her daughter's neck. As they hugged, my sister hushed a cry of appreciation, her cheeks the color of wishes. "But this is yours, Mom," Gia whispered. "You were wearing it last night." The pendant sparkled in the sunlight, glistening against her skin, resting over her heart.

Our mother straightened the necklace. "It means more to me now."

For the first time in forever, Gia felt light inside, her bones made of mist.

∽

One by one, my sister plucked pants and shirts from a dresser drawer and threw them into an open suitcase on the floor, while the Tampax box stared at her from its corner nest in the luggage. The morning had grown darker, the light now faded.

Luke strutted out of the bathroom, chomping on his toothbrush like a cheap cigar. "So, we can't really afford a honeymoon right now, but how do you feel about Aruba in July?"

"Hmm." Gia tossed a pair of jeans onto the pile of apparel.

"Hey, don't worry about the weather," he said, "Aruba is perfect. Nothing there ever changes."

"No, it's not that." She tossed her remaining clothes onto the floor, shut the drawer, and leaned back against the dresser. "Are we going to end up like my parents, Luke? I mean, what if I'm destined to be miserable?"

"C'mon, G." He dropped his toothbrush onto the bed

and took his wife's hand. "No one controls your destiny but you. After everything that's happened, believe that."

"I know." She toyed with her necklace and asked herself, for the millionth time, if our parents were supposed to be together. Or if our whole family was just one pitiful, terrific mistake. Our parents' divorce had convinced my sister that marriage was for suckers, that love hurt, that everyone kept secrets. When Luke proposed, she feared he'd eventually dump her, or that she'd fail him or their children. Gia hated our mother for the ruthless way she left Pops, never got over the sting. The day Mom walked out burned all three of us kids, but it scarred my sister the most.

Luke took her other hand, held both now. "I never told you this," he said, "but my folks separated for a year when I was a freshman in high school. Dad moved into a sad apartment across town for a while and then, before he even bought pillowcases, they got back together. I still don't know what happened, only that they figured it out somehow."

Gia squeezed his fingers. "Guess we all have our secrets."

"Maybe," he said. "But discretion is the better part of honesty." He smiled and kissed her on the lips. "I just made that one up, so if you wanna use it, you'll need my permission."

"Wow, that wasn't funny *or* clever." Gia held in a laugh, kneeled next to her suitcase and refolded a sweater. "I swear I will be nothing but honest with you, Luke Potter."

"Why do I feel like I might regret that?" Then he noticed the scrapbook peeking out from under a pair of Levi's. "Hey, babe, what's that?"

She brushed away the jeans. "Oh, my dad's gift to me."

After they sat on the bed, Gia opened the book. On the back page she found an old poem, crinkled and torn, familiar and forgotten. "God, I wrote this in Hopedale the day before Dev's funeral," she said. "But I remember throwing it in the trash, can't believe my father kept it."

"What's it about?" Luke asked.

"Nothing," she said. "It's embarrassing."

He leaned against her. "C'mon."

The scrapbook shook in Gia's hands, and she stared past its pages. "It's about not knowing anything, not knowing what happened with Devan, or with my parents. Not knowing how to move on, not knowing each other. Everyone in my family, we were like these helpless little things back then. Like life just did whatever it wanted to us, like it controlled us. And we all just sat there and let it happen."

"the unknowing"

drifting, floating, blown away, taken from the nest,
light and airy, silent, plain, not unlike the rest.
turning, spinning, fast and slow, where or when or why?
the wing clipped, the bird gone, The Feather in the sky.

clean and smooth reflecting, spotless, mindless, clear,
copy all in passing, any object near.
blurry, one dimension, a smudge, a print, a crack,
a twinning image vanished, The Mirror gazing back.

brewing, swirling, booming, stirring up the dust,
coming, going, fierce and loud, this torrential gust.
ruthless tempest, damage, doom, mashing cold and hot,
the calm remembers after what The Storm before forgot.

heavy, cold, unmoving, weathered by the time,
rounded, craggy, solid, dressed in moss and slime.
doorstop, weapon, paperweight, waiting to be thrown,
a lonely lifeless lump, hard-hearted is The Stone.

stepped on, over, and around, lapped up by the dog,
dirty daughter of the rain, blood of mist and fog.

stagnant, clueless, shallow, no current here will flow,
evaporating in the heat, The Puddle cannot grow.

drifting, spotless, swirling, stepped on by the time,
blurry, dirty tempest, spinning in the slime.
Feather, Mirror, Puddle, spawn of Storm and Stone,
The Unknowing, weak and ignorant, unaware, alone.

"But that's not you anymore." Luke fingered a spiral of curls beside his wife's cheek and let a tear slide, then he kissed her as if they were the only two on earth. "You brought your family together, Gia. You helped them."

"Maybe," she said, and got up from the bed.

When she dropped the scrapbook onto a wave of clothes on the floor, it landed with a muffled thump, while angst about our family's future flipped inside her stomach. In keeping Nana's secret about our grandfather's mental illness, my sister was an accomplice to the crime. She couldn't tell our father, didn't want to hurt him anymore. But wouldn't he want the truth? Didn't he deserve it? *I have to cover it up*, she thought, *pretend I never heard a word.* Lying was Gia's second nature. Or was it her first?

After extracting the box of tampons from under her clothes, my sister shielded it from Luke and slipped into the bathroom. She shut the door, removed the bag from the box, and shook the pills out into her palm.

"Hey, what do you need Tampax for?" Luke called

from the other side of the wall. "Something you're not telling me?"

Sitting cross-legged on the cold tile, Gia stared at the fentanyl in her hand. "Nothing you need to know."

Whatever Luke said next swirled into the air, flailed and flopped, then drowned with the flush of the toilet.

EIGHTEEN

Iris, or seasons

AGITATED IN A tight pair of boots, my mother huffed and scuffed while descending Cozy Cove's steep staircase, while Tom side-waddled behind her, lugging two large suitcases. At the front desk in the lobby, Helen checked Chrysalis and DJ Socket out of their rooms and hung their keys on a wall of pegs behind her.

"We'd like to settle up," Mom said to the innkeeper.

Helen halted her hunt for a random credit card receipt. "Oh, of course." She scratched her neck. "Was your stay a pleasant one?"

My mother plopped her key onto the desk. "Yes, fine." She'd reconnected with Gia and Russell, showed remorse for Pops and Nana Joan, but Mom's reparations with her family members didn't make up for the tally of complaints in her head: the ruined ceremony, the annoying power outage, the average meals, the pompous photographer, the shoddy flower arrangements, the tacky

DJ, the cramped bedroom. *God, I need to get out of these boots.*

"I'm glad you're satisfied." Helen's voice sounded itchy.

"Not completely," Mom said, pushing her lip out in an impressive pout. "It would've been nice if the closet in my bedroom had been usable. It was a major inconvenience."

Helen tilted her head and stood solid, no longer an impotent piece on a chessboard waiting to be toppled. "I'm awfully sorry, but that was Emma Hayle's room." She swiveled, hung Mom's key on a peg, and addressed the wall. "Out of respect for the girl's spirit, we've always kept that door locked." The frail woman waited a beat, faced forward, and placed her hands on the desk. "Just in case there's something in that closet she doesn't want us to find."

"Wow." My mother smirked and crossed her arms. "You are really something, aren't you? Why don't you just—"

"—make that your New Year's resolution." Tom stepped in, sweeping Mom aside and smiling at Helen. "You should keep that closet locked in honor of Emma," he said. "It's a marvelous idea."

My mother glared at Tom, her nostrils flaring, and jutted out her chin like a playground bully, begging the middle school weakling to bloody her nose. "Excuse me, Thomas."

Stomps and giggles tumbled down the staircase.

Two little kids, Katie and Maura, pranced into the lobby, throwing mittens at each other, while their wiped-out mother and father dragged behind them. The tired woman picked up a mitten and turned to Helen. "I'm sorry about this," she said. "And again, you and your husband are lifesavers. I don't know what we would've done without you."

Helen smiled and patted Katie on the head. "Well, it's quite all right," she said. "Thank you for staying with us and have a safe trip north. We hope you'll come back again."

"Oh, I'm sure we will." The woman placed a hand over her heart.

The girls galloped around the lobby on phantom hobbyhorses. But where was the third daughter, the older one with the ugly green dress? *Maybe she's in the bathroom*, my mother thought. *Or she forgot something in their room. Or she's waiting in the car. Or—Emma?*

The worn-out parents lifted their luggage, as if the bags contained anvils, and schlepped outside. On their parents' heels, Katie and Maura dashed onto the porch. Following the children, Mom reached out her arm and propped open the door. Then she stepped out onto the splintery wooden porch, into a morning alive with color.

The silly sisters spun and waved. "Bye-bye! We're gonna miss you!"

My mother tacked on a grin and waved back. "Okay, you take care now." She sighed and let her heavy hand fall.

Tom stole behind her as the girls skipped away. "Weird, huh?" He squinted through his glasses. "It was like those kids knew you."

Mom turned to go inside. "Yeah." She walked back through the doorway, as if over a threshold and into another world, one created from newly opened eyes. And the puzzle pieces she'd spent a lifetime scattering on purpose suddenly shifted together.

Helen curled out from behind the desk. "What a wonderful family that was." She turned to Tom. "And I thoroughly enjoyed meeting everyone in your family too."

"Nice to meet you as well, Helen." He doffed his herringbone wool fedora. "Everything was great, I mean, all things considered."

"Oh yes." Helen folded her hands. "Stanley and I offer our sincerest condolences. Joan seemed like a lovely spirit, from what we could tell."

Mom offered a sunny smile, one costing so little to give.

Just then, Stan ambled into the lobby. "Need some help with your things, Mr. Hyde?"

Tom opened his arms wide, clapped and kept his palms together. "Stanley, you are a scholar and a gentleman."

The men hauled the bags outside, along a shoveled walkway lined with walls of snow, while my mother stayed inside, thinking about the kids who had left, how cheerful they were. She flashed back to her childhood, to her grandmother's charity, when her family's fury was too tough for Mom to manage alone. To a time when Ruby Reed helped young Iris carry a load too ponderous for any child to bear.

My mother had constructed her life upon the snows of distress, and though she had experienced love twice, with Pops and Tom, she refused to *accept* love, convinced that the light of the universe couldn't pour through her—not exactly the way she was. From the start, Mom believed in her unworthiness, had no say otherwise, and as she grew older, it battered and broke her. But some light snuck in through the cracks.

༄

While Tom warmed up the Range Rover, my mother yanked on red leather gloves and waited in the foyer by the door. Then a voice hit her from behind: "Hey."

Mom jumped, wheeled around, and recoiled. "Oh, hello, Jake."

Pops stepped back, a safer distance apart. "Didn't mean to startle you."

"You didn't." A soft breeze snuck inside from a space under the door and played with her hair, bringing with it the scent of thawing memories.

My father had no bags with him, wasn't ready to go home yet. Sizing up his green and white sweater, an argyle turtleneck, the kind Pops would never buy for himself, Mom connected the context clues. *Anna Sikorsky.* The thought of my father in a serious relationship baffled my mother, depressed her and thrilled her all at once. The night before, after Pops told her about his affair, Mom nixed the notion he could've been lying and believed him in a blink, just like that.

At a gauzy window in Old Saybrook, I witnessed my parents, alone together for possibly the last time, and my soul ached for their loss, for my life, for our love that had gone like a song in the night. Nana's house moaned, as if riled by time, and the walls thickened. The gray veil that hung between me and the physical world grew a full shade darker, the clouded prism obscuring my view more than ever.

When my parents stepped out onto the porch, a ray of light caught Mom's slight smile, the very second before my father's frown formed. Flexing its muscles, the sun grew stronger and more virulent, like winter had gone to sleep twelve hours earlier and woken up in a better body. When Pops leaned against the icy wooden railing and peered out over the snow, my mother moved toward him, then stopped. And I watched as time burned off them.

What did Simone tell me before I chose the earthly realm over the heavenly? "It's not a question of this way or that, it's forging a way forward that incorporates both."

My mom dug into Pops, with eyes as bright and blue as the sky. *Something's wrong*, she thought. *Something's out of balance.* He wasn't wearing a jacket, but it was more than the cold that made him shiver, more than losing his mother the previous evening that bothered him. Mom recognized his weary and wary profile, an endearing expression that sought both acceptance and acquittal, a look she'd fallen in love with over thirty-five years ago.

She rewound the clock, replaying a scene in her mind: them at the beach, the July they met, her on his back as they waded into the ocean, wobbling and laughing, splashing in the rippling water. She'd washed her hair that morning and couldn't get it wet, but she trusted him, more than she trusted herself—he'd hold her up, he'd keep her dry.

Jake was so knowable then.

But on that porch, as all two-hundred pounds of his weight pushed against the rail, a mystery wore into the lines on his forehead, ambiguous, out of her grasp. And she yearned to know him again.

"I'm sorry about Joan," Mom said, moving closer. "And I'm sorry for how I treated you this weekend. I shouldn't have said those things to Gia, shouldn't have tried to come between you two like that." My mother drew near to Pops and touched his elbow. "I shouldn't have done a lot of things."

"No, you were right." He looked around for his cane. "Our family would still be together if it weren't for me."

She stayed quiet, wanting to be wrong this time, wanting to release the need that safeguarded her from the past, from her trauma: the need to be right. The man she once cared for—the man she still cared for, in another way—deserved better than her slant truths and petty criticisms. Diving into my father's eyes, Mom tried to find what she had left behind, beneath the drab cloak she threw over him all those years before. She finally cared enough now, and looked hard enough, to understand the weather of heartache under which Pops had traveled to get as far as he had. The gears in her soul shifted then, a change that went unnoticed, like the first falling leaf on the last day of summer.

"Look at me, Jake." Mom waited for his eyes to reach hers. "I was wrong. What I've done is unforgivable, but I hope you'll try."

Their lost love moved as a third person between

them, and she pined for him now, like she did before, a month or two after she left him, those nights she lay awake next to Tom, trying to bring back the exact sound of my father's laugh. She recalled my dad's wedding vows, the promises he made that Sunday in May by the jetty on Cornfield Point in Old Saybrook, his claims that she was his "reason and his way." But those kind words eroded, as fast as the years, while Mom dulled him down to a nub. She switched to another of his reasons then: the reason he stopped being himself and hid from the world.

"I need to ask you, Iris." Pops shoved his hands deep into his pockets, searching for a way to turn himself inside out, coming up empty. "Do you think about Devan much?"

The question arrived abruptly, but my mother responded, "I do." As her words landed, a blue heron flew in from the harbor—a sign I didn't send—and fluttered onto a tree stump across the road. He squawked, flapped, then settled. Mom stared at the bird and said, "But sometimes I forget our son isn't coming back."

The heron aimed his daggerlike beak at her, its bluish gray feathers ruffling in the breeze, garden hose neck coiled and bowed.

"I swear." She avoided my father's eyes. "I just forget."

But I knew the truth; she didn't *just forget*. She wanted to forget, tried to forget.

"Me too," my father lied.

After engaging in a clumsy hug, which had become comfortable, my mother looked again at Pops, behind his unkempt beard, at the person she once knew. She flicked his gray whiskers with her long nails. "Might be time for a shave, buddy."

Resting her hands on his waist, Mom stood face-to-face with her former lover, and in a moment constructed from each prior moment, she saw his younger self and a time when Jake told her she was the first woman to "speak to his blood," that looking into her eyes was like "being lost in heaven." She leaned in to kiss him, but Pops pulled back. She sucked in her lips, shook her head, turned away. *What am I doing?*

"You better get going," he said. "Never know when the weather will turn."

My mother's mouth twitched, and as she let out an awkward laugh, a curly strand of hair fell across her cheek. *Is our love still alive?* She longed to ask the question aloud, ached to announce her feelings for him, hoped to explain how she'd changed. *What's stopping me?* Pops was the only man who fully understood my mother; he knew her better than she did. In the beginning, her father's cruelty had hardened her. Then later, Tom blindly married a façade. But between those two men, for a glimmer of time, she let my dad chip away at her stony exterior and uncover the heart of a scared little girl.

"Please, let me know if I can help with Joan's arrangements." Mom's shoulders dropped, and she touched her throat. "You don't need to take on the burden by yourself."

My father shivered and nodded. "Thank you, Iris."

As clouds of warm breath mingled and hovered between them, my mother reached out, taking her ex-husband's frozen hands in her gloves. She said nothing, felt everything, and accepted a newborn empathy for their origin stories, their childhood wounds that found clever and destructive ways of getting attention. Mom saw traces of those stories everywhere still, but nothing firm enough to hold.

After she released her grip on him, Pops escaped the cold and went inside. As she stood alone, the morning sun swept away her sharp edges, lighting up the darkness inside her. My mother lowered her head then, regretting the words she couldn't take back, and the ones she never let out.

A whiz at wrestling wicked winters, Wickford had more than survived the overnight blizzard, emerging without a scratch. A fleet of plows worked like oxen around the clock, and the final flakes fell before sunrise. Now, judging by the clear roads alone, the storm may as well have been a rumor.

Hands at ten and two, Tom cruised the length of Main Street, and when he reached the end of town, he turned south onto Route 1. By his side, my mother stared out the window as the day rolled away. An echo of her former self, she didn't bicker about the music, or the directions, or how a detour sent them snaking through residential side streets.

Tom punched up a GPS app on his phone. "Never fear, my dear, Waze has never steered me wrong."

A robotic female voice replied, "In seven hundred feet, turn right onto Phillips Street, then turn left."

Tom saluted. "Yes, ma'am."

The GPS would help them avoid traffic, make good time, and find an alternate route home. But on her true journey, Mom would unfold a new road map, and she'd utilize a compass as well—one that was impossible to find, yet right in her pocket the whole time.

She thought of the affair she'd kept hidden, the secrets she buried, and where she was the night I passed away. She'd driven to the Berkshires with Tom earlier that Saturday, lied to Pops, took the minivan, said she was off to Philly to say goodbye to her ailing father; my dad had no idea that Lionel Reed had died the year prior. Before Mom headed out that day, she was supposed to pick up my allergy medications—albuterol and Singulair; the pharmacy had left her multiple messages. Now, nearly eleven years later, within the confines of the car, she shut her eyes and remembered my father calling her, saying I was dead, and her dropping the phone, and anguish swallowing her whole, and the pharmacy leaving another message the following day.

My mother couldn't go back and make different choices, but she could put a higher price on the time she had left, quit chasing what she couldn't catch, stop filling the void in her soul with "things." She considered telling my father the truth, apologizing, taking accountability for her negligence and the harm she'd inflicted. *Someday*, she thought.

If that day ever came, if she searched her conscience and tried to make things right, if she confessed to her mistakes, even if it caused Pops more pain, I'd forgive her. And I thought he might too. When I was alive, I wanted more from my mother, but now I realized she gave me what she could, in the only way she knew how. Whenever I moved on into the next world, I'd love her more, and I knew her love for me would grow. Trusted it would.

Tom fiddled with the radio, landed on a classic rock station, and sang off-key: "No one knows what it's like to be the bad man, to be the sad man, behind blue eyes."

Mom squeezed her husband's arm, took off her tight boots, and sucked in a cleansing breath. She fished her phone out of her purse and texted Pops: *Thinking we should hold another memorial for Devan. Maybe on the beach in March, on the anniversary.*

She gazed out the window, at the sun and the snow. "Spring will be here before we know it." But Tom didn't hear her over the music.

My mother was right, spring would arrive soon. In that moment though, on that morning, it was still the dead of winter. As she leaned back and closed her eyes, with the warmth of the day on her skin, Mom and I understood each other—and the true nature of the seasons. Winter didn't become spring, just as spring didn't become summer. Seasons existed individually, in separate spans of time. One could not arrive until the other was gone.

NINETEEN

Russell, or windows

IN THE FOYER, airy and bright, Gia and Luke held hands while my brother struggled with a stubborn zipper on his backpack.

"This…thing just…won't…cooperate," Russ said as he tugged.

Luke held up a finger. "Maybe if you—"

The zipper loosened, and my brother closed the pack. "Whew, there we go."

When Pops limped in with a duffel bag in each hand and his mother's pocketbook draped over him, Gia threw her arms around him. "Thank you again for being here, Dad. I'm so sorry about Nana."

Our father huffed and dropped the bags. "Yeah, of course, honey." He caught his wind and bobbed his head. "Hey, Luke, do me a favor and grab my cane in the library, would you?"

"Yes, sir, Mr. Jacoby."

While Russell slipped his arms into his backpack straps, Gia gave Pops a kiss on the cheek. "I love you," she said. "Promise you'll call when you get home. The roads look okay, but you always told me black ice is no joke."

"Will do," our dad said.

My brother hugged Gia and waved his phone. "Hey, thanks for the extra charger."

Our sister laughed. "Yeah, I love you too."

Father and son walked outside, and Russ loaded their things into the trunk of the Outback. He winced at how heavy our dad's bag was, smiled at the weightlessness of Nana's. Again, my twin wished he'd seen our grandmother before she passed, wished he'd said he loved her. He closed the trunk, amazed at how easily Gia offered those words to him and Pops. When did my brother last tell our father he loved him? *Tell him now*, Russell thought.

"Hey, hold up." Luke hurried down the driveway with the cane. "Sorry that took so long." Panting, he passed it to Pops. "It was hiding behind a chair in the corner."

"Thanks, son." Our father patted Luke on the arm. "Take care of Gia for me."

"I will, sir."

En route to Wickford Junction, our father sped down tree-lined streets, while skeletal branches swished past the windows, black lashes across the darkening day. Silence filled the car, then small talk—the Pats, the Celts, the snow—then silence again. The conversation was half-real, half-not, like the strange days after my death.

Rugged clouds moved in and covered the town. On a long stretch of road, a mile from the station, my brother and dad sat locked in a stalemate, looking straight ahead, into the distance, searching for a future they had to find together.

Our father coughed and glanced at Russ. "Still seeing that Dominguez girl?"

Since when do you care about Izzy?

My brother wanted to talk, but not about the woman who left him, or rather the woman he let leave. Should he bring up the vision he saw the night that I died? Or the dreams that he had? Or the voice in his head? Should he keep it all to himself, lock it away forever? He was choking under pressure, gagging again, doing what he did best. Like he choked at Tech, junior year, start of the season, when his coach put him in the rotation and Russ missed twelve straight three-point shots, never played another meaningful minute for the Red Raiders. Like he choked with Izzy, let her go to Poughkeepsie without stopping her, without even trying, without telling her how much he loved her, how badly he wanted to marry her. My brother was unreliable in crunch time; whenever he got a whiff of success, he cracked.

And now, with the clock ticking down again, Russ needed to tell Pops that I didn't blame him, and I yelled out my thoughts: *Tell him the truth. Tell him now!*

Russ wanted to shout: *Leave me alone. Leave me, please!* But he was tired of shouting, tired of fighting, tired of running away.

Then, from the top of a tall pine, a thick, snow-covered branch snapped and fell onto the icy road ten yards in front of the Outback. Pops hit the brakes, and the car skidded to a stop. The men got out, stood on opposite sides of the vehicle, and stared at the knotty obstacle.

"Think we can get around it?" Russell asked as the wind picked up.

"Nope." Pops reached into his jacket pocket and removed a green Boston Celtics winter hat, a Christmas gift from Anna, then he tugged it over his ears.

My brother chuckled. "Nice pom-pom."

Pops smirked. "Let's get this over with." He left his cane in the back seat.

As they dragged the branch to the side, my twin smiled, loved it when he and our dad worked toward a common goal. Like the summer before high school, when Pops ran Russ through offseason basketball drills in Nana Joan's driveway. For three hours every day, the middle-aged man fed my twin passes and rebounded for him, while I watched from the living room window. Our father had installed the hoop when Russ and I were toddlers, shot around with us as we grew. But I was terrible at basketball, all sports actually, stopped playing for good at nine years old, when I couldn't run five minutes without a twenty-minute break, or a puff from my inhaler.

After they cleared the road, Russell blew into his hands. "Okay, ready?"

Pops hobbled back to the car.

❧

In the Wickford Junction parking lot, the lonely Outback idled.

In the front seat, my brother rearranged the contents of his backpack, while on the radio, an old-timey disc jockey hollered through static. "We're going back sixty years, kids, and counting down the top songs from January 1963. Just heard the Earls with their only hit, 'Remember Then,' at number nine. Now it's on to number eight, by a fella who kicked off his showbiz career as a Mouseketeer. Here's 'My Dad' by Paul Petersen."

The crackly song split the quiet inside the car. Above the vehicle, perched like feathery gargoyles, two frozen crows clung to a sagging telephone wire, and the sun slipped behind a cloud.

Pops scratched his beard and scooted up in his seat. "Your train on time?"

"Amtrak app says so."

"Hmm."

Still stuck in my Old Saybrook prison, I wandered around from room to room, window to window, as my brother and father attempted to connect, and it killed me all over again. On the wall beside me, the Wheel of Time ticked like a bomb.

My brother turned down the volume on the radio, and Paul Petersen's voice faded: *When I bring him troubles to share, he's always there, my dad…*

"Thanks," said Pops. "I was just gonna turn that off."

"Hey," Russell said. "I gotta tell you something."

"You don't have to."

"Yes, I do," my brother said. "I, um, I know what happened that night."

"What night?"

"You know, I felt something when Devan died." Russell found a renewed bravery, from somewhere he'd never been. "Remember, I was at a sleepover for my hoops team that night, at Lucas Crawford's house. We were all in the basement, and I'd been asleep for an hour or something when I heard whispers. I opened my eyes and sat up, and Dev was right there. I thought it was a dream, but it wasn't. I was wide awake. I know I was. He was standing next to me, Pops, looking down, talking to me, saying that he was okay. And then he just disappeared, and I looked at my phone. It was twelve fifty-one, the exact time of his death."

Our father stared into the quiet.

Russell filled the space. "And I've had actual dreams, where I see you both in the car on the side of the road, and I hear Devan's voice all the time." My brother angled his body toward the old man. "For years he's been telling me to talk to you about the truth."

"Hmm, the truth."

"Yeah, his thoughts are in my head, playing on a loop." The words raced over Russell's tongue, all of them hitched together, like cars on a train. "I know what happened that night. I know the Focus ran out of gas, and you forgot your phone at home, and you had to watch Devan die in the back of some guy's SUV."

"That's ridiculous," my father said.

"I'm not crazy.

"I didn't say that."

Though I wasn't with him there in the car, my attachment to Russell was strong, and I tried to give him strength. I applied our twin telepathy and transmitted my thoughts. He had to tell our father the rest of the story.

"Devan's okay, Pops. He says he forgives you, and it wasn't your fault."

"That's nonsense." Pops glanced at the dashboard clock. "Train's gonna be here soon."

Russell rubbed his hands on his thighs and waited for our father to crack, for him to realize that his son was speaking the truth, for him to abandon his guilt. The two of them could've waited until eternity, but Pops wouldn't change; all the self-forgiveness on earth couldn't bring me back, and that was all he wanted.

Drained and defeated, my brother stepped out of the car. But before he shut the door, he took a deep breath and said, "Please, don't leave."

"Son, we both have to go."

"No, Pops," said Russell. "That's what Devan told you, those were his last words, on your way to the hospital, after the car stalled, before you got out and flagged down that stranger. That's what he said. Please, don't leave."

Those three words drove into Pops like screws. He slumped and looked away.

"Listen to me." Russell leaned in. "You have to stop blaming yourself." He hoped his appeal would bring Pops a measure of relief, thought if they both opened up, they'd break their pain into pieces. "We can talk about it. We can get past this together. But you need to let it go."

The crows cawed, and the train whistled. The old man looked up, stared into the windshield. "You don't understand."

My brother let the sentence breathe. "Understand what, Dad?"

"I'm tired of hurting, Russell, I really am." Tears fell from our father's eyes, and his words shook. "But sometimes, it's just that, I don't know, I feel like if I forget all the pain I caused, if I let go of all the blame, I'll have nothing left to hold on to."

"What do you mean? You have us. Me, Gia, Mom."

"But not Devan." Our dad turned his head.

"Wait," Russell said, but that was all he could utter. Nothing else came out. He'd said all he could, and more than I asked him to say.

"Safe home, son."

The air around him groaning, my brother surrendered and closed the door, then watched our father drive away. Left alone in the lot, surrounded by mountains of white, Russ stood near a tall statue of a cheery train conductor with two chipper children at his side. Bronze smiles stuck on their faces. Half-buried in packed snow, plowed in by city workers. All four of them unmovable, frozen in time.

∾

On the platform overhang, a string of skinny icicles wasted away.

Plip. Plop. Plip.

The day was warmer now. Still, Russell blew on his hands. Looking down at the tracks, he was unsure of which direction his train would arrive, couldn't tell south from north. His lungs were numb, and he had a hard time breathing, but despite the way our father left him, my twin felt strangely at ease. Like he was closer to the ground yet taller at the same time. *I'll call Pops tomorrow*, he thought. *Maybe visit him in a few weeks.* As Russ rubbed his eyes, the concrete under his feet vibrated, and a rumble thrummed in his ears. A light gleamed in the distance, and a lonely whistle cried. He'd be back in his dismal apartment by evening.

When we were young, everyone—teachers, relatives, friends, coaches—thought my twin was special, and they dubbed him "an original" although we literally shared DNA. No one was as handsome, or as athletic, or as virtuous as Russell Jacoby; he heard the story over and over; what he thought of himself didn't matter. Someday far in the future though, he'd discover his true identity, and all of ours, on his own. When he was ready, when the light came for him. Till then, I hoped he'd find the togetherness he needed in our family. Hoped he'd open up a restaurant like we talked about, fulfilled all of our dreams. And I hoped he'd get all the things he wanted for himself: an old colonial home in the suburbs, three kids, a yellow Lab, and Izzy.

From the bedroom we used to share, on the second floor of Nana's house, I glimpsed my brother standing at the station and felt like I was with him again. Our bond, though, would never be the same. No more visits, no more voices, no hauntings. By leaving him alone, I could help him more, and he'd remember me no matter what.

Russell wasn't by himself on the platform. At the opposite end, an elderly gentleman in a purple scarf sat on a bench with two adults and four small children huddled around him. My brother presumed the man was seeing his family off after a holiday visit, but none of them had luggage or bags.

The train approached, lurching to a stop, and the sliding doors opened in front of the group. Russell walked toward them and waited for the family to board, while the kids kissed and hugged the elderly man. "Goodbye, Grampy. Happy New Year!"

The woman straightened the man's scarf. "See you soon, Daddy. Love you."

Russell caught her eye and said, "I can help him from here if you'd like."

As her kids laughed, the woman smiled. "We really appreciate that," she said. "But he'll be okay on his own."

The man was feeble, balding, out of sorts. In his late eighties, maybe early nineties. My brother couldn't help himself, always aided others. *I can't watch this poor guy struggle.* Russell draped his backpack over his shoulder and grasped the old man's arm.

With a wry grin, the man faced my twin. "So, here we are."

Once they stepped inside the doorway, the woman shouted, "Hey!"

My brother spun. "Yeah?"

"Thank you." She moved a wisp of hair from her face. "You're very kind."

"No problem."

The door closed, and my brother guided the old man to a seat before settling in across the aisle. *Where's this guy headed? How will he manage? Why no luggage?* As Russ locked in on him, the man folded his hands and closed his eyes, swayed to an imaginary song. Like he was trying to remember something he figured out long ago.

"Tickets!" A conductor charged into the car, marched down the aisle. "Tickets, please!"

The old man patted his pockets, shrugged, and intertwined his wrinkled fingers again.

Russell counted ninety-six dollars in his wallet; he'd pay for his fellow traveler but prayed the man wasn't going far.

"Tickets, please! Tickets!"

My brother held out his own ticket while rehearsing a speech in his head, would smooth-talk a discount for his friend if he had to. According to Mom, Russ had "buckets of charm," and he was prepared to dump it all out for a stranger. But the conductor scuttled right past them, like they didn't exist, and took fares from three teens two rows back. *Huh?*

The old man looked at my twin and said, "Beautiful out there, isn't it?" He pointed over Russell's shoulder. "Sure is flying by awfully quick."

As Russell gazed out the window, the train quieted. No rumble below, no whistles or horns. Wheels glided smoothly, silently, and the chatter inside vanished. The whooshing scenery outside slowed, almost to a standstill. A cornfield waved in the wind; a river sparkled and flowed; a gaggle of Canada geese waddled in the snow, spread their wings, and took flight. My brother welcomed the calm, the easy give-and-take of his breathing, the letting alone of his body and mind. Alive to the strangeness of the moment, he looked into the sky, at a double rainbow arching across the horizon.

Then a soft sound, light and unobtrusive, a tapping in his brain, mixed with the peacefulness, and Russell chuckled. "That you, Dev?"

It wasn't me, and I didn't go to him then. Simone was right, my family had to travel their individual journeys by themselves, finding unique paths over the mountains of life on their own. But if my twin ever needed me I'd arrive, swift as a summer sun shower. If he listened with his heart, not his head, my small voice would settle inside and guide him. With a promise to only stay as long as necessary.

He dialed Izzy.

"Russell?"

"Hey, before you say anything, I want to apologize. I don't know why I freaked out, but you deserve more from me, and I don't want this to be the end, Izzy. This can't be over."

"I don't want it to be."

"You don't? Oh, you don't. Well, I don't either."

"We can talk about it when you come visit. How was the wedding?"

"Wasn't quite a Hallmark movie, but I talked to my father about some personal things, stuff I wanted to say for a long time. Still don't know how he feels though."

"And how do *you* feel?"

"Like I finally did the right thing."

"You did."

"Um, you know, I was just thinking that when I come

see you upstate, maybe I could stay for a while and check out the Poughkeepsie restaurant scene. I mean, if your job's going well and you have the room, and you're cool with that. What do you think?"

Izzy said nothing, and it was enough of an answer.

My brother hung up envisioning a different way forward, where life would be all right even if his dreams didn't come true, where he wouldn't fear the unknown. It was as if my death had pushed him out of a plane, and for a decade he fell, fighting with gravity, screaming and thrashing, until, just now, he realized there was no earth. He wouldn't overthink every decision, he'd take a broken-wing approach. Whatever happened in the days ahead, he'd live in each moment, and let life play out however it played out.

He plucked the rubber band on his wrist, and it broke. Across the aisle, the old man tugged on his purple scarf and laughed.

TWENTY

Jake, or choices

Pops pulled off Plum Bank Road.

The snow around his house was deep, but someone had shoveled and salted the driveway, the sidewalk too. He threw the car into park, slouched in his seat, tugged at his beard, breathed heavy. What Russell told him at the station banged around in his head, and he couldn't shake it out. *Not my fault? Stop blaming myself? The kid has no clue.*

My father snatched his cane and got out of the car, opened the rear door. He took out his bag but left his mother's things. Unsteady with his steps, he started up the driveway. When he reached the sidewalk, he slipped and fell on the bricks, his bag and cane flying out of his hands and into a pile of snow. He clutched his lower back. "Shit!"

A shout came from the road, cheery and concerned. "My lord, Jake!" Pulling Dewey on his leash, Anna hurried to my father. "You okay?" She laughed as the dog licked his face.

"Fine." Pops pushed Dewey away.

Anna plucked his cane out of the powder and wiped it off. "Need some help? How was the wedding? Do you like Gia's husband?"

With each question, Pops felt colder and wetter. "Dammit," he mumbled, propping himself up, while the frozen bricks stung his gloveless hands.

"Oh, wait," Anna said, depleting my dad with untiring affection. "Where's your mom?"

"Staying with Iris and Tom for a few days." He got up, didn't brush himself off, then headed toward the house without his cane, wincing with every step. *Why lie to Anna about Ma? Why lie to Iris about Anna? Why?* Like endlessly rolling waves, his regrets lapped onto shore, one after another.

When he was five feet from the door Anna yelled, "Hey, silly! Forget something?"

"Ugh."

She hurried up the walkway with Dewey, unhooked his leash, and handed it to Jake. "I fed him an hour ago, and he just peed." Anna paused, tried to meet my father's wayward stare. "If you're up for it in the morning, maybe the three of us can take a walk on the beach, and you can tell me all about the weekend. Supposed to be a warm one tomorrow."

Pops grumbled, and Dewey rubbed up against his leg.

❦

After dumping his coat and hat onto the floor, my father latched the door and tracked muddy snow across the linoleum. He ignored Dewey on his heels, opened the fridge, and grabbed a Bud Light. When he cracked open the can, the hissing of pipes, perhaps, from somewhere down the hall, clanged in his ears.

As afternoon shadows crept into the corners of the kitchen, Pops settled at the table, huffing hard, the beer trembling in his hands. He hung his head and leaned back in his chair, sensed me then, felt me near. I saw the red in his eyes, heard the thump in his chest. Then he lost his breath—like he had lost everything else.

When the doorbell rang, my father wiped his brow, and didn't stand. He peered over his shoulder, at Anna's face in the window, then beyond her at a world dressed in white. She mouthed a quick comment, but he couldn't make it out through the glass. He was stuck in a stifling solace, like being trapped inside a snow globe.

Another voice came to Pops then, soft and invisible. Not Anna's, mine. Our time together ticking away, I'd be leaving him soon, but I needed to reach him. Using all the energy I had left, focusing harder than ever, I rapped on the door of his heart. Since my death, he'd rejected my efforts to communicate, doubted me for years. For a decade, when I tried to break through to my father, I'd say, *I'm still here*.

Now I whispered, *I have to go*.

And finally, this time, he let me in.

The gray veil around me lifted, the shroud over the house disintegrated, and trickles of light pressed through tiny cracks in the windows. When I died, I should've ascended into the heavenly realm, should've accepted the reality of my death, and my life. Should've let it all go and moved on. Now, was it unfair of me to ask Pops to do the same?

Anna tapped on the door glass and called out again. My father rose from the table, pushed his chair to the side. He hobbled out of the kitchen and into the living room, past the broken clock. As Dewey and I followed, a powerful golden glow lit up the ceiling and walls. The windows cleared and brightened, scratches and stains disappeared. Pops stopped at the foot of the staircase, turned and glared. "Stay, Dew!"

When I tried to touch my father's shoulder, a dazzling shaft of light blasted through the roof and shined down from the top of the stairs. Someone called my name, then several voices, then a choir. The light wrapped me in its wonderful warmth, and I saw my grandmother. She looked no older than Gia's age, and she stood with a handsome young man at the end of a brilliant tunnel. "Come, Devan," Nana said, smiling at me with lively eyes. "It's time."

Fraught with determination, my dad and I climbed to the second floor. When we paused for a moment on the landing, the light beckoned me, and the voices called again. But I turned away and followed Pops into his bedroom. From inside the glowing tunnel beaming down through the ceiling, Nana gestured for me to join her. "Don't be afraid, I'm here for you, honey. We're both here." The man next to her spread his arms, and I recognized his soul: my grandfather, Elliot.

Pops went to the closet, grabbed the box of keepsakes, dropped it on the bed. When he flung open the box, my childhood spilled out: a Polaroid of me and Russ dressed as pirates for Halloween, a love letter I never sent to a third grade crush, an apology note I wrote to Pops after I "borrowed" one of his ties for a school play, a picture I drew of our family surrounded by giant trees. Slouching alongside the bed, my father hid his face with his hands. Directionless, lost on a lonely path in the tangled forest between his heart and mind, he screamed to himself, *I can't do this anymore!*

He began to sweat and wheeze, couldn't think straight. A funeral procession marching in his brain. The framed photo on his nightstand, the one of him reading to me as a kid, sat mute. Then a knowing voice called, not his, not mine: *Go now. Slip into another life.*

As he hunched over, the voice grew louder, and an idea unfolded—as Pops prayed it would—a welcome arrival that bore into him, an understanding that changed him. His mother's death and the truth about his father had upended the snow globe of his life and caused a chaotic flurry, a blinding storm that clouded the image of who he was and kept him from seeing who he hoped to be. *I don't want to do this!*

I shouldn't have tried to interfere with his life, or anyone's. Shouldn't have forced Russell to confront him. If I hadn't meddled, my dad would've moved on in time. Would've gotten over his pain. I didn't mean any harm. *I'm so sorry, Pops.*

His cell phone buzzing, Gia calling. He didn't pick

up. The phone rang again, and he tossed it aside. It rolled off the bed, onto the floor. He went back to the closet, feeling warm and faint, reeling as he pulled the shoebox off the top shelf. And he stood there, shaking, for what felt like hours. I was beside him but couldn't help him. Not now, or ever.

❧

Jake Jacoby was six years old the last time he saw his father. They had played catch in the yard on a perfect spring day. They ate supper with Joan: fried chicken, green beans, and baked potatoes. Afterward, the son apologized to the father for breaking the watch he'd been playing with earlier in the afternoon. And that night, when young Jake went to bed, his father told him the story of the man who lived inside his dreams. "Now you listen good, EJ."

"Yes, sir."

When my father awoke the next morning, his dad had gone.

But Elliot, Sr., was with me now, surrounded by a beautiful, forgiving light. Together, from the bedroom window, we watched Pops shuffle onto the back deck. "Soon he'll understand," my grandfather said. "And he'll know how much I love him."

Pops threw open the sliding door, stumbled down the steps, and staggered onto the beach. Snowdrifts swallowed his calves, and spikes of icy air shot into his windpipe. The silvery sky, the color of being stuck between breaths. He carried the shoebox but wore no jacket, held no cane.

A thousand summers, past and future, slumbered under his shaky feet.

Dewey galloped out of the house.

As a boy, I wished away the winter, prayed for spring to rush in and turn snow into water, let me play on the sand, swim in the sea. My father, though, taught me to wait and be patient. "Winter," he'd say in his fatherly way, "is a time to leave things alone, let them hide." But now on the beach, as he battled the cold in his heart, he recalled what he couldn't forget, the mistakes he couldn't unmake. And as memories of me tried to slip through his fingers, he held on and wouldn't let go. *It's all too much.*

I whispered in the wind, *No, don't give up.*

He fought through gusts of shattered images, the good times and bad our family shared, the loving and the leaving. *What have I done, Devan?*

Dewey darted around him, almost cut his legs out.

"Get back home!" Pops cried and flailed.

The dog bounded through the drifts, encircling his friend. Gulls flocked to the scene, some alone from beyond the marsh, some in low swift ribbons along the coastline, all with urgency in their pumping wings. Pops muttered and huffed, neither apologized nor accepted forgiveness for what he did, or didn't do, the night of my death. Russell's knowledge of my last moments: now an unforgettable reminder of my father's greatest failure. How could he face his surviving son, or himself, again? How could he separate truth from belief?

The rising tide swallowed the beach. After stumbling just twenty feet from the house, Pops reached the water.

At the frozen shoreline, he shivered and stared at the dropping sun. On that very spot, he and I saw day flip to night a hundred times, the sky exploding with color as if painted by angels. Now, in the dying light, the wakening pale moon lurked over my father's shoulder, and shadows moved across the water, going wherever shadows go. As his knees weakened, Pops looked out at a world beyond the horizon that wouldn't let him pass, that forced him to find another way around. No false salvation, no retreat into illusion.

At the window in the bedroom, with soothing light all around me, I watched my dad alone on the frozen beach. My grandparents were there too, imploring me to depart with them, to cross over into the heavenly realm. "I can't go yet," I said.

Simone joined us then, more of a real person now than she ever seemed before. More beautiful and recognizable, as if we'd met in a past life. "You're ready," she told me. "Soon, this chance will be gone."

But this is all my fault!

In the creeping dusk, Pops dropped to his knees. And as the snow eclipsed his shins, the lighthouse beacon conducted a search and gave way to a shivering silence. The sun inched toward its destiny, and the endless years ahead of him were empty of time. My father opened the shoebox, eyed the pistol. Blinked hard. *What am I doing?*

An ocean of light flooded the house. Simone took my hand, and we moved toward a bright tunnel filled with great love, drawing me closer to the spirit world and away from the ghost world, farther from my father. Expanding outward into infinity, Simone and I had no boundaries. Everything was within us, awareness, vastness, spaciousness. Her voice was inside of me; we were the same. We were the creator, and the created.

Wait! I stopped, shielded the light, and tried to break into my dad's thoughts. *Pops!*

He denied my cry, reached into the box, removed an object he hadn't held for sixty years: his dad's wristwatch, the vintage Timex with the black lizard skin strap, the watch my dad broke when he was a child. In his palm, the timepiece was another busted memory, flimsy and forgotten, the hands stuck on 3:14. He wound the watch slowly, examined its face, unmoving and cracked. As he fitted the strap around his wrist, Dewey bobbed and yelped, intense and aggressive, his snout hovering low to the ground. Pops saw glimpses of his father then, heard bits of what Nana told Gia, smelled the lie his mom carried for ages. Like his dad before him, mine had lived inside a never-ending nightmare.

Then from the box he took out an old photo, crinkled and faded, one of him and his father holding fishing poles by a river, smiling for the camera, Elliot, Sr., crouching next to his six-year-old son. For my dad, the people in the picture were strangers, a boy and a man he couldn't recall.

I watched my grandparents disappear into the brilliant tunnel, traveling beyond and behind the earthly realm, where I hoped they'd await my arrival. Basking in the light with Simone, my spirit danced, and energy soared, and my consciousness merged with hers. She looked into me, and I perceived her like I hadn't before. She was more than a familiar aura, more than my usher, guide, and ally. After all our time together, I recognized Simone as her true self, as the soul I'd always known—and the sister I never knew.

The beacon bent its beam across the sound, and my father peered into the horizon, at the last curving sliver of day. He held the pistol unsteady in his frozen fingers, his face more haunted than afraid. Fate had bludgeoned him, his will to go on bloodied and busted. He looked at the watch on his wrist. The wind blew hard. He lifted the gun to his temple. The cold steel stung his skin. He didn't flinch, ignored the pain, ignored it all, and shut his eyes.

"Jake!" Anna yelled from her deck. "What on earth?"

When I heard the call, I hesitated, afraid of abandoning my father, and the bright tunnel before me narrowed. Drifting away in the distance, Simone motioned for me to follow. "Now, Devan," she said, her voice and thoughts fading.

I looked back at Pops. One last time. *Please. Don't. Leave.*

Then a blast and a scream, silent and serene, echoed across the water. The gulls deserted the beach, flying off for safer skies. On a cloud of snow, Dewey whimpered and lay beside my dad, stayed long after the sun fell into the sea. And after I went into the light.

"It's okay, Jake, I've got you."

THE BEGINNING

UNDER A RED morning sun, at the end of August, Plum Bank Road teems with activity.

Backhoes rattle, dump trucks hum, and bulldozers chug as they unload dirt, transport gravel, and push new earth into the marsh. On the other side of the street, on a thin strip of sand behind a weather-beaten house, a woman and her four-year-old granddaughter hold hands and carry yellow plastic buckets.

The woman picks up a shell, hands it to the girl. "How many have we found, Ellie?"

The girl pokes her nose into her bucket. "Ninety million thousand and forty-eight"

"Holy cats, that's a lot." The woman lifts the brim of her straw hat, takes a peek at the girl's stash, counts only four shells. "Why do you think all those snails left their homes?"

"I dunno."

As they stroll the small beach, little waves creep

closer to a three-foot-high cinder-block wall that stands between the deck of the house and Long Island Sound. The woman scans the near-barren shoreline and sighs. "Can I tell you a secret?"

"Yes!" Ellie shrieks. "And I promise not to tell a single person in the whole wide world."

Her grandmother smiles, crouches, and faces the girl. "Next summer, when you stay with me, I'm going to have a brand-new house."

Ellie's excitement fades. "Aww, but I like this one."

"Me too but, here, look." The old woman puts an arm around the girl and points into the distance, along the curved coast, where dozens of homes have been demolished. Of the few that remain, the sea laps onto decks and back steps. "These houses will be gone soon, but they're building new ones high on a hill on the other side of the road, where the marsh is now."

"Why?"

"The water is getting too high, sweetie."

"Will the ocean take you away?"

"No, I'm not going anywhere, Ellie." The woman taps the pink daisy on Ellie's purple bathing suit, tickles the flower over her heart. "I will always be right here."

The sun's low rays set the beach on fire. Ellie scoops a handful of powder-soft sand and lets it fall slowly through her fingers. She giggles, then screams, "Look, Nana Pearl!" She leaps into her grandmother's aching arms as a hermit crab scampers between them.

"Wow." Pearl pulls down the brim of her hat and smiles at the creature. "You know, my mother said that when she was a little girl, this beach used to be really, really, super-duper big, and thousands of crabs would scurry around looking for shells."

"Whoa, cool." Ellie says. "Did your mommy live in this house too?"

"No, but when she was your age, she visited her nana here every summer."

"Really?" Ellie skips around her grandmother, swinging her bucket, while her tiny footprints form a ring of love. Her dark, curly hair and big brown eyes mimic Pearl's, when she was a girl, once upon a time.

"Yes, really." The woman lifts her gaze toward the attic window, the one that always reminded her of a ship's porthole. "Your great-great-great-great-grandmother moved into this house over one hundred years ago, and it's been part of our family ever since."

The girl draws a circle in the sand. "Before even you were born?"

"A long time before that." In her mind, the woman revisits the past. "This house is twice my age."

"Two, three, ten." Ellie counts on her fingers, bites her lip. "Does that mean you're, like maybe, two hundred years old?"

"Don't get fresh, young lady." Pearl fakes a frown, and her knees creak as she bends over and picks up her precocious granddaughter. "Oh my goodness, you're getting so big."

Behind them, a seagull perches on the wooden rail of the deck, while construction vehicles in the marsh continue to chug and hum. And as the tide rises, Ellie plays with a double-heart pendant on a gold chain around her nana's neck. "This is so, so, so pretty."

"Well, if you're really good," Pearl says, "I just might give it to you someday."

Ellie wraps her warm legs around her nana's waist. "Would you give it to Mommy instead, if she was still here?"

"Probably, but then she'd give it to you."

"Do you know why she had to die?"

Pearl squeezes Ellie tighter and breathes in the salt air. "I think that when your baby brother was in your mommy's belly, her heart got too big because it was so full of love for her family."

"Daddy called it, um, an idiotic carpentry."

"That's right, an idiopathic cardiomyopathy." Pearl smiles and puts her granddaughter down. "Now, do you want to know another secret?"

The girl grabs the old woman's wrinkled hand, shakes and tugs. "Yes! Yes! Yes!"

"Okay, okay." Pearl pauses, grateful for the little fingers holding hers. "Well, this secret is extra special." She leans over and whispers, "Both of our mommies are guardian angels together in heaven, and they're watching over us all the time." Pearl hangs onto Ellie's hand for a moment, then lets her go, watches her wade into the water, up to her knees.

"Oh, Nana, I forgot to tell you something." Ellie splashes and laughs. "I heard scary noises in the house last night."

"Don't worry, it's nothing to be afraid of," Pearl

says as a breeze brushes the late-summer warmth off her shoulders. "Probably just the wind whistling, or the old pipes knocking."

"Well, I think it's a ghost." The girl twirls in the sea, arms out wide. "And it's a man ghost, and he has a big white beard."

"Hmm." The woman stares out at the horizon, past the twirling girl and the rippling water. "Do you think he's a nice ghost, or a mean ghost?"

"Um, well," Ellie says, "I think he's a very mean ghost who wants to be nice, but he can't because he's so sad."

And the sun shines on and on.

When the heart truly understands,
it lets go of everything.

—Ajahn Chah

ACKNOWLEDGMENTS

If I were to thank every single person who helped me write this book I could, well, write an entire book. My typed-out fingers are really sore, and I assume you all know who you are, but here's an abridged version of the story…

Introduction: *Life*

To the people, places, events, experiences, feelings, and thoughts that have molded me, influenced me, and directed me through each phase of my fifty-six years: you always have been, and always will be, my greatest teachers.

Chapter One: *Love*

To my family—wife Jackie, son Caleb, daughter Lucy, sisters Cheryl and Linda—who have loved me unconditionally and accepted me (the kids had no choice) for who I was, who I am, and who I need to be: you hold a piece of my soul.

Chapter Two: *Devotion*

To all of you who read this book, or any of my others, and to those who have supported me, encouraged me, and cheered me on as a writer: you are the reason I keep going.

Chapter Three: *Appreciation*

To Mike Labrie and Mark Nadeau—who offered their homes as I tried to capture the souls of Old Saybrook, CT, and Wickford, RI, on paper—and to all my friends from Massachusetts, New Jersey, the NBA, the Aging Bulls, and around the world (settle down, everyone) who have been in my corner since the beginning and, hopefully, till the clock stops ticking: you are incomparable, invaluable, and irreplaceable.

Chapter Four: *Dependability*

To Sam Nadeau, Dave Ethan, and Quincy Hampton—the players behind the best book trailer in the history of You-Tube—who provided their unique talents, and a shared willingness to help: you are almost unthankable.

Chapter Five: *Trust*

To my editors—Will Allison, Jessica Powers, and Jennie Cohen—whose abilities humbled and comforted me as we brought the Jacoby family's story to life: you made me, and every word I wrote, better.

Chapter Six: *Gratitude*

To my beta readers—Cindy D'Altorio Sherman, Andrea Soulellis Erickson, and Dave Chmiel—who helped tailor an early draft of this book, and who probably spent twice as much time scratching their heads as they did reading: your brand of generosity should be taught in the finest schools.

Chapter Seven: *Inspiration*

To Ann Geer, a beloved and dearly missed presence, a soul who inspired everyone she touched, who showed us how to live, love, and die with grace and strength: you have changed me forever.

It'd be selfish of me, and incredibly understated, to say that Ann was a close family friend. She was what we all should be: a servant of the world. Ann maximized joy, didn't fear death. She told her daughter, Beth, that her greatest sadness about dying was that she wouldn't be able to tell her family "what happens next."

From her backyard on Lake Champlain Ann famously kept her "Lake Log," snapping photos of approaching storms, capturing the tangerines and lavenders of sunsets and moonsets, noting the changing colors of the water as the lake breathed the seasons in and out. She's a part of those colors now, always changing, always glowing, always lighting up our skies.

Recently, she passed in her sleep on what would've been my twin brothers' sixtieth birthday. What a gift for them. I imagine another realm where my parents and brothers welcomed "Annie" (as my father called her) to a never-ending celebration, a blessed and blissful reunion of souls.

Conclusion: *Hope*

To my parents—Robert and Cynthia Gagne—who believed in life and in people, who taught my sisters and me that every struggle results in hope: you are why I wrote this book.

My folks died a long time ago, but only after they fulfilled their purpose on earth, this time around, as Bob and Cindy. I wonder where their souls are now, in what dimension, or in what other bodies. What new lessons have they learned? What struggles have they survived? I wonder when I'll see them again, or if they send me signs, or if they're always with me.

I wonder, but I don't need answers.

My mother and father showed me there's more to life than waiting around for whatever comes next, more than demanding to know why the past played out the way it did. It's about the time we have now, here, they'd say. More time for love, devotion, and appreciation. More people to depend on, trust, be grateful for and inspired by. More reasons to hope.

Thank you, Mom and Dad, for teaching me the difference between giving up and moving on, quitting and changing, acceptance and tolerance. Thank you for showing me that nothing is impossible, that no path is unfindable, and that there's always a light in the darkness.

Questions and Topics
for Discussion

1. Much of *The Unknowing* takes place in the author's idea of the afterlife, where souls choose between the ghost world, the spirit world, or reincarnation. How do you think the Jacoby family saga would have unfolded had Devan chosen anything other than remaining earth-bound in the ghost world?

2. The death of a child is perhaps the most horrific experience a parent can imagine. How do Jake and Iris deal with Devan's death differently? Which of them is more to blame for the tragedy, given the roles they each played? Should we always forgive others when they make mistakes that hurt us? What kinds of mistakes do you find unforgivable?

3. We all grieve differently and in our own time. Who in the Jacoby family deals with grief in a healthy way? Who deals with it in a self-destructive way? Besides losing Devan, what else do some of the characters grieve?

4. In the novel's opening scene, Nana Joan compares snail shells to souls, referring to the theory of reincarnation. Later at the inn, the Ouroboros engraving alludes to the eternal cycle of death and rebirth. How are these two references similar? How are they different? What significance do they have in the overall story?

5. Why is it often difficult for family members to forgive each other, even when they want to mend their relationships and move forward?

6. Hanging on to negative emotional attachments can limit our personal growth and cause unnecessary suffering. Why do we find it challenging to let go of our grudges, tensions, guilt, blame, and so on? Why is it crucial to "let go" when we're approaching death? What are some hang-ups you wish you could release in your life?

7. The seasons and the weather play major parts in the story, as if they are characters themselves. What do you think they symbolize? Do they hold individual meaning for each member of the Jacoby family?

8. We can find referrals to spirit guides—connectors between the physical and spiritual realms—in various cultures and religions. In the book, Simone is Devan's spirit guide, or "soul usher." What necessary wisdom does she share with him? If she is an all-knowing entity, why wouldn't she recognize and deny Devan's suspect motives for remaining earthbound from the start?

9. Was Nana Joan right or wrong for lying to Jake about his father? Do you think hidden stories can be more powerful than shared ones? Why?

10. What choice does Jake make at the end of the story? Is his decision ambiguous or clear? When that scene is over, someone says, "It's okay, Jake, I've got you." In your opinion, who is that person?

11. No matter how dark the road, the power of hope can light the way to salvation and a brighter tomorrow. What kind of hope shines through at the end of the novel? How does the "light" that comes for Joan, Emma, and Devan represent salvation? How do other characters find a brighter tomorrow?

12. We all lament the past and worry about the future, even as friends, therapists, and self-help books urge us to appreciate the present. Who in the Jacoby family is most saddened by the past? Who fears the future? By the end of the story, who is most prepared to accept and appreciate the present?

13. Ghosts are often associated with haunting or being trapped in a specific location, whereas spirits may be more ethereal and capable of moving freely. What role does Emma Hayle play in *The Unknowing*? How do her needs and motives differ from Devan's? What prevents both ghosts from ascending into the spirit world?

14. Gia wrote her poem, "the unknowing," during a low point in her life—after her brother's death and in the midst of her drug addiction. How does what's happening at a particular moment in our lives affect our worldview? What else does the word "unknowing" represent in the story? What does the title mean to you after finishing the book?

15. Like the rest of his family, Devan hides a secret, waiting until later in the novel to tell the reader that his family loved him "too little" when he was alive. Do you sympathize with his decision to stay in the earthly realm? Why? Does his big reveal make him an unreliable narrator?

16. Gia is one of the most courageous characters in the book, brave enough to invite the family to her wedding and confront her nightmarish past. Where did she find the strength to be honest about her faults and mistakes? Why can't her parents do the same?

17. Many readers detest Iris, finding her completely unlikable and unsympathetic. But Jake describes how she was a kinder, more loving person when they first met. How do you think her growing up in an abusive family affected her personality? How did her childhood pain find its way into her adult life? What are some ways in which we all internalize negative behavior and struggle with unresolved trauma?

18. Is it better to make decisions based on rationality or intuition? Throughout the story, Russell must choose between listening to his head or his heart. How is he pulled in different directions? Why is it important for him to alter the way he views life? How can we all find the balance between thinking logically and emotionally?

19. Each member of the Jacoby family finds him or herself in a different emotional place at the end of the story; their experiences and growth shape the novel's narrative. Which character changes the most? Which one changes the least?

20. *The Unknowing* is filled with symbols: the Wheel of Time clock that Jake built, Iris's double-heart necklace, Gia's oyster shell tattoo, and the rubber band Russell wears on his wrist. How does each of these things represent the main themes of the story? What other symbols are prominent in the book?

Made in United States
North Haven, CT
03 June 2023

37326780R00183